I0645533

Man in a Cage

A novel

Patrick Nevins

Print ISBN: 9781088034026
Ebook ISBN: 9781088034033
Library of Congress Control Number: 2022906036

Published by Malarkey Books, August 2022.

Cover design by Angelo Maneage.
angelomaneagethewebsite.com

Typesetting by Alan Good. *Man in a Cage* is set in Munson, a typeface created by Paul James Miller that combines elements from Clarendon with the style and look of a nineteenth-century typeface called Consort.

malarkeybooks.com

For Lucy and Will, my little reading bugs.

Preface

Man in a Cage is a fictional account of American naturalist Richard Garner's first research trip to Africa. Many details of the fictional Garner's life hew to accounts of the real Garner's life, while others are pure invention. Likewise, all other characters, as well as places and events, with a basis in reality are used imaginatively.

A note on the language: Richard Garner conducted his research on primate speech in the late nineteenth and early twentieth centuries, a time when racist pseudosciences such as phrenology and polygenism prevailed among scientific communities. While the fictional Richard Garner's narration at times reflects that racism, I hope readers will find *Man in a Cage* an indictment of it.

Chapter One

My gorilla, Dinah, is not long for this world.

She was a vigorous little creature until this recent turn, as robust as the day I purchased her in Gabon. But despite the great care I have taken with her, from a West African jungle to the Bronx Zoo, I fear she is resigned to the same fate as the other two gorillas who have survived passage to America: a slow, pathetic death by starvation. God bless Mr. Engelholm, the zookeeper who has appointed himself Dinah's nurse. Mr. Hornaday's doctors have prescribed fresh air, so every day you may find the keeper pushing the pitiful ape about the zoo grounds in a baby carriage. She peers out from under the thick blankets that are necessary to keep her body warm and returns the incredulous stares of visitors with an emptiness that betrays her suffering. The illuminating factor behind her dark eyes is all but extinguished.

Engelholm brings some levity to the scene by pretending to mistake the ape for a human child. "Do you want to see the pretty buffalo?" he asks in baby talk. To the ape's blank stares he replies, "Hang it! You're a gorilla, not a baby!" The act always elicits a laugh, but what the audience will not be allowed to see are the vain attempts by Engelholm and Hornaday and me to remove Dinah from the carriage and return her to her cage. She cries and fights—it is the most she moves anymore—until we set the carriage inside the cage and allow her to emerge from it on her own time.

Only a few weeks earlier, Dinah showed none of these signs of resignation. Quite the opposite. Upon the arrival of a young lady from *New York World*, Dinah had knuckle-walked eagerly to the reporter, and the reporter, who had never been up close with an ape before, readily accepted the animal into her arms.

"Oh, you are a big girl!" she said.

The reporter, carrying Dinah like a child, followed me to the concrete room in back of the cage where the gorilla lived during inclement weather and sat upon a stool. Dinah sat upon the young lady's lap, sounding off with low grunts, while the reporter interviewed me—if it could rightly be called that. From the start of my career in Gabon, many of the men who have reported on me have been transparent in their aims at tearing me down, but I could not guess this young lady's agenda. She showed little interest in what I had to say about the gorilla's language; as I expounded upon the subject of my life's work, she held her ear to Dinah's muzzle—and whispered back into the ape's ear! They were conspiring schoolgirls, and I a learned pedagogue speaking to the ether!

I wandered away and let the girls do as they wished. My thoughts drifted across the Atlantic to Africa. Had not Europe done enough to that continent? An abominable slave trade. Christianity. And now war.

"Professor," the reporter called out. "Dinah says that in New York, the sun stands no chance, and the moon is only a memory."

"Why, Miss, you've not only mastered Dinah's language—in mere minutes!—you've also discovered that she's a poet!"

"Her words thrum like the rivers of Africa. Her breath is the jungle's mist. It does not require a skilled interpreter to discover that she wishes to know why she must remain entombed in concrete when you return to her forest."

"Miss, you may exploit Dinah and me for your little society piece, as I now see that's what this is all about. But could you do me one favor? Africa is being ravaged by Europe's greed. I would not describe to a lady some of the violence I have seen carried out against its natives. And now the continent is being ravaged by Europe's war. White generals are arming Africans and marching them into battle. Marching them into death. I've seen war, and it isn't pretty. And for what are these Africans fighting? For the generals' masters' right to keep stealing from their lands! When the war is over, the Africans who have survived will have to trade their rifles for whiplashes! Unless they turn their rifles on their generals! So you may tell Dinah that she is better off here. I aim to return to Africa as soon as the war allows and pick up my studies, if the whole continent hasn't been laid to waste. Now could you put that in your little article?"

The reporter's countenance had shed its girlish smile and all vestiges of cheekiness. I felt ashamed for having unleashed the storm of my thoughts on the girls' sunny conversation.

"Tell me," I said softly to her, "what else has she told you?"

She whispered to Dinah; the ape's lips fluttered against her teeth. The reporter gave me a sympathetic smile. "She is an enigma. Perhaps we are not meant to understand her."

The *Times* has reported that Dinah is improving, but I have no faith that her appetite will remain and she will make a complete recovery. Nurse Engelholm's heart will break.

Mine has already been broken. Twice. My chimpanzees, Susie and Moses. Susie, like the gorillas, succumbed from my failure to adapt her to this country's climate. And Moses. You must ignore the lies that have been spread about me and trust that I am being forthright when I tell you of the unfortunate circumstances I met in Equatorial Africa.

My acquaintance with those chimpanzees dates back over two decades to my first African expedition to study the languages of apes—the science to which I remain devoted. My association with Mr. Hornaday and the Bronx Zoo may have long ago eclipsed my reputation as a scientist, but supplying primates to Hornaday's zoo is merely a means to an end: It provides the funds necessary to continue my studies in Gabon. In the last twenty years, I have spent more time in my house there than in America; were it not for Dinah's case, and the war, I would be there this very moment.

The notion that monkeys and apes possess languages similar to the languages of men was inspired by a visit to Cincinnati's zoological gardens thirty years ago. I had by that time devoured Charles Darwin's works and taken a great interest in man's primate cousins, so upon learning that Cincinnati's zoological gardens boasted one of the country's few primate collections, I took Maggie and Harry to that city for a vacation. On the day of our arrival, the elements had conspired to produce a sweltering heat that encouraged languor in nearly the whole menagerie. The alligator, in spite of his size and spiked flesh, failed to inspire fear as he sprawled on his belly, forepaws tossed back; a few visitors wondered aloud whether he was alive. The hyena slept like a bored hound, his head occasionally twitching as if he dreamed of Africa. The pair of grizzlies, at least, lumbered their great, soft bodies around their pen, though they looked as if at any second they would collapse into a pile of fur. Maggie was quite cool toward the animals, humming and huffing only cursorily; Harry, who was ten at the time, joined in with the contemptible youths who yelled at every new species they encountered as if their commands would induce the creatures to perform. But I did not discipline him, for I doubted I would have behaved much differently in his position. There were no zoos in my youth.

The heat could not dampen my excitement for the Monkey House; when we came upon the Moorish building, I trembled at the prospect of finally meeting these wonderful creatures I had before only seen illustrated. Upon stepping inside, I faced the shifty darkness occasioned by moving from sunlight to shadow; I held Harry's shoulder for fear of his becoming separated from us. Enclosures, lit only by skylights in the domed roof, encircled us. Vague shapes moved inside of them. I tried vainly to force my eyesight to correct itself; in due time, though, I could see various monkeys in positions of retreat, nesting in their branches, high and to the rear of their enclosures, fingering the steel-wire lattice. They were incredible! They walked gracefully along branches on their hands and feet, and occasionally one would swing to another branch, its suddenly lengthened form producing a fresh series of rude calls from the gathered children. A group of pink-faced rhesus monkeys instilled in me the belief that they, of all the animals I had seen that day, formed the most sophisticated social group. There was not a single behavior that made this impression, but rather a combination of small gestures, which may have escaped the attention of less-observant visitors: One monkey bared his teeth, but made no sound, at a larger cousin. This cousin did not return the bared-teeth expression, but narrowed his brow in a show of force that affirmed his dominance. Such humanity in that tiny face! Always the monkeys were mindful of the whereabouts of their cage mates. And a shine in their dark sclera showed that they watched their watchers. No animal would strike me as so human-like again until I returned to those zoological gardens years later to see chimpanzees.

"Incredible," I said. I let go of Harry and moved closer to the lattice. "Don't you think, Dear?"

Maggie had taken hold of Harry's shoulders, though her countenance suggested not a mother protecting her child, but a child seeking succor in her father.

"Please, Richard, not so close."

"Don't worry, Dear. We shall stay on our own sides of the cage. Won't we, fellows?"

"Look, Daddy—that one is painted!"

On the other side of a solid dividing wall in the rhesus monkeys' enclosure slept a single mandrill whose red and blue face was remarkably brilliant. A few other boys had caught on to Harry's discovery and began yelling at the creature to awaken.

"Frightful," Maggie said.

The mandrill answered the onslaught by raising a single eyelid, setting off a chorus of screams with one portentous, glazed sclera.

I returned to the zoo alone the next morning, wishing to observe the monkeys undisturbed by throngs of children. Maggie had left the Monkey House somewhat undone by the experience, especially the hellish jungle portrait projected by the mandrill's eye, so she and Harry remained at the hotel for breakfast. I was among a small number of visitors that morning and, as I had headed straight for the Monkey House, was able for the first time to study primates in the solitude necessary for scientific observation. I was richly rewarded. The rhesus monkeys swung freely and playfully, having forgotten yesterday's torments. One dropped to the floor and skittered to the dividing wall, where he made me aware of a feature I had not noticed before: an opening just large enough to admit a monkey from one side of the enclosure to the other. The rhesus looked through this doorway onto his neighbor, who this morning was pacing, knuckles drawing him forth impatiently. The rhesus then baptized me in primate speech: His mouth formed an "O," and a low growl rumbled in his throat. He was calling to his cage mates. His growl drew their attention, for at once they turned their faces toward him, seeking further information. The mandrill paid no attention to the call, but his pacing grew faster, and to my astonishment, his war paint increased in brilliance. The red of his face grew brighter than my waistcoat. I was in awe of this transformation—but the rhesus watchman had a very different reaction. The pitch and volume of his call increased and the very shape of it changed into what struck me as a new call. He repeated this second call several times, sending the other rhesus monkeys into a panic marked by high squeals. It was then that I hypothesized that the calls were not only distinct in degree—as some scientists would still have you believe—but in meaning; the calls were not purely emotional, but contained specific information—in this instance, that the mandrill's mood was dipping, as shown by his brightening colors. Look out fellows!

If only there had been a way to capture the rhesus monkeys' calls for scientific study!

My interest in Mr. Darwin's work had come during the course of my teaching career. After the war, I put myself through the Jefferson Academy for Men in Blountville, Tennessee, and began my career as a teacher of human biology. By this time, Darwin had long been known for his *Origin of Species.* Natural selection was held as a sacred truth by enlightened men and even much of the general public—even Christians who were not slaves to dogma. It was the appearance of his *Descent of Man* and the subsequent public arguments regarding the development of language that caught my attention. I held with Darwin's claim that language, like species, evolved. Early man likely uttered sounds based upon instinct and, later, onomatopoeia. Those men who were able to harness these utterances to enable their survival in the prehistoric world would have passed on their developing use of language and its attendant brain and vocal organ development. Those iterations of men whose speech remained weak failed to warn each other if a region's hunting was poor or its winters freezing. Perhaps most deadly, they failed to warn each other of imminent predators. Bears and big cats. Other men. I think it is likely that the greater races of men murdered the lesser races, driving them to extinction. (After what I have witnessed in Africa, I hope we do not repeat our ancestors' course.) Over millions of years, as the best men proliferated—and the weaker ones died out—so too did the best brains and vocal organs and utterances. The languages of ancient civilizations rose in place of the grunts of barbarians. Natural selection applied to languages just as it did species.

Opposing Darwin was Professor Max Muller, who would have us believe that in some prehistoric age, primitive languages blossomed forth in men around the globe—quite miraculously, it would seem! True-cause doctrine would have any rational man ignore Muller's assertion of some language-making instinct, now vanished, but the professor did have his supporters. Muller also asserted that language was the "barrier" that separated man from animals—an idea that would not have gained any ground with me even as a child, when I had seen around my family's general store so many dogs bark out their dominance and whimper their submission, and would have been utterly shattered by my observation of Cincinnati's rhesus monkeys.

I found a kindred spirit in Professor Georges Romanes, who supported Darwin's claim regarding language and natural selection. Just a few years after my experience with rhesus monkeys, Romanes argued that those animals that understood words—think of a dog that responds to the command "sit"—had minds that, in varying degrees, edged toward the ability to use words. Of course, a dog's vocal organs limit its range of vocal expressions, but in man's primate cousins, there existed the possibility of articulate speech. Romanes had the same thought; he studied a chimpanzee in London's Regent Park zoological gardens and distinguished between her expressions of affirmation, dissent, and gratitude—quite elementary compared against my later discoveries, but he must be credited with getting there first! I admit to burning with envy upon reading about his work with the chimpanzee. It would be another two years before I could build upon it.

What bearing did these arguments about animal language have on the origin of man? If language, and thus reason, were proven to exist in man's primate cousins, there stood proof of evolution. If chimpanzees were in possession of a rudimentary language, and therefore in possession of the requisite brain and vocal organs, they were in a state of evolution that the races of men had once passed through. The debate over evolution could be put to rest for all time! I had lived with the notion that if I effected the right change in my life, an important secret would be revealed, and I had become increasingly convinced that the secret was connected to primate language. This conviction brought me to attaching myself to the Smithsonian Institution. Washington has since been Maggie and Harry's home, though hardly ever mine.

After school let out, I would walk home and join Maggie and Harry for an early dinner, then catch a horsecar to the Smithsonian's grounds. As evening came on, the sharp red sandstone of the Castle's towers seemed to rend the darkening sky. To the east stood my destination, the Castle's proud younger sibling, the National Museum. Between the Museum's twin towers of brick, Columbia held her motherly hands over the sweet heads of Science and Industry, maidens bearing a heavy volume and an ancient sextant, respectively. Walking under the pure marble, I felt the hand of Columbia, too, offering her protection as I embarked on a scientific mission whose methods were not yet clear even to me.

I used my position as an esteemed secondary-school teacher to gain access to a variety of materials related to animals and language. Curator Frank Baker would grant me admission to the Museum and direct me through its halls to the materials I sought. I would examine the skulls of rhesus monkeys one evening and scrutinize photographs of Mayan glyphs the next. I admit to becoming a bit lost in that trove of scientific delights, and found myself in the position of having to explain the ends toward which my means were aimed. I had been neglecting Maggie and Harry, to whom I owed some justification for the long nights I spent in the catacombs of the Smithsonian. And Baker threatened to deny me further access to certain materials. His hand was stayed only by Assistant Secretary Charles Walcott—but even he wanted to know the design of my amorphous research.

My saving grace was the anthropologist Jesse Walter Fewkes. In the summer of 1890, Fewkes used a phonograph to record the speech and songs of Maine's Indians. If a scientist could use the phonograph to study the primitive speech of America's savages, then it followed that an intrepid thinker could use the same technology to capture the speech of monkeys and apes—for I was convinced they possessed it. The previously mysterious purpose of my life was revealed, and the secret it would throw like a light upon the world was the proof of evolution. I presented my case to Walcott and Baker and was granted the opportunity to transport their phonograph to the Department of Living Animals and record the speech of the rhesus monkeys there, as long as my scheme was satisfactory to the department's director.

This would not be an issue, as I had visited the department several times and made the acquaintance of its founder and director, Mr. William T. Hornaday. The department was really a makeshift zoo located behind the Castle. Hornaday had begun with a dozen animals collected on a trip out west, but he was constantly purchasing or being given new animals, and now they numbered in the hundreds. Their homes were hastily constructed and haphazardly laid out wire pens and steel cages and a wooden shed hidden in the Castle's shadow. It must have looked simply odd at first, but now it had set in like a stain on the institution's grandeur. Crude as it was compared to, say, the zoological gardens in Cincinnati, it did attract visitors. I had brought Maggie and Harry there several times during our first few months in the city, but Maggie had demanded I not take Harry back after the bear incident. One of the zoo's three black bears scaled their pen and pulled himself to the roof of the shed where, to the terror of visitors, he paced and considered whether he ought to leap and make a meal of one of us. He decided against bodily risk and lowered himself back into the pen. Hornaday later informed me that the bear escaped regularly—a fact I did not repeat to Maggie! The menagerie badly needed the new home that Hornaday had recently fought for and won: The zoo was to move to a proper zoological garden in beautiful Rock Creek Park.

I found Hornaday walking amongst his buffalo family. Though he was a couple years my junior, he appeared older; perhaps it was the effect on my mind of his record as an explorer, carved out in the Everglades and Borneo. He also was distinguished by his short, neatly combed gray beard. His upper half was that of a gentleman of the Smithsonian, but his lower half was caked in mud. I had admired him before I made his acquaintance. Once I met him, I quite liked him.

I paused a moment before entering and removed my bowler. Standing at that gate was like standing at the threshold of a church; you automatically assumed an air of reverence whether you were a true believer or an agnostic. Only a few years earlier, Hornaday had conducted a sweeping survey of the American West and concluded that the buffalo, which had once roamed those lands in the tens of millions, were now virtually extinct. Hornaday and a team had returned from their trip with the half-dozen buffalos required to make his American Bison habitat for the National Museum. The animals had been hunted—and Hornaday himself had taken the great bull of the group—in the name of science and, paradoxically, preservation, but I dared not imagine what Hornaday must have felt in reducing their numbers even by this slight amount. The giant glass cube that held the finished habitat was a window on the

West in its primitive glory, the bulls vigilant against Indian hunting parties while the little calf feeds. The party returned with no living buffalos. Hornaday's captive family was a gift.

Upon being noticed by Hornaday, I passed through the gate and stepped across the muddy pen.

"Have you taken an interest in buffalo?" he asked, stroking the tufted hair of the beast that had lumbered between us. It was the father; the mother and their two calves grazed nearby. Hornaday looked wistfully at his charge. "I preferred stuffed animals to living ones for so long."

Such was Hornaday's way of speaking that even a declarative statement such as this struck the listener as an imperative. I searched for the glass of an eye in the massive head of the animal that faced me, and having found it, looked into it for a moment, for I was sure Hornaday wanted my attention there.

"But taxidermy doesn't preserve an animal—only the image of it," he said.

After a moment I said that my request concerned some of his living animals and explained the design of my experiment.

"I can't imagine what good will come of that," he said. "But you have my permission to proceed."

"I aim to study the speech of various monkeys and apes, both in zoological gardens—and in their native lands."

"I've seen the orangutan in Borneo."

"Yes—I've read your book."

"Upon meeting one of those fellows, one needs no further convincing of Darwin's theory of evolution."

"Then why did you have to kill so many of them?"

"Do you not study the skins and skeletons in the museum every night?"

"Yes, I know the scientific value. But why so many? What was the final count? Over forty?"

"You have an odd way of requesting favors, Mr. Garner."

I returned us to the topic of Darwin, arguing that while erudite men like ourselves accepted the theory, there were multitudes who required further proofs. And that I aimed to show an affinity between apes and men via their shared faculty of speech.

"I expect to find that the various species have languages of a higher or lower type depending on their overall capacity for thought."

"Capacity for thought?"

"Speech is thought. And the phonograph is the scientific instrument with which to measure it."

Hornaday shook his head and laughed. "Frank Baker's right—you really are a pain!"

"Well, you're a taxidermist!"

"Do you want my help or not, Mr. Garner?"

"Yes. I'm sorry."

"You really intend to go abroad to study these animals?"

"Yes. Africa."

The phonograph was delivered to Mr. Walcott's office in the Castle and placed on his desk. I was like a child on Christmas morning, barely able to stay my hands as Walcott removed the polished-wood top and demonstrated how to attach the brass horn. Mr. Baker allowed himself inside Walcott's office as Walcott was teaching me how to operate the machine. Baker slunk into a chair with a great sigh. The middle-aged curator seemed to have acquired some new complaint upon our every meeting. Either Mr. Hornaday was right, and I was edging Baker toward his grave with my constant requests, or the curator was trying to shake me. Walcott, however, always met me with kindness and carried himself with grace. He had a ring of fine, gray hair around his bald head, and was clean-shaven, and on that clear face I imagined the future being written. I will always admire the man.

"Shall we test it?" I asked.

"Are you afraid our phonograph isn't in working order?" Baker barked.

"Sure," Walcott said. "Speak into the horn."

He began cranking the handle, rotating the cylinder. I trembled at its slight hissing. I was speechless!

Walcott spoke in the even tones with which he would always treat me: "This is Charles Walcott, Assistant Secretary of the National Museum. It is August 12, 1890, and I am here with Mr. Richard Garner, who plans to record the sounds of monkeys in the Department of Living Animals. Is this correct?"

I leaned into the horn.

"I will document for scientific study the speech of the park's various monkey species. That is correct."

Baker, who had watched us contemptibly to this point, pushed himself from his seat and approached the horn.

"Richard Garner is a fool whose ideas are the stuff of a Jules Verne novel."

Rather than remain at the Museum that evening, I returned home to share my wonderful news with Maggie and Harry. They were seeking relief from the heat in what little breeze and shade graced the porch of our little home. Harry was reading *Treasure Island* for the hundredth time.

"You remember the monkeys from the zoo?" I asked Harry. "The little pink-faced fellows?

I'm going to capture their voices on a phonograph cylinder!"

"Can you bring a phonograph home to listen to it?"

"I'm afraid I'll have to carry out my studies in the museum. Perhaps you could join me at the zoo for my experiment?"

"That zoo is wretched," Maggie said.

"It's a temporary affair. Mr. Hornaday will soon have a marvelous zoo."

"Then you may take Harry back."

I gave Maggie a glare, and I'm a monkey if she didn't return it with her own outsized eyes. *He's not a boy anymore*, is what I meant to convey; I could read in her countenance only a plea to possess him a bit longer. Harry must have sensed the struggle, for he rose from his chair— it still surprised me when he straightened himself out and was two inches taller than me— and retired to his room with his book.

Maggie is burdened by the unfortunate feminine trait of heating and cooling much too quickly, so when I sat down beside her, I was not surprised at her reaching out to take my hand in hers. Her eyes—little emeralds is what I thought of them—met mine sweetly.

"It's nice to have you here," she said, her words now in a cooler register. "You spend too much time in that strange museum."

I weighed my words carefully. Maggie deserved to know my mind, for I had uprooted her and Harry so many times in pursuit of my scientific interests—finally bringing them to Washington for the express purpose of having the nation's greatest scientific materials at close hand—and my interests had not yet yielded anything of value. I supported them on my modest teacher's salary. The days and nights I spent at the Smithsonian must have seemed to Maggie an indulgent hobby. But was I not progressing toward a life of scientific achievement? Was the Smithsonian men's permission to experiment with their phonograph not proof of a budding career in primatology? Would my purpose go unfulfilled?

"I know it may not seem as if my work is worthwhile. But you must trust that I'm on the verge of making a real impact in the natural sciences."

Every part of Maggie collapsed: shoulders, cheeks, emeralds.

"I do not see it, Richard." The heat had returned to her voice. I felt it in her palm, too, for she did not let go of my hand. "You know what I see? You coming home talking of big dreams, but smelling of buffalo dung."

"Edison's machine is going to lead to a real breakthrough. I'm confident the study of primate speech will yield proof of evolution."

"I know we are not a churchgoing family. But there's no need to boast about it."

"I will not shrink from the truth, Dear."

"Nor will I: We have lived in this awful city for a year, and your promise of improving our lot here has remained just that—a promise."

"That is changing, Dear."

"A promise wrapped in buffalo and monkey dung!"

My initial attempt at recording primate speech tested my patience, but proved a useful exercise for my subsequent work. Some primates will chatter and cry freely until the moment I begin cranking the phonograph, at which time they become silent as monks. There is no point interrogating them. One must simply wait, hand at the ready, for them to resume their talk.

Joining me that morning—quite to my surprise—were Mr. Walcott, Mr. Baker, and assorted other men whose attachments to the institution were driven by passions other than my own, but whose curiosity drew them to the zoo to discover my purpose. There was also a reporter from the *Washington Post*. Who had alerted him to my experiment? Walcott? He seemed too pragmatic to call the press before he was certain there would be some result to report. Baker? I suppose he could have been certain of my failure and sought to embarrass me.

Time seemed to have stalled in the morning's sticky atmosphere. The rhesus monkeys sat in clusters and exchanged bared-teeth grins, but made no sounds. These silent conversations were mirrored by the side conversations of the gentlemen around me, whose words evaporated in the gauzy heat before reaching my ears. We are wasting our time. This man is a fool. Surely these were the conclusions I was not hearing. The men faded away, until only Baker, Walcott, and the man from the *Post* remained, and then they, too, left the scene. I believe this was the only time that a reporter had nothing to say about my doings.

Of course, upon my being left alone, the monkeys began to speak a little. I was able to catch only a little of their speech, but one word in particular proved very valuable in convincing Walcott to allow me to continue my studies. I had to wait only two hours to capture it.

The rapid approach of dark clouds did not escape the attention of at least one of the monkeys, the little fellow I had taken to calling Prince. He leapt to a high branch and scanned the skies. His sudden movement having captured my attention, I was able to see him nearly tremble with anxious thought just before a cry burst forth. The high-pitched bark was repeated several times to his brothers before I remembered what I was there to do and began cranking the phonograph. From his perch, Prince dropped to the dirt, just opposite the phonograph on the other side of the steel lattice. Quite unprompted by me, he cried the same word into the horn, allowing me to capture this important utterance.

I carried the phonograph back to Walcott's office and played back this word and the others I had captured.

"What an interesting use of Mr. Edison's invention!" Walcott said.

"And exactly how do you propose to translate this squealing?" asked Baker.

I argued that slowing down primate speech would allow one to analyze it and discover its phonetic features.

"The phonograph," I claimed, "is a microscope for sound."

I felt, upon saying this, that I truly was ushering in a new age of scientific discovery.

"But," argued Baker, "how will you discover the meaning of it?"

As I had returned the phonograph unharmed—and I think Baker had doubted my ability to do even that—I was allowed a second session the next morning. Only Walcott and Baker would join me. On this day, the skies were fair. The monkeys chattered and cried to each other like children in a park. But as I prepared the phonograph beside their cage, they fell silent.

"Stage fright?" Baker said.

I began to turn the crank in reverse, which would produce at normal speed the rhesus speech I had recorded the previous morning. I did not know the effect this would induce in the monkeys, but I could not have been more pleased at the outcome: Upon hearing the voice of Prince crying from the horn, the monkeys pricked up their ears and rapidly ascended the branches to the upper reaches of their cage to peer at the sky. A cacophony of cries rained down—within which I could not be sure I heard Prince's word repeated—surely produced by the contrast of hearing what I concluded was a warning of approaching thunderstorms and the proofs of a clear sky and gentle breeze.

Baker frowned. "So you've succeeded in scaring them with their own shrieks. That should produce an excellent paper."

"You recall yesterday's storm clouds? One of these fellows uttered that word as he watched those clouds gather."

"'A storm's brewing, boys,'" Walcott said. "That's what the little fellow was saying."

"That's my preliminary conclusion."

Baker was less convinced.

"Proves nothing."

Mr. Walcott was so impressed by my demonstration with the rhesus monkeys that he did not hesitate to allow me to borrow the phonograph for subsequent experiments. I chose for my next subjects the park's spider monkeys.

Physically, spider monkeys are the shadows of rhesus monkeys; these spindly and languorous creatures would deserve our pity if they only knew how cruelly nature had slighted them!

I was able to capture some of the spider monkeys' speech, though the preliminary results of my research suggested that the spider monkey's language, like their very beings, is of a low order in the ranks of monkeys. But what my initial study of spider monkeys yielded was the first of many successful experiments with mirrors. Experiments such as these require my entry into the animals' habitat. On this morning, Mr. Hornaday allowed me into the spider monkeys' cage, which I entered without trepidation. The spider monkey is a low, but gentle, creature, and I had no fear of being on the same side of the steel lattice as him. Acquainted to the presence of Hornaday, the spider monkeys likewise had no fear of me; they continued to sit in their perches and occasionally swing from branch to branch, such as their small cage allowed, to find a new spot in which to sit, undisturbed by the strange man below. One curious female even dropped from the branches and skittered over to examine me. I squatted to her level and greeted her in low tones. She sat within arm's reach; I slowly extended my hand and petted her slight shoulder, and for the very first time had close contact with a primate (save humans, of course). I have grown quite used to petting and even carrying monkeys and apes—but I can still recall the thrill of feeling her coarse hairs yielding to my fingers, of sharing a touch with one of man's less-evolved kin.

I spent the remainder of the morning recording the spider monkeys' speech and observing their reactions to a small mirror. I have found, beginning with the pathetic spider monkey, that monkeys without fail take their reflections to be other monkeys. Depending on the natural disposition of his species, a monkey will either attempt to speak to, caress, or otherwise engage his new companion. Often, he will search behind the mirror for him. To their credit, most monkeys are diligent in their searching. And none have exhibited any signs of mental anguish over the puzzle, save for the female spider monkey with whom I had shared contact—and that was entirely my fault.

As the morning was leaning toward the noon hour, a few boys had come to see Hornaday's animals. Satisfied with my morning's work, and knowing that the boys would make real scientific study impossible, I packed up the phonograph and reached for the mirror down in the dirt. The mirror slipped from my fingers and shattered upon the ground. The female, alarmed by the crash, turned and saw some piece of herself in a sliver of glass only a couple of inches long. She grabbed the shard and, upon giving it a closer look, gave a terrifying series of shrieks. The alarm drew Hornaday—but also a crowd of mean-spirited boys, who laughed at the spectacle of the poor beast and the scientist and keeper attempting to calm her. She must have viewed the shard as a portal between herself and the monkey on its other side, for she held it at different lengths and angles, trying, I believe, to allow safe passage for her friend. When she flipped the shard over and lost sight of the other monkey, she gave a mournful cry. Upon finding her again, her calls returned to their anxious state, and she laid the shard down and tried one contortion after another, turning herself in circles in between, in a search for a way to join her friend on the other side of the mirror.

Hornaday armed himself with a broom to sweep up the remaining shards and bat away other curious monkeys, while I spoke solicitously to the distraught female. In spite of the boys' shouts, I was able to gain the monkey's attention long enough to cover the shard with my shoe. She cried several times before retiring to a corner of the cage, exhausted and pathetic over the loss of her friend.

Mr. Hornaday later praised my handling of the situation, though it turned out to be a backhanded compliment—a suggestion that I was a fine handler of primate life, as long as it were caged. We were in his church—the buffalo pen. The beasts lumbered between us. When I accepted his compliment with no more than a nod, he explained his true meaning.

"In the wild, you won't be able to simply walk up to an ape and interview him."

"That is why I shall make my home among them."

Hornaday laughed, earning my glare.

"I'm sorry, Mr. Garner. The truth is that if your plan is realized, I will be quite jealous."

"William T. Hornaday, jealous of me? I'm the one who should be jealous. You've been up the Orinoco River delta, to the hills of India, deep inside Borneo."

"Yes, that's all true. But I never was able to follow the trail of Du Chaillu. I was set up to go—before I traveled to any of those other places—but my uncle talked me out of it. He was afraid it would have killed me. We'll never know. My mettle was first tested in the Florida Everglades."

"If you're worried I don't have the constitution for an expedition to Africa, know that my mettle has been tested, too. In the war. The Third Tennessee Mounted Infantry. What's more, I was captured and imprisoned. Twice!"

"Captured twice? Good for you, Garner! I was too young. Though the war did kill one of my brothers and chewed up and spit out the other."

Hornaday was entitled to a pause out of respect for his brothers, and I observed it, silently admiring the buffalo.

"But with all due respect," Hornaday began, "do you really think you ought to be venturing to Equatorial Africa? Considering your lack of experience?"

"What experience did you have when you first set out for the Everglades?"

"The experience of being half your age!"

I was allowed more sessions with the phonograph throughout the fall. But by springtime, I had attracted the attention of Secretary Langley, whose thoughts about my use of his institution's scientific equipment were a mystery to me. Mr. Baker's contempt for me could only have been a negative influence upon him. Mr. Hornaday, while always willing to help, remained skeptical of my pursuits. And Mr. Walcott's enthusiasm was beginning to wane. I felt I had to bring the institution something quite special to repay them for their generosity, and I had exactly the right study in mind.

The stateliness—the grandeur—of the Castle affects every man who approaches its doors. Its massive tower is a sentinel over the Smithsonian's growing domain. The smaller towers along its walls offer protection to the treasures held within. The dome in its center suggests to the viewer something from the Far East. It is as if the Smithsonian contains the entire world: It is the ultimate map, bestiary, and collection.

For the curious visitor, it is thrilling.

For the fledgling scientist seeking its favor, it can be terrifying.

Though the Castle by this time served mainly as an administrative building—many of its materials having been moved to the National Museum—these effects cannot be denied.

It had taken little courage to request of a curator—even one as cranky as Baker—to see up close some of the materials. And Walcott, being an evolutionist and a perfect gentleman, made conditions easy for me to inquire about using the phonograph. But I felt quite nervous regarding my newest request. I worried it would require Langley's involvement, and I had no guess as to his feelings regarding my work.

Walcott welcomed me to his office and inquired after my latest session with the rhesus monkeys.

"It went very well, thank you. Though I'm starting to attract a crowd. Would that people knew when to make themselves scarce!" I regained an earnest countenance before continuing. "I have lately been thinking that you—that the Smithsonian—deserve something more than cylinders of monkey speech for your generosity."

"That is exactly what we have been thinking."

"Then perhaps this proposal will appeal to you. The Cincinnati Zoological Gardens have recently acquired two chimpanzees. I think it's time my studies reached beyond monkeys and included the speech of the higher primates."

Walcott sighed and turned toward his window.

"And I suppose you will require our phonograph to accomplish this? Mr. Garner, we were thinking it's time you publish some of your findings." He paused and narrowed his eyes at me. "Mr. Hornaday tells me you want to study primates in the wild. Is this true?"

"Absolutely. I don't think a true study of primate speech can be done without it."

"Then you need to publish your findings here first. The Smithsonian doesn't send enthusiastic amateurs into the field, only bona fide men of science."

Walcott trained his eyes on mine to convey one of two beliefs: Either I would always be an amateur or it was in me to become a "bona fide" man of science. In that moment, I believed he felt the latter.

"Let me take the phonograph to Cincinnati, and I promise you will see my results in print."

"I'm sorry. Publish first."

Chapter Two

Thus began my relationship with Mr. Samuel Sydney McClure. Only a few years earlier, McClure had innovated the newspaper syndicate and in a short time become, through his diligence at finding interesting writers, America's literary tastemaker. He has acquainted America with Rudyard Kipling and the evolutionist Professor Henry Drummond, among many other great minds. And he proved to be exactly the man to spread my work among the public. Among publishing men, McClure is as fine a man as one could wish to know. As far from that scabrous Labouchere as one can get.

I wrote to McClure in New York with an abstract of my research in Washington and was received quite warmly. He urged me to write an article boldly proclaiming the implications of my work. He found my claims for simian speech too qualified in early drafts, and would-not seek to publish my article until I had cast off my doubts and bared my theory before the educated readers of the world. That is how "The Simian Tongue" came to be published in *The New Review*, prefaced by a statement to the effect that I was willing to suffer the ridicule of those whose dogmas disallowed the reality of articulate speech in monkeys and apes and the conclusion that man, in his evolution, had once passed through a similar phase of rudimentary speech. And suffer I would.

The article appeared in June and earned attention beyond my greatest expectations. Newspapers around the country spread my ideas among their readers. The *New York World* suggested that my theory had been the talk of every known tongue save the simians'!

In the months prior, I had stayed away from the Museum. I spent the time with Harry, mostly fishing. The sport, and the getting there and back, afforded us hours to talk, though I got very little out of the boy regarding his plans for the future. I did not discern much interest from him when I spoke of monkeys and apes and Africa; if anything, his searching green eyes and the flattened line of his mouth expressed a mild disbelief. *Oh, I'm going, my boy*, I wanted to say. *Perhaps you will join me when you are a man.*

In the evenings, I wrote in our den. My work often kept me at the desk late into the night; on those occasions, Maggie would squeeze my shoulders and kiss my cheek before retiring to bed. She never complained about my staying up, for she was simply glad to have me at home rather than at the museum. It tore at my heart, her slight—yet strong—hands on my shoulders and back; in her touch I wanted to feel encouragement, but read over and over that she was holding me in place. I may have been wrong; perhaps she did mean to encourage my scholarship. There's no point in asking her now. Given my feelings at that time, upon completing "The Simian Tongue" and even upon its appearance, I remained at home in the evenings with her and Harry. But it soon became clear that my new celebrity—though that word degrades the scientific value of my research—was the collateral Mr. Walcott needed to send me to Cincinnati with the Smithsonian's phonograph.

I returned to Walcott's office with *The New Review* in hand.

"I hope the article is satisfactory to you," I said, laying the magazine on Walcott's desk with a flourish.

"Congratulations, Mr. Garner."

To my embarrassment, Walcott did not pick up the magazine; it was evident he had already read it.

"*The New Review* was an interesting choice."

"It was Mr. McClure's suggestion."

"It's not where the best scientific work is debuting."

"But people are talking about it! What good is my work if it's hoarded among a coterie of scientists?"

Walcott laughed. "There's a lot of good in scientists conversing with each other. But I'll grant that it's impressive how your experiments have captured the public's imagination. It's critical where you take this momentum."

"As I suggested in the article, I expect it to take me all the way to Africa."

"Let it take you to Cincinnati, first."

After an absence of seven years, I returned to the Cincinnati Zoological Gardens, not as a husband and father with a budding curiosity about primates, but as a scientist equipped with a revolutionary theory and a fine scientific instrument on loan—however reluctantly—from the Smithsonian. I had thought this was all I needed to gain entry to the Monkey House in the hours before the zoo opened. But upon my arrival, phonograph in hand, the keepers at the gates refused to admit me until they had cleared my request with the primate keeper. The primate keeper, however, refused to come to the gate. "Do you not know who I am?" I asked, only to be refused again. I sat down on a bench in front of the gates and removed my jacket, as the morning was quickly heating up. I was soon joined by some mothers with their young charges.

A boy of no more than seven inquired after my case, against his mother's requests to leave me alone.

"It's quite all right, Ma'am."

I explained to the boy that the case contained a phonograph and pulled the horn from my jacket. A subtle flexing around the boy's eyes suggested a deepening of his curiosity. He ran his fingers along the brass.

"Can you play some music?"

"No, this phonograph is for recording the speech of the chimpanzees inside."

"What can they say?"

"A great many things, I'm sure."

"Mama! He says the monkeys can talk! The monkeys can talk, Mama!"

The mother furrowed her brow at me, checking my wish to correct the boy regarding the differences in monkeys and apes.

When the gates were finally opened, I inquired after the primate keeper again. I was told by a ticket seller that I would find him in the Monkey House.

"That's eminently useful," I said.

I moved through the gates, but was stayed by the ticket seller's hand.

"You'll have to pay just like everyone else, sir."

I would find the primate keeper no easier to deal with than those implacable types I had already suffered that morning. He was as large as a circus strongman and kept the chimpanzees under a close watch, as evidenced by his hesitation to allow me inside their enclosure. He was familiar with my article, though, and relented upon seeing the phonograph assembled. He stroked his waxed mustache, searching for the words with which to dispatch me to the apes.

"Chimpanzees are many times stronger than their size suggests," he warned. "If there's any harm going to be done, it will be to you or your machine."

"I'll take my chances."

The chimpanzees were simply the most amazing animals I had ever seen. There was a male and a female, and the pair, sitting in their enclosure and curiously watching my entrance, shared an affinity with man and woman that simply does not translate in illustration. Their bodies were dense with black fur and their brown faces were much wrinkled, but the expressions upon them, the quick turning of the flesh around the eyes to suggest inquiry—to suggest thought!—were the mirror of the expressions belonging to the boy at the gates, the keeper, you and me.

"Hello," I called to them.

In a moment, they had acclimated to my presence, much as they must have acclimated to the presence of their keeper, and returned to their business of grooming each other. The female, who was called Lucy, was picking upon one of the male's shoulders, working her way across his broad back. Though humans do not groom each other, the affinity with human gestures was not lost upon me: The delicate finger work suggested Maggie's knitting; the gentleness suggested her caresses as I worked at my desk.

The chimpanzees were not eager to make contact with their new human visitor, and there would be only the briefest of touches between me and Lucy during my visit. But my skin bristled as if between us moved the ghosts of our common ancestry.

Guests quickly filled the Monkey House, stuffing it with chatter that would surely spoil any attempts to record the chimpanzees, so I recorded my observations of the animals' behavior in a notebook, waiting for a quiet moment. The chimpanzees did answer some of the children's awful calls with brief bouts of hooting, so my hopes of filling a cylinder with their speech increased; I only needed them to keep speaking after the children were gone.

Soon, my wish was answered, and I was able to capture several words from each chimpanzee. I expressed my pleasure to the keeper, who remained unmoved but willing to allow me into the enclosure the following day for further research.

The chimpanzees sung me to sleep that night.

In my hotel room, I played the cylinder over and over, attempting at times to write the words in a notebook. My initial study suggested that the chimpanzee's vocal apparatus is similar to man's, and subsequent investigation has supported this view. This being the case, it is easier to represent a chimpanzee utterance in print than, say, the utterance of a rhesus monkey, though it is still quite challenging. I closed my notebook after a while and only listened to the chimpanzees speak. I selected a single word—having no idea of its meaning yet—and practiced forming it with my own voice. It required great diaphragmatic effort and resulted in a low, tired hoot. I practiced this single word, viewing myself in a hand mirror as I spoke, then listening to the word on the cylinder to check my ability in the chimpanzee's tongue. I did this until late into the night when my lungs ached.

The next morning, shortly before the zoo opened, I barged past the ticket sellers claiming an important appointment with the primate keeper. The keeper would not appear until the opening hour—a tactic that had no justification except asserting his position! Seeing no need to satisfy that small man's ego, I walked right up to the chimpanzees' enclosure and set down the phonograph. I wrapped my fingers around the steel lattice and spoke the word that I had spent the previous evening practicing.

The male chimpanzee paid me no more attention than he might pay a barking child. But Lucy, upon my third or fourth sounding of the word, turned her head toward me curiously. Upon another sounding of the word, she bounded toward me and clasped the lattice, placing her brown fingers over mine. Her touch was utterly human!

She spoke the word back!

I thrilled at the realization that this was surely the first time that a man and an animal had spoken to each other! We volleyed the word several times, banishing the ghosts from the room, leaving only the two of us survivors. Our lines had parted millions of years ago and evolved to make us *Homo sapiens* and *Pan troglodytes*, and we stood together, fine representatives of our respective species, and reconnected those lines via our shared speech. No two diverged species had ever completed such a circle! My part was only mimicry, but I was confident I could discover the word's meaning.

I returned to the Smithsonian emboldened. I played the cylinder for Mr. Walcott and shared with him my notes and the story of speaking with the female chimpanzee and the promise of a new article. To complete my new article, I argued, I must see all the chimpanzee and gorilla skulls in the National Museum.

Walcott accompanied me one evening to the room in the museum where the primate materials I sought were held. He opened for me large steel cases that contained the skins and skeletons of several monkeys and apes. Though we were in search of skulls, the brown and black furs drew my attention. On my second day in Cincinnati, I had entered the chimpanzees' enclosure and petted Lucy's shoulder as we kept up our "dialogue." She regarded my hand casually, as if it were the hand of her mate. I sought to replicate the touch I had shared with my animal cousin, but the furs were cool and yielded to my fingers—rather poor simulacrums.

We selected a chimpanzee skull and a gorilla skull and set them on a table for observation. The bleached skulls with their jaws set nearby could not speak to us, yet I knew there was much they could yield. Walcott and I handled the skulls, first in an intuitive way, and later taking measurements. We had begun to compare notes when it occurred to me that we were missing a vital piece with which to carry out our study.

"We need a human skull," I said. "Surely you can round one up."

Walcott raised an eyebrow in agreement, then asked to be excused for a moment.

He returned a short time later, human skull in hand. To that unknown man I am eternally thankful! Walcott and I worked into the night, putting together our two heads—or should I say five!—until I arrived at a theory: The vocal power of a vertebrate correlated to the angle at which its spine met its foramen. The vertical spine of man passes into his skull at ninety degrees, and man possesses superior vocal powers; in the rest of the animal kingdom, the angle grows greater, and the powers of speech lessen. In a reptile, the spine meets the skull at 180 degrees, and his vocal powers are no more than squeaks and hisses. From this theory, I deduced that, after man, it was the chimpanzee rather than the gorilla who had the most complex vocal ability. Walcott nodded thoughtfully, as if to affirm the validity of my theory without committing to it with too much force.

Over the following months, Mr. McClure published more of my articles, and Mr. Walcott extended my privileges with the Smithsonian's phonograph. Walcott had been very good to me. As an unpublished, fledgling scientist, I had been allowed to impose on his curator and zookeeper. But there was a growing tension between us as my writing continued to appear in periodicals and newspapers intended for mass audiences—for that was McClure's business model: The more markets to which he sold my work, the more his syndicate profited—and did not cross over into the scientific journals. I think his firm belief in evolution was one reason he allowed me to carry out my studies. But I like to believe there were deeper, more personal, reasons.

We had both overcome modest beginnings and suffered great adversity. Walcott did not come from wealth; he had lost his father when he was very young and never finished high school. But he taught himself enough about fossils to become a professional collector. And how he had risen in paleontology! Besides being the Assistant Secretary of the National Museum, he was also a member of the U.S. Geological Survey, of which, shortly after our dealings at the Smithsonian Institution, he would become director, a post he would hold until becoming the Smithsonian's current Secretary. He was happily married, but he had lost his first wife in the bloom of their marriage. I could not imagine what it would have been like to lose Maggie when we were just starting our family. Nor was I born into wealth, but into a middle-class family in Abingdon, Virginia. The outbreak of war, however, would ruin us. After

Emancipation, I ran away to join the Third Tennessee Mounted Infantry. I was fifteen and full of fire. My heart told me I should fight to protect my birthright, though I ought to have listened to my head and stayed home to help my parents during that tumultuous time. I will never know whether staying would have changed anything. I am not ashamed to tell you that I was scared upon finding myself in battle. I did not want to die; nor did I want to suffer terrible pain, as I had heard so many young men did. But I was neither killed nor injured when some of my regiment was captured at Bull's Gap. I handed my rifle over and was taken to a Union prison, but was released because I was no more than an unarmed boy. I rejoined my regiment and was captured and released yet again! The second time, I returned to Abingdon and found that my family's general store had collapsed. Situated as it was on the Virginia and Tennessee railroad, the store supplied many plantations and mining companies; when those enterprises began to fail under Emancipation, the general store followed suit. My father yielded to the great weight of it and put a revolver to his head. (A uniquely human solution, is it not? Imagining a future in which death is preferable to life. I don't think any other animal ever opts for taking its own life.) My mother liquidated his estate to pay off debts, then moved north. Rather than remain in poverty and despair in Abingdon, I set out on my own and completed my education.

I admired Walcott and believed he admired me. But even if I were unequivocally correct, what I had in mind for my continued study of the chimpanzee tongue required an investment I was not sure he was willing or able to give.

We spoke one fall night in the museum, a mounted chimpanzee skeleton hanging between us, our earnest study over for the night.

"I'm afraid you know what I've been working toward asking you," I said.

"And I'm afraid I can't stop you from asking."

"It's the next logical step. I've exhausted the captive supply. To prove the presence of language in the chimpanzee—to offer proofs of evolution—I must go to Africa."

"I agree. But Langley doesn't like controversy. If your work weren't so well known, I might be able to do something for you."

"You delayed me because I hadn't published; now I've published too much?"

"I'm not sure engaging Samuel McClure's services was the wisest choice. Thanks to him, the public is convinced that you talk to monkeys. And the scientific community has no doubt that you believe your research is indisputable proof of evolution. Neither of which please Langley. He won't be any part of it."

"There's a book in the works that should clarify things."

"That's wonderful. But I'm afraid it doesn't change the current state of things."

I fingered the chimpanzee's jaw.

"I'm not expecting the Smithsonian to fully fund an expedition. I have written to Mr. Edison regarding my work with his invention, and I expect he will provide me with a superb phonograph. And I expect to secure some loans."

I explained to Walcott that I planned to take out a large life insurance policy and name all of my backers as beneficiaries. Should I perish in Africa, they would all profit. Should I return, the publications and lectures that would follow would easily allow me to repay the loans.

"That's quite a scheme," Walcott said. "I suppose McClure is in on it?"

"He's going in for the biggest share."

That winter, I visited Mr. McClure in New York to discuss the publication of my first book. I had expected McClure's offices to be a storm of stenographers and telegraphers, but I instead found a small suite of rooms in the Morse Building, a dignified foil to the *Tribune*'s massive office across the street. In the suite's main room, I was welcomed by the bespectacled office manager, Mr. Phillips, and two ladies,

Mrs. McClure and Ms. Roseboro. Mrs. McClure escorted me to her husband's door; we found him holding up a finger to stay us as he finished reading the manuscript in his hand.

"Who is this, Dear?" asked McClure.

"Professor Garner."

"Come in, Professor! We've been expecting you!"

I sat down and was treated to a flurry of questions about the train and whether I had brought a phonograph and when did I think I was headed to Africa. I answered respectfully but quickly, as I was far more interested in what McClure could tell me. I had to bear many of the man's pet stories before he returned to the subject of my work: He had, as a boy growing up in Ireland, been first impressed by the power of the press by the impact of the news of Lincoln's assassination on a gathering of men in his village's general store. Later, he came to love literature by way of the short stories and serialized novels that appeared in the newspapers he read while attending high school in Indiana. He said he judged tales not with his mind, but with his solar plexus. That was the test, he claimed, for the stories he selected for syndication: Did it pull on something inside of him? He urged this test in his wife, who from the syndicate's start had been her husband's greatest supporter, and the rest of his small staff. My work with primates, though scientific rather than literary, had had the right effect upon McClure.

The sudden movements of McClure's excitable face sent his eyeglasses jumping up the bridge of his nose and held the tuft of hair atop his forehead at attention as if it were electrified. He kept an intense focus on me, though his eyes betrayed the hatching of plots in his quick mind.

"You're an enthusiast, Richard."

"An enthusiast?"

"Yes. In your mind, you're already in Africa. Your mind is fixed upon that end so firmly that, for you, the future is the present."

"I have felt for many months that I will find my way there one way or another. Though I am still unsure exactly how it will come about. But, yes, I do feel as if my course is already decided—as if I were setting foot in Africa tomorrow."

"You know who were great enthusiasts? The abolitionists."

"Abolitionists? I'm certain I don't follow the comparison."

"You see, their aims must have felt impossible, but they ignored those feelings and persevered until they were successful. You may be just as impractical in your own way—yet your impracticality is your strength!"

He then permitted me a few questions regarding the publication of a book and answered that if we met the publisher's deadline, I could expect to see it in the early part of the coming year.

"*The Speech of Monkeys,*" he said. "Those four words will leave no doubt in the public's mind of your thesis."

The prospect of my work coming to fruition in a book that would enlighten men of modern sensibilities about our primate relatives—and disrupt the dogmatic thinking of our less-enlightened brothers!—elated me. I relaxed in my chair and smiled at McClure. The publishing man, however, deflected my smile with a lowering of his great brow.

"You're not as young as I imagined you, Professor."

"I have had a long career already as a teacher."

"Are you sure you're up for the task? Africa, I mean?"

"I'm certain of it."

"And your family?"

"My son is nearly grown. And my wife will not be joining me. Not yet, anyway."

"Equatorial Africa." McClure shook his head; whether gorillas or elephants or cannibals treaded through his mind, I did not inquire. "Probably for the best. Did you read Stevenson's South Sea letters?"

"Yes, from time to time. Those were wonderful stories."

"Stevenson was to return from his travels and conduct a lecture tour. Like you, he was going to take a phonograph. His lectures would be enhanced by the sounds of the seas crashing against the shores and the peoples speaking and singing in their native tongues." McClure paused and gazed at something upon his desk—though I believe his concentration was trained on the object of his mind's eye: Stevenson aboard his yacht, sailing toward his Pacific adventures. "I invested quite a bit in him."

"I expect to survive," I assured McClure. "And if I don't, you'll profit anyway."

"That's true. But I'd rather be your agent than your beneficiary. In the long run, you're worth more to me alive than dead!"

Mr. McClure promised to whip up a storm of promotion. He imagined that early sales of my book, along with my life insurance scheme, would get me to Africa. For the expedition to be a success, I was still depending upon Mr. Walcott to pull through for me with some Smithsonian dollars and Mr. Edison to provide a phonograph.

My itinerary in New York included a visit to the Central Park Zoo. Walcott had allowed me to bring the phonograph to record capuchins, a species I had not yet studied. McClure, never one to miss an opportunity for promotion, invited a writer from *Harper's Weekly* to report on my visit. The story would prove a great teaser for my African adventure, McClure had said. And, in what I considered a rare misstep on the publishing man's part, he also invited a palmist to take part in the proceedings.

The Central Park Zoo is truly a menagerie rather than a zoological garden; its creatures are confined in small pens and cages, arranged with little regard to design, set against the Arsenal, an imposing brick block. Today, the menagerie's cages and grounds are in such a state of decay that it shrinks in the shadow of its elegant sibling, Mr. Hornaday's Bronx Zoo, and it was not in much better shape in 1891. The reek of dung rivaled that of the Department of Living Animals.

In front of the Arsenal was a large hall with twin chimneys and multiple dormers; it was this structure that invited all classes of New Yorkers to the grounds. The front of the hall was lined with cages of steel bars, and it was inside one of these cages where the monkeys I sought lived. It being early and cold and wet from a recent snow, there were scant visitors; my trek across the slippery walk toward the cage was noted by only the assembled animals. A giant polar bear lumbered around his pool. A double-humped camel raised his lazy eyes at the hurried visitor. I was stopped by only one animal: A small building on one side of the hall was marked by doors of an unusual width and height, and from one of these emerged a great elephant. He was marked by his sloping forehead and straight tusks as one of Africa's forest elephants. No fence lay between us. No keeper was in sight. Even as I feared a proper skewering, I was pulled toward the beast. When the great elephant took a couple of long strides, it was revealed that one of his ankles was bound by a heavy chain attached to the elephant house. Reassured of relative safety, I slowly approached him. Up close, his hide resembled a beech tree; upon reaching out and stroking it, I found it to be bristling. Alive. Africa thrummed under his flesh. I closed my eyes and was transported there. In a jungle dense on all sides, gnarled roots below, sun-flecked canopy above, thick trunks on either hand, a path was cut through; to my back lay my past, ahead lay my future, and I knew without hesitation which way to march. The elephant, used to human contact as he was, did not even flinch at my touch. His trunk searched among the dirt for the hay his keepers had spread. If he regarded me at all, it was with tolerant indifference.

I conducted experiments with the zoo's capuchins over a period of several mornings, capturing speech that was vital to the completion of my book. The reporter, accompanied by an illustrator, and the palmist appeared on the second morning. The reporter was kind enough to limit his intrusions to moments between experiments, and the illustrator worked so quietly I forgot about him. The palmist, a young man whose close-cropped hair and mustache and curious way of speaking did not easily give up his race, was a constant nuisance, as he frequently would begin cooing to the monkeys as soon as I started turning the phonograph's crank.

Finally, I invited him to enter the capuchins' cage with me and do whatever McClure had sent him there to do.

To his credit, he joined me inside the enclosure without hesitation. He squatted and invited a monkey to sit before him. The white of the monkey—his head and shoulders—seemed to relax on his dark body. The palmist gently took the monkey's miniature black hand and began an examination of the palm. What on Earth did he expect to learn? He began whispering to the monkey. At first, I could not understand what he was saying, but it soon became clear he was telling the monkey its fortune! Did this carnival freak expect he could close the circle between species that easily? He didn't even ask for my assistance as an interpreter—though if he had I would have laughed in his swarthy face! He was encouraged by the way the little black cap upon the monkey's head shifted, suggesting the creature's interest in whatever ridiculous things the fool was saying. But the monkey quickly grew bored with the exercise and jumped away. The palmist took this opportunity to describe to me some information about the contours of the monkey's palm and its similarity to our own palms. I saw the reporter writing in his notebook. This was regrettable. Before the palmist left, he read the fortunes of two other monkeys. They would enjoy a long life in the Central Park Zoo; there was someone in Africa whom they each dearly missed, but their loved ones were safe in the jungle. This was remarkable; I had thought capuchins were a South American monkey!

Upon leaving the enclosure, the palmist thanked me for allowing him to read the first ever monkey fortune.

"They seem to have enjoyed it," I said. "And I think they believe in their fortunes as much as I do!"

I returned to Washington to enjoy the holidays with Maggie and Harry. First, however, I visited Mr. Walcott's office to return the phonograph. Walcott asked me to sit down, for he had good news.

"Secretary Langley is permitting me to provide you with some funding."

"That's wonderful!"

"It's not as much as you had hoped."

"Anything at all will help."

"You will have to acquire a phonograph on your own."

"I'm sure Mr. Edison will come through."

"And you will have to bring back more than cylinders to satisfy Langley. Some specimens for the museum. Maybe a live one for the zoo. Langley and Hornaday have locked horns over the proposed zoo. Perhaps your delivering an ape will be a welcome distraction."

"I shall not disappoint."

In my brief absence, Maggie had suffused our home with Christmas spirit: the sweet and savory smells of apple pie and ham; candlelight twinkling in every room; Harry had put up a tree. It had long been Maggie's insistence that we enjoy the holiday time, for I always had a break from teaching, and, she argued, all children deserve a Christmas. Every Christmas Eve, she took Harry to a service at a Methodist church, for that was the denomination she and I were raised in, though I had long ago rejected it as superstitious nonsense. I know that as a boy Harry enjoyed the spectacle of the service. I suspected that for at least that one day he held the man on the cross in some reverent light. Though he was in his last year of secondary school—practically a man!—he still indulged in Christmastime, and I did not doubt he and his mother would be attending a service.

I found them in the kitchen. I went to Maggie and kissed her.

"Oh, Richard, I missed you." She held me in a long, warming embrace.

"I was barely gone," I insisted, pulling away.

"Welcome home," Harry said.

I shook Harry's hand and complimented him on the fine tree.

"How was New York?" he inquired.

"Dreadful, actually. The buildings are so tall as to never admit the sun, and the streets between them are clogged with humans of every stripe. The smell of horse dung is tenfold what it is in our own city."

"That I can scarcely believe," said Maggie.

As we enjoyed our dinner, I told them about my meeting with the excitable publishing man and the odd palmist who had purported to read monkeys' fortunes. Maggie was genuinely excited to hear the news that Mr. McClure was making an author out of me.

"Your students should feel lucky to have a teacher who's published his very own book."

"My students! My book is meant to resonate with the world's naturalists, not with schoolchildren. I expect it will fall upon the scientific community with a crash!"

"You really think so?" Harry's tone was optimistic, as if he looked forward to being proud of my accomplishments, but I still took his question as an opportunity to expound upon my proposal.

"Primates speak. Their speech is lower, of course, than even the lowest humans, but I have no doubt of my claim. And Edison's phonograph can be applied to the study of their speech. I don't wish to appear immodest, but this is an insight that cannot be dismissed."

"It does seem extraordinary," Harry said.

"And McClure predicts it will support my studying wild apes."

For a moment Maggie and Harry were silent.

"Wild?" Harry asked.

"Yes. In Africa."

On Christmas Eve, Maggie and Harry went to a service, and I, as always, politely refused their invitation. It was fortuitous that I did, for that day the mail carrier delivered the *Harper's Weekly* with my profile. I set aside the manuscript pages I had been proofreading to see the public's newest picture of me and my work.

That evening, Harry retired to his bedroom to read, and Maggie and I sat in the den drinking egg nog. The *Harper's Weekly* lay on her lap. She could not hide her anxiety over Mr. McClure's prediction that my book should get me to Africa: Her emerald eyes and delicate hands would not settle. Finally she made her mind known.

"You don't really intend to go through with this, do you? Please tell me it's all just talk."

"It's not just talk, Dear. I fully intend to go through with this."

The illustrator, besides portraying me recording the capuchins in Central Park, had ventured to draw me sitting inside a cage of steel bars pointing a phonograph toward a gorilla twice my size, while another approached from the rear of the cage. In the distance, an elephant raised its trunk, thrusting his tusks like great spears.

"Go anywhere you like to look at monkeys in zoos, take as long as you need—but Africa? You'd be away for such a long time—and it sounds terribly dangerous."

"Where I plan to go is a French colony. A place to holiday, for heaven's sake. I'll take you there sometime."

"A holiday in the jungle?"

"As for when I'm in the jungle, I'll be protected by the cage I'm going to build."

"But you'll have to get there and build it first. You could get yourself killed. I'm tempted to pray that your friends at the Smithsonian will keep their purse strings tight. I'm sorry—but that's just how I feel."

"I am afraid it's too late for that."

"Oh, Richard!"

"Surely you recognize the importance of my work? Would you have me hand it over to some other scientist?"

"We never asked you to become a great scientist."

Chapter Three

When Mr. Hornaday questioned my mettle for Equatorial Africa, he did not take into consideration the great test of merely arriving! Tendering my resignation—against Maggie's strong wishes—and bidding goodbye to my family were only the first hardships. Maggie and Harry accompanied me to the train station, and after giving my son a firm handshake and asking that he take care of his mother in my absence, I spoke to my wife in what privacy the bustle of the station allowed. "My Dear, you must know that I know that embarking on this journey means sacrificing the blessings of the home you so lovingly make for privations the likes of which I cannot yet fully appreciate. But I must endure this sacrifice if I'm to bring the world proofs of evolution. Don't think of my course as leaving you, but of going toward my destiny." Maggie's pleading, pathetic eyes did not soften, did not express admiration at my speech, but only deadened, their green fading to gray. I embraced her and kissed her. "I promise I'll return."

I boarded my carriage for the first of many privations: a train to New York; an ocean liner to Liverpool; further trains to Edinburgh and London. My supplies remained in storage—at an exorbitant cost—so I had only some tobacco and a few copies of *The Speech of Monkeys* with which to pass the time. Many times I opened my book to the dedication page, where I had, at some length, honored Maggie. I hoped she would find some succor in it. As for me, my senses were wrought bare by all manner of Yankee and English dialects and an unchanging gray landscape. Would that I could not stop and continue for Gabon, for the soft, primitive tongues of the natives and the soothing, lush palette of the jungle; for the Eden where I would live among the apes! But I had business in Edinburgh and London before returning to Liverpool to board the ocean liner that would take me to my destination.

Upon learning of my African expedition, the British Association for the Advancement of Science invited me to give a lecture at their annual meeting in Edinburgh. I admit to feeling a bit overwhelmed upon entering the main hall and seeing the swarm of distinguished gentlemen, but shortly after I had handed my coat and hat off, I was warmly greeted by one of the association's council members, the naturalist Professor Snowe. Snowe was a slight, bespectacled gentleman several years my senior. His deferential smile and pleasant tones quickly earned my trust.

"I have a strong interest in apes, as well," Snowe informed me, "and look forward to what you report from Africa."

"Thank you, Professor. And I look forward to sharing my recent work in America and my objectives for Africa."

Snowe then introduced me to Professor Conwy Lloyd Morgan. The longest beard I had ever seen on a man of my age distinguished Morgan. His mouth lay hidden behind it—but rather than diminishing him, this feature exaggerated the visible portion of his face, his dark eyes and strong nose, granting him authority before he even spoke. When his beard parted and his deep voice emerged, his power increased.

I noticed in the meeting's program that I was scheduled to present my lecture in two days.

"Professor Snowe, I am afraid I have business in London on the morning I am scheduled."

"That is such a shame, Professor Garner," said Morgan. "I was looking forward to your lecture on simian speech."

"Surely we can rearrange the schedule so that I may present this afternoon or tomorrow?"

Snowe's quick mouth moved anxiously. "Let me confer with the council, Professor."

While I awaited the council's decision, I attended several zoological lectures. Though the social habits of spiders were nothing of great interest to me, it was exhilarating to be present among the learned men of the association. Between lectures, I became acquainted with many fine naturalists—though I want to qualify that statement: They were fine observers and thinkers, but they owed a great debt to the men who collected the specimens they studied. Yet the collectors were merely footnotes—if even that—in their lectures. When these armchair scientists wished me well on my African expedition, I was bitten by the feeling I was being humored. Why, they must have wondered, had I not engaged someone else to sit in the jungle and crank a phonograph?

The only lecture worth mentioning here was Morgan's. In his lecture on comparative psychology, he laid down a new law, which at first seemed quite reasonable, as it suggested a method for achieving truths about animal behavior between Professor Muller's claim that language was a threshold animals would never cross and Professor Romanes' claims about the richness of animal minds. Morgan's law suggested the kind of thorough experimentation and observation of which I saw myself a practitioner. He claimed that naturalists must be careful observers of both animal behavior and of their own mental processes; great care must be taken in interpreting their observations. I was fully with the professor until he reached his conclusion.

"Animal behavior should never be interpreted as the outcome of a higher mental faculty if a lower mental faculty will account for said behavior. The professional scientist should never conclude that he is seeing in an animal's behavior *reason*, when trial-end-error offers a satisfactory explanation. Nor should anyone read anything concrete or abstract in an animal's vocalizations, when an involuntary cry of emotion suffices as explanation."

My estimation of Morgan and his law collapsed as I felt this last statement to be pointed at me. Among the claims I had expressed in my work were that apes and monkeys made sounds that were quite voluntary and that all voluntary sounds were the products of reason. It required great will power not to stand up and defend myself.

Instead, I retreated to the main hall to regain my composure.

In a moment the empty hall would fill as the crowd from Morgan's lecture spilled into it. Smug fools. I was at least happy to see Snowe—until I registered his regretful countenance.

I inquired as to what he and the council could do.

"I'm afraid it's quite out of the ordinary. Surely you can extend your stay one day?"

"I have very important business in London. The acquisition of a phonograph and the recording of apes in Regent's Park. And I really can't postpone those, for then I must return to Liverpool to board my ship for Africa."

"It seems you have overscheduled yourself, Professor," said Morgan in passing.

"I can leave a manuscript of my speech for a proxy to read at the already appointed time," I suggested.

"I regret that's just not done, Professor," said Snowe. He looked at me with great sincerity. "I wish there were something I could do. I truly do, Professor."

I stayed my tongue again—I literally bit down on it. I presumed that Snowe was behind my invitation, but now he—and perhaps the entire BAAS—seemed to be under the sway of Morgan's buried lips. They struck me then as a league of weak-willed armchair scientists to whom I owed nothing. I left the meeting to go to London the next morning.

The following day, I had a meeting with Mr. Henry Labouchere, publisher of the English journal *Truth*. I had at that time no reason to regard the publisher with any suspicion, nor do I believe Mr. McClure had any inkling of the trouble he was setting me up for. Labouchere, upon welcoming me to his offices, seemed a dignified man of letters; he was a few years my senior and a head taller; his long beard was turning a nearly transparent gray. As befit his stateliness, his voice commanded his listener's respect, though, curiously, his every inquiry concluded with an extended note, which instilled in me the first anxiety over his intentions.

"DuChaillu discovered the gorilla. Hatton and Cookson have brought us palm oil and ivory. What do you believe there remains to discover in western Africa?"

"My thesis, which is made clear in *The Speech of Monkeys*, is that monkeys and apes have their own languages. Those species of a lower order, say, the spider monkey, have only the most rudimentary speech. Those of a higher order, like our close relative the chimpanzee, have a more complex language. It is that language I intend to study in the wilds of Gabon."

"By what means will you study wild chimpanzees?"

"The construction of a cage deep inside the jungle, where I can observe them in relative safety."

"Relative safety?"

"The cage should protect me from most of the jungle's threats."

"Gorillas?"

"And leopards. Only a charging elephant could dismantle the cage."

"And its occupant?"

"I suppose so!" McClure had urged me not to shy away from the threat of danger in interviews. "And I plan to record chimpanzee speech for study using a phonograph."

"Very interesting. Supposing you are able to prove your thesis—there are implications for our knowledge of man. What will you say?"

"That evolution is indisputable. That men evolved like other primates. That there once existed a species from which men and apes diverged."

"Those are bold claims, Professor. I will be very interested in your experiences in Africa. I am sure there will be many eyes on you."

Having not the goodwill of Secretary Langley to borrow the Smithsonian's phonograph for an extended period, nor a timely reply to my inquiry to Mr. Edison for his sponsorship, my next objective in London was to acquire an instrument from the Edison-Bell Phonograph Company. I expected no trouble in the matter, as Edison had been so enthusiastic about my work. But upon my arrival, the manager, Mr. Moriarty, claimed to know nothing of Edison's promise to supply me with a phonograph.

"Then telegraph him at once," I demanded. "Tell him Professor Garner is in London awaiting the promised instrument."

"I shall do no such thing."

Moriarty must have been roughly my contemporary, but his face seemed folded many times over in pain, and his words came out as befitted such a monstrous countenance.

There was not a phonograph in sight, though the top of an oak case, its handle in need of repair, sat on his desk like a paperweight, enticing me.

"Perhaps you do not understand. I am Professor Richard Garner. The primatologist."

"I know who you are. But current sentiment toward your experiments with monkeys do not give you license to walk into my office and demand a phonograph."

"I am not demanding a phonograph based on my social currency, but on the promise of Mr. Edison himself."

"I am aware of no such promise. I will, however, accept actual currency."

I stormed from Moriarty and telegraphed Edison—a telegram that, for unexplained reasons, never earned a reply. I sought additional funds from Mr. Walcott, but was rebuffed. Mrs. McClure also informed me that she and her husband could not advance me the funds. I had no choice but to return to Moriarty with a more solicitous approach, which I did the following afternoon.

"Perhaps there has been a misunderstanding," I said. "I am sure Mr. Edison intends to reimburse you the cost of the phonograph and cylinders."

Moriarty was silent. The creases in his face did not soften.

"You may bill the Smithsonian."

"No."

"Samuel McClure."

"No."

"I will pay you myself when funds allow."

"I do not give out phonographs on credit."

I leaned into Moriarty, conspiratorially.

"There are orangutans in Regent's Park whom I plan to record before departing for Africa." I whispered, "Give me a phonograph on credit, and I'll allow you to join me for this research. To bear witness to scientific history in the making."

Moriarty whispered back, "I may go to Regent's Park any day I please to hear monkeys babble."

"Fine! I'll demand that the Smithsonian pay you and await the phonograph's arrival in

Gabon. And orangutans are *apes*, not monkeys!"

I could afford neither the time nor the anxiety of waiting around my hotel for the phonograph situation to change, so I visited Regent's Park with a new series of experiments to conduct with the orangutans.

Hornaday's orangutans! Upon seeing Regent's Park's pair of apes, I was drawn back to my reading of Mr. Hornaday's adventures in Borneo; I had been thrilled by his tale of tracking the apes deep into the wild, eyes trained upon the trees where he sighted the orange men of the forest ever so briefly before their escape into the foliage, until finally coming close enough to take a shot. That I would soon be tracking the orangutan's African cousins, joining myself to Hornaday and DuChaillu, made my spine crackle. Though the only thing I planned to aim at the apes was a phonograph's horn!

In London's zoo, I would have to settle for viewing orangutans in the most artificial conditions I had yet seen apes or monkeys. Fearing that those animals from the tropics would perish of chills in the English atmosphere, the zookeepers kept them in rooms with no access to the outdoors. No steel bars or lattice allowed the animals to breathe fresh air, or the sun to

kiss their faces. The orangutans' room was constructed with few windows—and small, I suppose so they would not admit an orangutan's
passage should he break the glass—and appointed with few branches for climbing. I
pitied the apes.

Then I marveled that I might be in the very
room in which Mr. Darwin had first encountered our ape cousins half a century ago.
Shortly after his voyage on the *Beagle*, at the
start of those two decades over which he would
labor on his theory, Darwin had paid visits to a
pair of young orangutans, Jenny and Tommy.
My observations of chimpanzees—as well as
what I would soon observe about the orangutan—mirrored Darwin's experience with
these apes. When Jenny was denied an apple,
her tantrum and subsequent sulkiness were
recognizably human; when she was spoken
to—told to quit sulking and she would be rewarded with the apple—she complied. (Obviously, she inferred the command, Darwin
speaking our language and Jenny possessing
her own.) How the encounters must have encouraged the young scientist in his revolutionary thinking!

I selected for my subject the orangutan Jim.
This little red fellow was estimated to be about
five years of age, and had not yet developed the
large cheek pads and throat sack that his more
mature cage mate exhibited. While the older

orangutan brooded in the upper parts of the branches, Jim swung down to me and engaged with my experiments as if he too needed something with which to occupy himself while waiting on an important turn of events. His acrobatic grace in the branches was lost upon his reaching ground level, where his awkward gait more closely matched his simple countenance.

Jim proved to possess the mental abilities of a human infant, insofar as he could succeed at the tasks I set him to, which might, for example, aim to determine his ability to discern quantity. I had on other occasions given a primate three marbles to play with, and after several minutes, placed two of the marbles inside a box with a hole just large enough for them to insert one hand; the other marble I used sleight of hand to hide in my vest pocket. The animal would then reach inside three times, the first two times retrieving a marble, and the third time searching anxiously before giving up and satisfying himself by playing with the pair of marbles in his possession. I saw no other conclusion than that the animal could count at least as high as three.

Jim was immediately successful at this counting experiment. Then he did something I had never before seen: He returned a marble to the box, as if it could find its wayward brother!

"Very good, little fellow!"

The experiments supported my claim that monkeys and apes were in a state of evolution that the branches of men had once been chained in. They possess the cognitive faculties—the raw materials—that civilized man possesses in the highest state of development.

Jim and I worked together for two mornings. I had found by that time that you cannot wait until a zoo has opened to the public to study its primates; a scientist cannot concentrate due to the constant interruptions, and the primates are turned resentful of all humans by the actions of only a few peanut-throwing idiots. After running through all my experiments, I returned for an additional morning—still without a phonograph—just to listen to Jim speak. What little he had said during the previous mornings I had not tried to record in written form, for that usually proved to be a useless exercise. On this final day, I tried to coax more speech out of him with the only thing in my trunk that I had not brought to the park: my banjo, Pearl. It had never occurred to me to try this with any of the primates I had visited in American zoos, but I had packed the instrument in my trunks bound for Africa to see what its effects might be on wild apes.

I seated myself on a concrete bench and began to pluck out "Swanee River." Is there truly any sweeter sound? Childlike Jim swung down to investigate. He stared at the instrument for a moment before slowly reaching out to touch its neck. This disturbed my playing, which I did not mind terribly; when he let his brown fingers up, I resumed. I am not much of a singer, but I did not think Jim would mind if I sang a little to him. I think he rather enjoyed it. "Is your heart weary, too, for home?" I asked him. I began to pluck out and sing the final verse, Jim occasionally muting the banjo with his fingers, which he seemed to enjoy—so much so that I began to laugh.

My laughter was broken by the screams of a dozen of the orange men. Above us, the elder orangutan had erupted in a piercing shriek. His awful, echoing cry was matched in fierceness by the bared teeth that threatened me from between his great cheeks.

Jim retreated into the branches. I returned my banjo to its case and retreated myself—and carried that terrible, foreboding scream all the way to Africa.

Chapter Four

Gabon! After more than a month at sea, the ocean liner brought its passengers within view of the majestic African coast: A paradise of beaches kissed the Atlantic; a backdrop of thick jungle thrilled those who, like me, were seeing the mysterious continent for the first time.

The first sign of civilization appeared as the ship arrived in the port of the capital city, Libreville. Several plain buildings sat behind the beach there, many of which were several decades old, as white men had long traded with the coastal Mpongwe tribe. Among the tribe's exports were slaves captured in the interior—a practice that had gone on since the first Europeans landed on the coast centuries ago. The French, however, had outlawed slavery in their colony in 1848. Unscrupulous Europeans had continued the practice with the all-too-willing Mpongwe until a year later, when a French ship intercepted a vessel loaded with slaves. It was these slaves who, upon their liberation, founded the "city of the free."

Forty years later, Libreville was a city of some eight thousand residents, a blend of French bureaucrats, English and European traders, and the Africans who lived and worked among them and generally adopted their white neighbors' dress and manners. Behind the old buildings of the original trading post were newer structures, clearly French in design. But in keeping with the primitive continent on which they were built, they were unostentatious: The architects had shown restraint in the size and intricacy of the pediments and cornices. I would find the architecture reflected the commissaire's attitude toward Africa.

Commissaire Brazza welcomed me to the colony. While a team of African porters stored the crates that contained the materials from which my cage would be constructed and my other supplies, Brazza invited me to join him and another guest, the French naturalist Alfred Marche, to dine at his home.

The commissaire's home was, of course, the grandest of the newer structures. Brazza, who was unmarried at this time, had appointed the place sparsely, though; the large foyer contained only a side table decorated with a single wooden statue of a man in a loin cloth and a headdress. A sitting room into which I peeked contained several bookshelves and a few fine lamps, but only one tribal piece, an oval wooden mask with a semi-circular headdress and miniature shoulders and arms extending from it, hung upon a wall. The dining room also contained only one piece, too; the female version of the statue in the foyer glimmered in the sunlight streaming in from the wide windows on the west side of the home. I speculated that each room was, in Brazza's mind, protected by a single African charm. But surely Brazza had been given hundreds or thousands of such gifts by the peoples he had befriended. I wondered whether there existed a museum's worth of items in a cellar. If I were a superstitious man, I would wonder if the pieces in such a collection would pool their powers to ensure Brazza's longevity, or if they might, like their respective tribes sometimes do, find themselves at war and deliver the commissaire his doom.

I should have been in awe in Brazza's company, for he, like Du Chaillu, was a storied African explorer, but he had such a calm demeanor that it inspired ease in everyone in his company—even the vervet that perched upon Marche's shoulder throughout the meeting. His appearance was a striking collection of paradoxes, beginning with his habit of going about barefooted, yet dressed in a finely tailored white linen suit. He was tall, yet gentle; bearded, yet boyish. And though he possessed more knowledge about Equatorial Africa than most men, he was endlessly curious about what secrets it might yet yield.

"Where does your itinerary take you, Professor?" Brazza asked. In another paradox, his voice instilled confidence in his listeners, even as his speech stumbled between Italian and French accents.

"Cape Lopez, then the Lake Nkomi region."

"Ah, the Nkomi tribes." Brazza smiled wistfully, as if recalling some pleasant encounter with those peoples. "You are also likely to find yourself among the Fangs. Do not let their name—or appearance—frighten you."

"I'm grateful for your work befriending the tribes of the interior. My work would be quite difficult without your diplomatic efforts."

Brazza's approach to colonizing Equatorial Africa was to befriend each tribe as he traveled deeper into the interior by way of the Ogowe River. He celebrated his new friendships with fireworks as he won the western side of the Congo for France, while Henry Morton Stanley dynamited his road through the eastern side in taking it for Belgium. When Brazza's expedition did occasionally turn deadly, it was due to long-standing tribal conflicts or the deprivations his men suffered from such a long time in the tropics. Violence, for Brazza, was to be avoided at all costs; for Stanley, it was routine.

"Diplomatic efforts," huffed Marche. "I had nearly forgotten about all that."

The handsome Marche exuded authority even as he spoke under his breath. He had been a member of Brazza's first journey into Africa, an often brutal three-year affair.

"Be glad the commissaire's not joining you," Marche said. "For he would have you stare at the same river bank for two months while he became best friends with every man in the local village. As if learning the names of every man's wives and children were a prerequisite for planting the Tricolour! What was your philosophy, Pierre? If you tread lightly enough in the African's affairs, he won't notice he's being conquered? Oh—and he would interrupt your work to play emancipator!"

"But slavery has long been outlawed here," I said.

"It is not like in the United States," Marche said. "Though America's Great Emancipator was murdered, the rule of law ensures the freedom of its former slaves. At least it's supposed to. Gabon's emancipator enjoys life in Libreville, but his brutish subjects still enslave each other!"

"Gabon is a peaceful colony, mutually beneficial to its white and Black inhabitants," Brazza said. "Should you witness slavery here, it would be an anomaly. If you want to see institutionalized slavery, go east to King Leopold's Congo."

"Yes, yes," Marche laughed. "Were you to believe the rumors, every Black man in the Congo Free State has had his hands lopped off for insubordination!"

"Time will bear out that conqueror's atrocities."

Marche laughed; I gave him an inquiring look.

"You see, Professor, what the commissaire won't admit is that every white man in Africa is a conqueror."

I could not believe the cheek with which Marche treated Brazza; Marche was a fine naturalist—he'd spent recent years in the Marianas discovering new species of birds and a curious mammal he called the stink badger—but his host was an officer of the French Navy and the commissaire of a large colony. The naturalist clearly harbored ill feelings from the Ogowe River expedition of over a decade prior.

"Perhaps you would be interested in the work I intend to carry out in Gabon," I said to Marche.

"I understand your work is listening to monkeys talk," he said.

"My objective is to study the languages of apes. Chimpanzees, specifically."

Marche reached into a bowl of dates, taking a few for himself and tossing one back to his monkey.

"You really believe they possess the faculty of language?"

"Absolutely. I've observed several primate species in America's best zoos, and unless their keepers are extremely clever teachers, I believe that they have languages of their own."

Upon Marche's vervet squealing something from his shoulder, Marche asked, "What's he saying?"

"That he absolutely agrees with me."

Marche laughed. "I'm sorry, Professor, but it's hard to swallow. I've seen many of these animals in the wild, and I've never had any reason to suspect that their grunts and howls are anything more than ways of gaining each other's attention or giving warning. Purely emotional. I've never heard two chimps converse like you and I."

"I'm sure you haven't. But with all due respect, I believe there is more to the apes' speech than you suggest."

"Do you care to weigh in, Pierre? I believe you're the only one present who's had a monkey named after him."

Brazza smiled as he shook his head no.

"I did not discover the DeBrazza Monkey," Brazza informed me. "It was simply named in my honor. I have no theories regarding whether they or their cousins talk to one another. You men are the scientists."

"Well, Professor, I wish you luck in your continued endeavors with Mr. Edison's invention. Would you mind if I took a look at the machine?"

Marche's query preceded the longest pause in the evening's conversations. Brazza interrupted the silence with a non sequitur that proved to be the best piece of advice I would receive on my expedition.

"I will pass onto you these words of Dr. Livingstone: If a man goes with a good-natured, civil tongue, he may pass through the worst people in Africa unharmed."

Commissaire Brazza accompanied me to the custom house, one of the newer structures inside of which I would have one of surprisingly few interactions with French bureaucracy. Upon entering the custom house, we surprised a young Frenchman slouching behind a desk. The bureaucrat abruptly stood at attention and gave Brazza a cursory nod before curtly demanding the manifest of my crates. Brazza and I sat in chairs opposite the desk while the bureaucrat entered notes in an oversized book.

I whispered to Brazza, "I believe he's drunk."

"Investment—of all types—in the colony has been slow."

I expected the contents of the manifest—namely, the materials from which my cage would be constructed—to elicit some curiosity, but upon finishing his notes, the bureaucrat simply said I was to build no permanent structures.

When asked if I had any personal effects, I listed the contents of my trunks, of which only my rifle and revolver warranted a response. I paid the steep fees, feeling a bit like I had been robbed. The bureaucrat dismissed me with a slight upturn of the corners of his thin mouth—an attempt at cordiality.

"I am sure you noticed the absence of a phonograph on my manifest," I said. "I assure you that you will be informed upon its arrival."

"I noticed no such thing."

After satisfying the French authorities on the matter of my two firearms—a useless exercise, given that one would never be fired and the other would go missing—I was led by Commissaire Brazza to the Meridien Hotel. I retired to a well-appointed room and spent the evening studying my maps of the region. My quite-flexible itinerary had me acclimating myself to Gabon's heavy heat in Libreville for a brief time before taking a steamer down the coast to Cape Lopez and then into the Fernan Vaz region; I had settled on exploring the borders of Lake Nkomi.

"You'll find your chimpanzees there," Brazza assured me the next morning at breakfast. We were joined again in his home by Marche and his vervet. "You will also find the hospitality of the Holy Ghost Fathers."

"I beg your pardon?"

"The Holy Ghost Fathers. The missionaries of St. Anne's. When you need respite from the jungle, drop in on them."

"I have provisions for six months. I should not need their hospitality."

"Should you visit them," Marche said, "it would be wise to keep your cards close regarding the nature of your work."

"Are the missionaries troubled by naturalists?"

"Not at all. Missionaries of all stripes fancy themselves naturalists. I understand Father Buleon is quite curious about monkeys and apes. But I doubt he would take kindly to anyone whose purpose is to prove human evolution."

"On this point, I agree with Alfred," Brazza said.

"I understand."

"Sound theory, mind you," Marche continued, "just keep the talk of it between you and your chimps."

"I'm beginning to think you don't take my work here seriously."

"I've read your book. Your use of the phonograph to document the utterances of primates is impressive. But your work . . . ." Here Marche searched the dining room, exasperated, and his sudden movements sent his vervet jumping across the table and into my lap. His tail flitted about like a snake—the tail being the last part you can tame.

"Your work isn't scientific."

"How can you suggest such nonsense! I expect such offense from the legions of armchair scientists—like those fools in the BAAS. But not from you, a naturalist who has spent years suffering the deprivations of Africa and the Philippines. Does spending time in the field conducting experiments and publishing the results not qualify one as a scientist?"

"Come off it, man! You claim to be going to the jungle to record apes, but you've got no phonograph! And your doctorate was conferred on you by Samuel McClure!"

The sobriety and ease with which Commissaire Brazza treated all things seemed to subdue all of Libreville; in the middle of the afternoon, I could stand in front of the hotel and hear nothing save the breaking of waves on the beach. The capital was the port through which Europeans came and left the French colonies and attracted a coterie of wealthy tourists, but I suspected the tourists, stifled by the tropical climate, remained in their rooms for much of the time. I believed I would find the real noise and bustle in Gabon's trading center, Cape Lopez.

For a number of days, Brazza detained me in the sleepy capital by constantly forgetting to help me obtain passage for my supplies on a steamer. I am certain this holdup was not intentional. And at first I enjoyed the invitations to his home and the hours of conversation on Equatorial Africa and its peoples. There was much to be gained from the explorer. But at a certain point I became anxious to begin my own explorations.

Finally, Brazza assembled a group of porters to load my materials onto the *Ballay*. He also gave me the name of a man from the English trading company Hatton and Cookson who would be on board, and from whom I could seek information regarding the lake region.

Mr. Marche had left Gabon by this time and did not take his vervet with him, for the little monkey was bouncing across the crates as the porters loaded them onto the steamer. The porters shooed the creature into the arms of a passerby. This passerby caught my attention: His well-formed torso and arms bare, a long cloth skirt tied around his waist, he was a Mpongwe and the first true African I saw. He must have been a guide in the service of one of the traders, and on his own way to Cape Lopez and beyond. He smiled as the vervet crawled across his shoulders. The little monkey seemed pleased as well, having attached himself to a man of familiar coloring. It struck me as the most natural thing, the savage and the monkey playing together—for was not the bridge between men's lowest types and the animal kingdom's highest types but a short one?

The *Ballay* provided more than adequate accommodations and society. My cabin, though narrow, was well furnished, and the meals were of the same quality I had found in the hotel and at Brazza's. On deck, a veritable garden of languages were spoken. The atmosphere was that of a European holiday: Gaily dressed ladies and gentlemen traded stories as the sublime, verdant coast passed by. Upon making my acquaintance, many of these ladies and gentlemen inquired about my experience in Gabon so far. Mr. McClure, by seeing that *The Speech of Monkeys* was published in America and England, had made my expedition a favorite topic of conversation on both sides of the Atlantic before I had even set foot in Africa. "The society here strikes me as very well-read," I exclaimed, garnering much delighted laughter. "But my scientific work will begin in earnest upon reaching Lake Nkomi, where I have it on good authority that chimpanzees are abundant."

When I turned the subject to the trader, Mr. McLaughlin, I was directed to the bar below deck. In contrast to the colorful, sunlit deck, the bar was all muted light and men in khaki. I politely interrupted one of the tables around which the khaki men sat and introduced myself, but earned only a stern report in German that I failed to understand. I asked the barman if he could direct me to McLaughlin. He nodded toward the lone man seated at the bar, a gentleman a few years my junior. I say gentleman because he was wearing a fine wool suit and a sharp bowler, and his mustache was precisely sculpted; one would not place him immediately as a trader. He was still as a cornered animal, but there was subtle movement about him: Fingers of cigar smoke wrapped around his face; the ice in his drink collapsed as it shrunk. The effect was not unlike that of the jungle in darkness: obscure, trembling, foreboding.

I introduced myself and explained that Brazza had recommended I seek his counsel.

"Have a drink?"

As preparation for the ascetic life I faced in the jungle, I had not had a drink since a brandy I enjoyed during my first meeting with Brazza, so I asked for soda water only. McLaughlin was silent as the barman fetched my soda. He did not seem eager to make conversation, so I tried plying him by complimenting his suit.

"You must be a fine trader, indeed. Do you ever trade in primates?"

"I have."

There would come a time when McLaughlin would treat me with forthrightness and not measure out his words with teaspoons. Now was not that time.

"Commissaire Brazza suggested I would find chimpanzees in abundance in the Fernan Vaz region. Do you concur with his conclusion?"

McLaughlin lifted his glass to his lips.

"You do know of which ape I speak?"

"I can recognize a chimp."

"I'm sorry—it's just that confusion about primates isn't uncommon among the lay community."

"You'll find chimps there."

I ventured to ask more of this inscrutable trader. "And what is it that you seek?"

"Gorillas. Though I'm not seeking conversation partners."

I laughed to try winning even more of his confidence.

"I don't expect to be able to converse with the apes—not right away anyhow. I hope with my research to show proofs of evolution."

"A remarkable theory."

"And a highly misunderstood theory. You know, it is not accurate to say we descended from apes; one could just as well say the apes descended from us! We simply share a common ancestor."

"Are you seeking the Missing Link?"

"That is misunderstood as well. There isn't one species that existed between humans and, say, chimpanzees. There were likely many species that descended from our common ancestor, all of them lost forever."

"Misunderstandings aside, it suggests that man wasn't made in the image of God."

"I don't dare presume to know the image of God."

The *Ballay* arrived in Cape Lopez the next morning. After a short visit there, I would board the steamer again and head further down the coast to Lake Nkomi. Upon our departing, McLaughlin suggested, like Commissaire Brazza, that I seek the hospitality of the Catholic missionaries at St. Anne's.

"The jungle is a brutal," he said. "You will appreciate their succor. Though I cannot promise they will appreciate your mission at Fort Gorilla."

Unlike Libreville, which, for all its quietude was Gabon's hub of French officialdom, Cape Lopez was a trading center dominated by English and European traders and native peoples. The houses, inns, and trading posts were plain in style; the beaches and jungles were not so far off as they were in Libreville. The upper reaches of the encroaching jungle scraped the sky; in the spaces between buildings, the jungle floor revealed itself as a shadowy maze, exhilaratingly close. No more did an ocean separate me from my objects of study.

Cape Lopez's inhabitants seemed rather untouched by the colonial government. In fact, there appeared to be no central authorities among either the white or Black peoples there. This lack of centralization conferred kingly power to money and goods. The traders provided the natives with all variety of English and European wares in exchange for ivory, rubber, palm oil, and aid in hunting. From inside a trading post, I witnessed an Englishman attaching a watch to a Fang's cloth skirt. (You can tell a Fang from his teeth, which are sharpened to look like, well, fangs. Brazza had said not to fear these savages, but my nerves pricked like a dog's hackles when I saw those chiseled, animal teeth. It has long been believed that the Fangs are a tribe of cannibals.) The men spoke amiably in the native's primitive tongue, little of which I understood. The trader's well-worn jungle outfit, tanned face, and untended mustache, and his ease with the savage all suggested that he was a veteran of Equatorial Africa. When the Fang left, I asked the Englishman about the deal that had just been brokered. He explained in his sandpaper voice that the

Fang, whose name was Mbye, would be assisting him on a hunt for gorillas.

"Your Smithsonian Institution will pay up to two hundred dollars for such a prize."

There was certainly much to be gained from the study of the skeletons and furs of apes; but if such a premium were placed on those materials, then what price should the voice of an ape command? Secretary Langley obviously didn't think it was nearly two hundred dollars, or else I would have had my phonograph many times over.

The Englishman, whose name was Wolfgang, inquired as to my business in Gabon. I introduced myself and elicited a wry smile from the trader.

"The man who speaks to monkeys! Do you really wish to teach a gorilla to speak?"

"Nothing could be further from the truth."

Wolfgang was very interested in my work and terribly misinformed about my intentions, so we dined together in one of the rude lodges where traders boarded. The brisket and coarse bread and sweet potatoes more closely aligned with the diet I intended to maintain in the jungle than did the fine meals in Libreville, though I was given beer to wash it down before I had an opportunity to refuse. The open windows allowed the fecund breeze to waft across the tables and the flies to orbit our plates. I wished at once to be deep in the jungle in my cage, rather than explaining my plans.

I had straightened Wolfgang out regarding my intentions in Gabon and learned a great deal about the post that was my layover before venturing to the shores of Lake Nkomi. In the decades before the French had colonized the region, trade with the natives had worked in the same manner: From the port that would eventually bear the name Libreville, white traders sold their wares to coastal Africans, who then sold the wares for a profit to a tribe deeper in the interior. Commerce being a language which even the lowest of humans understands, that tribe sold the wares, earning their own profit, to a tribe even deeper in the interior, and so on. The further an African lived from the coast, the more he paid for white men's goods. Ivory, rubber, and palm oil moved in the opposite direction, gaining similar markups, making them quite expensive for white traders. And no tribe dared trespass on a tribe closer to the coast to earn a higher profit; such transgressions of the trade route could result in war. But that had changed.

Wolfgang explained the breakdown of African rule in Gabon with this story: About a decade earlier, just before Brazza was appointed commissaire, a Scottish trader had presented a luxurious armchair to a Nkomi chief. Whether or not it was the Scot's intention, the

Gabonese ruler, King Oyembo Onanga, felt greatly snubbed. Onanga imprisoned the trader in a rude hut in his village. Word of the trader's imprisonment traveled from the chief's village to the French authorities, at which point the colonists forced Onanga to surrender his sovereignty. With the fall of Onanga, it became customary for each tribe to rule itself without regard to a central authority such as the king had been. And Brazza has allowed the tribes to keep sovereignty. Though no one knows what happened to the armchair!

"So we traders started braving the interior and establishing factories—trading posts. Enough adventurers, including Brazza, had visited the interior and lived to tell the tale, so what was holding us back? The tribes there had been paying too much and selling for too little, so they were eager to deal directly with us. And all a trader had to do to gain their trust was to mention Brazza's name!"

The white man, he claimed, still had to deal with the natives on equal terms in Gabon. And though Brazza's name was excellent currency, you had to be careful negotiating with a native. Besides the existence of several tribes, there were countless clans of each, and since the armchair fiasco, each was self-governing. The new system had created competition among them, which could create dangers greater than venom or fever.

"I once paid the council of an Eshira village for the right to hunt on their land, and in the course of my hunting, quite accidentally stepped onto the property of a rival Eshira clan. The rival clan was not open to negotiation; I was relieved of my bounty—including a fine gorilla!—at spearpoint."

"How frightening!"

"It wasn't frightening, really. I was armed to kill gorillas; I could've easily escaped a few Eshiras."

"Then why'd you let them take your goods?"

"Can you imagine the French response if traders started slaughtering natives? Brazza claimed the region for France by befriending the natives, not enslaving and murdering them as the Belgians do on their side of the Congo. He won their trust and keeps it to this day. And we both should pray that Paris doesn't relieve him, as I'm afraid they will."

"Why is that?"

"Brazza is good for the English. Hatton and Cookson, and our rivals, Holt, flourish under Brazza's free trade."

"Why doesn't Brazza give control to French firms? Isn't the point of a colony to enrich the country to which it belongs?"

"That's not Brazza's philosophy. He takes the long view: Develop Gabon and the French Congo, let the free market work, and in time, everyone will flourish: French, English, African. Maybe he's right."

"It certainly benefits you."

"Yes. Because French firms would rather wait for men like me to be thrown out than to compete with us!"

"Are they wrong to wait?"

"Depends on what you mean. They may not be wrong to wait for Brazza's dismissal, since that could be soon. But they are surely wrong—in another sense—to wait for Gabon and the French Congo to be wrested from the hands of the natives. That will likely result in chaos."

Wolfgang explained how the Belgians had put their colony in the hands of concessionary companies. Not being satisfied with having a monopoly on trade, these Belgian companies seized ownership of the region's natural resources. The demand for ivory and palm oil was always great, and now there was an increased demand for rubber.

"Pneumatic tires," Wolfgang said.

"Come again?"

"Your vulcanized rubber tire filled with a tube of air. Makes the tire better able to absorb shocks. Apparently, these things are making bicycling a regular way for folks to get around. I've never tried it, myself. I would rather square off with a hungry lion than take my chances on a penny farthing!"

"Quite right!" I said. "How do men mount those contraptions?"

"Well, those things might be history soon. I hear what's called a 'safety' bicycle is the new thing. I've a cousin in Coventry who rides a Swift. The machine's wheels are the same size—much smaller than the penny farthing's giant wheel. And he rides upon pneumatic tires. Takes the thing to his cobbler's shop every day."

"You really believe there's to be an explosion in bicycling?"

"It's already happening, from the news I hear of the Congo Free State."

The companies, Wolfgang continued, imposed heavy taxes upon the natives, payable in goods or cash; but the natives could not afford the taxes even after backbreaking weeks of collecting rubber and ivory and palm oil. Those who refused, it was said, were tortured or executed. If the rumors were true, villages were being decimated.

"It sounds as if the people of the Congo are being exterminated for the sake of bicycle tires."

"Exactly right. Belgian capitalists are getting rich. You can see why Paris would like to get rid of Brazza."

I conjured an image of one of these so-called "safety" bicycles. It seemed a trifle—not something I would have imagined catching on, but so it was. Brazza had accused King Leopold of "atrocities"; and Wolfgang, whose network of traders ran deep in Equatorial Africa, supported this view with talk of torture and executions. I had no reason to doubt them. And I could not reconcile the two facts—the bicycle and the suffering. No man—of any race—ought to suffer torture or death for a bicycle—or one thousand bicycles.

"Is this imminent?"

"No one knows. It might not be for years; it might be tomorrow. But when it happens, the English, the Germans, any trader who isn't French will be forced out. I doubt the new regime will be friendly to American naturalists, either, so you better make your ape records quickly."

"I haven't even received my phonograph!"

"I wish I could help you, Professor. But I'm in my own race with Paris—and another with a trader named McLaughlin."

"I met him aboard the *Ballay*."

"I don't know which is the worse opponent!"

"I wish us both luck," I said, raising my glass to toast.

"To luck," Wolfgang said. "With luck and the help of the little Fang, I'll get my gorilla yet!"

Wolfgang insisted we have another round of beers.

"You know the worst thing about losing that gorilla to the Eshiras? Seeing that Irish bastard McLaughlin come into the factory with it the very next day!"

Knowing of nowhere better to go, I took a room at the lodge. My trunks remained in the hold of the *Ballay*, which would leave the following afternoon, so I had nothing to occupy myself with except Cape Lopez. Having enjoyed two glasses of beer at dinner, I saw no harm in returning to the dining room for a nightcap.

I enjoyed a whiskey by myself, watching a tableful of Norwegians singing a song whose words I did not understand but whose sounds were proud and boastful—and perhaps slightly melancholy. I watched and listened like an anthropologist and ached to have my phonograph. Cylinders were precious—but surely this song was worthy of one!

Indifferent to the Norwegians, McLaughlin sat at the bar drinking alone, in the same cool manner he had on the steamer. He was heading back into Fernan Vaz, rather than out of it, so he must not have had much business in Cape Lopez. Our eyes met briefly—then my smile began to quaver and I returned my attention to the Norwegians.

In my room, I became restless. My agenda for the following morning was to telegraph Mr. Walcott and Mr. Moriarty to inquire about the status of my phonograph. Otherwise, I had nothing to do. I thought I might try to pick up a few of the native's words.

From my window, I saw that the evening light had burnished everything with gold, so I left my room for a walk on the nearby beach. Not far from the lodge, a weather-beaten board-walk followed the roaring Atlantic, and I traversed this boardwalk for a time as the sun set. There being some young Orungu men on the beach, I removed my socks and shoes and approached them. We did not speak each other's language, but managed to carry out a little trade nonetheless. They showed me several balls of rubber they had rolled, for which I had no real use except kneading in my fingers. I demonstrated the proper way to fill a cigarette paper with tobacco, roll it, and smoke like a gentleman. The young men were delighted, so I gave them each a paper and a pinch of fine Virginia tobacco in exchange for a ball of gummy, black rubber. We smoked together—a common tongue being unnecessary for the enjoyment of this sublime moment.

The countenance of the young man opposite me was suddenly charged with fear. I turned around to see what beast was upon us and found myself relieved and frightened at once: A white man, stripped completely nude (not even wearing the modest covering of a savage!), was approaching us from down the beach. His feet went suck-suck as he kicked up pockets of sand;

his knuckles grazed his thighs, as his arms hung limp from hunched shoulders. But his eyes—rather the stern cheekbones and forehead that enclosed them—were unmistakably McLaughlin's.

The fool was drunk out of his mind.

I am sure he recognized me, for he stopped suck-sucking toward us and let out a simian howl.

The natives scattered in a trail of smoke. I held my ground. McLaughlin howled again. I think he wanted me to answer, but I would not give him the satisfaction.

I bade him goodnight and made my way back to the boardwalk, the sound of my feet in the sand echoed by his as he continued to menace the beach.

At breakfast, I told Wolfgang about the incident.

"Are you sure it was McLaughlin? I've never known him to be anything but perfectly cool."

"I thought so. It was growing dark, though."

"Whether it was or not, you needn't worry about him. He's a clever trader. And fair."

"I suspect he doesn't care for my mission in Fernan Vaz."

"He may not."

"He suggested I pay a visit to the mission on the lake."

"And you should. St. Anne's is on the mouth of the Rembo Nkomi, right next to Hatton and Cookson. And it's an excellent hub from which to venture into the jungle."

"Are you a Catholic?"

"No, Anglican. Don't worry—you'll find them very welcoming. Father Buleon is rather interested in apes, so I imagine you two will get along quite nicely."

That afternoon, I boarded the *Ballay*. I was outfitted for the jungle, having traded my waistcoat, suit, and bowler for a khaki coat and trousers and a pith helmet, all from the Jaeger Company, the same outfitter who supplied Mr. Stanley on his mission to find Dr. Livingstone. There were fewer people on board—mostly traders and some native guides—as the steamer was headed into the lake and toward the Hatton and Cookson factory for which Wolfgang and McLaughlin were agents. At this factory, the English agents would pay advances to their African liaisons, who would in time return with an abundance of ivory, rubber, and palm oil. Some of the traders, like Wolfgang and McLaughlin, would take leave of the factory for periods to go into the jungle to hunt. The earnest faces of the traders forced me to consider a new worry: The reports of traders' guns would frighten away the chimpanzees I wished to peacefully observe. I had planned on circumventing St. Anne's, given Mr. Marche's warning, but I decided on the steamer that I should seek Father Buleon's help in restricting hunting around my camp.

We left the Atlantic and entered Lake Nkomi. The traders, inured to the beauty of the lake and its verdant shores, had congregated in the steamer's bar. I relaxed in a chair on deck and marveled at Gabon's natural beauty. Beside the majesty of the green walls that lined the lake, lush islands broke the lake's surface. Often, the boughs of the trees on one island reached toward their neighbors on another and formed grand arches. In the shadow of one of these arches, the steamer, the water, the air—all was held captive by quiet. On the other side of the arch, the sun and the afternoon's attendant soundings returned.

Wolfgang joined me on the deck and passed me a whiskey. "Cheers, Dick!"

I asked Wolfgang's opinion of my seeking Father Buleon's help.

"He certainly has leverage with us traders. Yes, I think he'll grant you a parcel of the jungle near the mission from which you can be free from hunting parties. I told you, he's quite fond of apes. I cannot imagine that you two won't become great friends."

"That's a relief to hear."

Wolfgang leaned toward me to whisper, though there was no one else on deck.

"You don't have to worry about McLaughlin or me ruining your phonographic recordings with gunfire. We're in a bit of a race, you see. Regent's Park desires a gorilla. And they will pay a princely sum for one."

"I wish you luck in your quest. It's a rare thing to remove a gorilla from Africa without its perishing."

McLaughlin appeared on deck then, sober and outfitted for the jungle. He unhurriedly approached our chairs.

"And I worry about your competing against McLaughlin," I added. "He has a way of appearing at the most inconvenient times."

Wolfgang turned around and laughed.

"Morning, Irish! I was just telling our friend the professor that the next time he visits his orangutan friends at Regent's Park, he'll also get to meet the park's new gorilla, courtesy of yours truly!"

McLaughlin smiled wryly.

"You will certainly have an advantage if you recruit Professor Garner. I have only a net to capture a gorilla, but the professor has the power of rhetoric."

Chapter Five

As the *Ballay* plunged deeper into Lake Nkomi, the lake opened up and spread its many fingers into the African jungle. Toward evening, the steamer came upon the mouth of the Rembo Nkomi; on its right bank was the Hatton and Cookson factory, a long, low building with a thatched roof, almost African in design. Further in was St. Anne's Mission. As the sun faded behind the steamer, the mission was increasingly shrouded. A short road, lined on both sides by mango trees, led to the mission's church, which towered over the grounds. The church was not many years old, but the pale coral stone from which it was built gave it an aged look, as if the Church and Gabon had a far longer history.

Upon departing the steamer, some of the traders and their native guides headed west, toward Hatton and Cookson. Other traders and their native guides were met by a young priest. The priest spoke to the gathered crowd in French, German, English, and at least one African tongue. I understood that he was directing the men who did not live at Hatton and Cookson to a couple of the mission's dormitories. These men then followed the priest up the road toward the mission. McLaughlin, bearing only his rifle, walked alongside the priest. Behind the traders, their native guides carried their supplies. Some wore heavy packs upon their shoulders; a few pairs hauled trunks between them. Wolfgang, sensing that I was a bit lost in all of this, stayed behind. With him were Mbye and another young native.

"I'll introduce you to Father Buleon," Wolfgang said. "But first, let's get your things."

"It's quite a lot, mind you."

"That's why I recruited Olago for you," he said, slapping a hand on the second native boy's back. "He's Nkomi. Speaks English quite well. When he's a bit older, he'll be a fine agent for Hatton and Cookson. But for now, he'll be a great help to you."

I studied the boy and found his skin to be remarkably lighter than his native brothers. He gave a timid smile, as if he were hiding something terrible he had done.

"Very well," I said.

Wolfgang's Fang and my Nkomi removed my trunks from the steamer while Wolfgang escorted me up the road to the mission. The remaining sun burnished the church; its movement seemed stayed so that all who approached the church from the lake would pay heed to its prominence. Beacon of Christendom or watchful eye: That was to be decided by each man who followed the road to the mission's shelter. At this hour, there was not a soul on the grounds, which added to the mystery. Besides the church, the mission grounds were comprised of two more large stone structures: Just west of the church lay the three-story mission building, which housed Father Buleon and the associate priest and the brothers, and to the east lay the two-story convent. Surrounding each of these structures were several low, plain buildings that shared the pale stone of the other structures, but nothing else. These were the dormitories; the men's and the women's lay in the shadows of the mission building and the convent, respectively. Forming a perimeter of several acres between the mission's structures and the jungle were plots of coffee and cocoa.

Wolfgang led me to the mission building, which was plain in design. Its only notable feature was the third floor's construction: The top floor was smaller than the other floors, allowing for a covered deck around its perimeter.

Wolfgang and I entered the mission building's foyer, where brothers rested on couches and in chairs. The brothers smiled politely, but did not inquire as to our business nor move to make us welcome. A young Nkomi attendant dressed in khaki pants and white shirtsleeves came to our attention, instead.

"Is Father in?" asked Wolfgang.

Being attended to by this Black child brought to mind memories of being waited upon by slaves in my youth. My father being a respected proprietor, my family was occasionally invited to the homes of wealthy plantation owners. To my young eyes, the slaves carried out their duties contentedly. Happy darkies thankful to be freed from their former savagery was the narrative I recalled. The young Nkomi attendant struck me in the same way—content, even dignified. I cannot say exactly how he did—perhaps it was in his stride, or perhaps it was in the way his eyes met Wolfgang's unflinchingly. But there was something else in his stride and in his eyes—the intimation that his determined look was a mask. I reflected back on those contented plantation slaves and wondered if their deferential countenances also were mere masks. Slavery was the best condition for them in America at that time, but surely it was borne with indignity.

The Nkomi bade us follow him upstairs to the third floor. Here was another open area with a couch and several chairs and, in one corner, a desk containing a French telegraph machine. A gentle breeze blew through the mosquito netting hanging across the wide windows. Wolfgang and I followed the Nkomi to the open door on the north side of the room. Behind a large wooden desk sat whom I presumed to be Father Buleon studying sketches of chimpanzees. Though I had been told of his interest in apes, it surprised me to actually see him engaged in their study. And so earnest was he in his study that he either hadn't noticed our appearance in his doorway or had not bothered to show that he had. His age was difficult to determine; his hands, one of which held a single sketch while the other took notes, seemed strong with youth, but his long, wispy beard lent him an aged countenance.

"Ozounge," the Nkomi said, gaining Buleon's attention.

Buleon raised his head from his work, and I saw for the first time his eyes. They were as contradictory as the other details about him that I have described: They were a soothing pale green, but he fixed them upon you with intense concentration.

"Thank you," Buleon said gently, dismissing the Nkomi with a nod. "Gentlemen, please sit down."

"Greetings, Father. How are things?"

"Quite well, Mr. Wolfgang, thank you."

Buleon turned his eyes toward me, eliciting an introduction from Wolfgang.

"I have been expecting you, Professor. I, too, am interested in the region's apes. They are fascinating creatures."

Buleon and I discussed in what direction from the mission I would find the best conditions for setting up my camp, and he promised that no traders would hunt within the vicinity. Everything was arranged without discussion of the specific objective of my research. In fact, Buleon seemed eager to share his own "observations" of gorillas and chimpanzees in the lake region. He handed me a journal that I expected was filled with his rudimentary notes.

"I am setting out for the Eshira people tomorrow. Among my interests in the Eshira is their language. My journals"—he indicated the journal in my hands—"are all that have ever been written of it."

"A naturalist and a linguist." Whether Buleon heard the note of dismissal in my voice, I made no effort to hide it. "When do you have time to convert the heathen?"

"It is a journey of about three days up the Rembo Nkomi, then another three-day's march into the jungle. Perhaps you will join me? It would provide an opportunity for us to share our knowledge. And we are likely to see apes."

"That is generous of you."

I was eager to set up camp, now that I was in the lake region, but there was the nagging issue of the missing phonograph. It would take some time before the phonograph could be shipped from Libreville to Cape Lopez to St. Anne's, and as far as I knew it had not yet arrived in Libreville. If Mr. Walcott had not had any success convincing Mr. Langley of the true value of my mission, there was a good chance it had not even left London. It seemed I could not pass up this opportunity to venture into the jungle with Buleon.

"Yes, I think I will join you. Thank you."

"Terrific!" Wolfgang said. "Mind you to note the location of any gorillas."

Wolfgang and I thanked Buleon and got up to go find our lodgings. At the door's threshold, Buleon addressed me one more time:

"There is a story that long ago, a French bishop was so shocked upon visiting a captive chimpanzee that he said to it, 'Speak, and I will baptize thee.' But of course, there are no baptized apes, are there?"

After I settled in to one of the dormitories, Father Buleon gave me a tour of the mission. The evening meal having ended, the mission was now bustling with Africans. The boys and men dressed in khaki pants and white shirtsleeves, and the girls and women in plain khaki dresses. Many of them smiled and greeted "Ozounge" as they passed; a few even smiled deferentially at his guest. As we walked past the dining halls and toward the edge of a coffee field, Buleon explained the mission's role in the colony. Commissaire Brazza, he claimed, had invited the Spiritans there to evangelize the interior's peoples. In all the hours I had spent in conversation with Brazza, not once had he spoken of any religious affiliation, and he had agreed with Mr. Marche that I not raise the issue of evolution with the Spiritans, so his support of the missionaries perplexed me at first. But as Buleon continued to speak of the commissaire with reverence, I began to understand: Catholic missions were a sign of France's superior culture, and their efforts at civilizing the natives would advance Brazza's vision for a flourishing trade partner.

We returned from the coffee field by way of the convent. A solitary sister, the first I had seen, blacked out a sliver of the coral stone. I could not see her face for the angle of her habit. I thought: What a strange figure she must be to the Africans! What a contrast the sisters cut against the bare-breasted Gabonese women of the villages deep in the jungle! There was no clearer symbol of white civilization in the entire mission. Everything else—Bibles, crosses, vessels of holy water—were mere totems by comparison.

"And how do the natives receive your proselytizing?"

"Most are former slaves, freed by Commissaire Brazza or purchased by us. Others come to us freely, from their villages or the terrors of the Congo Free State. They welcome the Word of God."

Even when conversing with me in English, Buleon referred to the mission's charges—from children as young as seven to men and women past forty—as "les enfants": the children. Les enfants were being formed into Catholic Christians through the experience of the mission: They attended Mass; labored in the coffee and cocoa fields; and crowded into the men's and women's schoolhouses for their studies.

"Are any vestiges of their former lives allowed? Besides the forced labor?"

Buleon turned his green eyes on me and smiled.

"Professor," he laughed. "Do you think the Father of Slaves would allow forced labor in his colony?"

"I suppose not," I had to concede.

We crossed over to the men's dining hall, where we and a few of the brothers were served dinner and claret by another native boy. "Merci, Luke," the brothers said as they were served.

When the boy had returned to the kitchen, I asked whether all the mission's "children" were renamed.

"Paris does not throw money at missions. We must raise much of our own funds."

"Thus your coffee and cocoa plantations supported by free labor. We tried that in America, you know?"

"The cost of freeing Luke from his master was paid by a wealthy Frenchman. It was allowed that the child's benefactor could give him a Christian name."

"Wolfgang informed me that it is customary for your guests to make a contribution to the mission upon their departure."

"Contributions are welcome."

"Then you may count on me to reward your hospitality."

Returning to the issue of the mission's relationship with the colony and France, Buleon praised Brazza for his efforts as the mission's liaison to the Ministry of Foreign Affairs.

"Commissaire Brazza not only supports our evangelizing work; he also supports my studies as a naturalist."

"You consider yourself a naturalist?"

"I am in the employ of France's Museum of Natural History."

I nearly choked on claret, so surprised was I by Buleon's declaration, for I never would have guessed an esteemed museum would trust scientific work to a missionary. In spite of this, I was aware that the statement elicited a stern glare from one of the brothers, a stout young man with a short, oily beard.

"Much as you are in the employ of the Smithsonian Institution, correct?" Buleon inquired.

"Yes, exactly. They are generously backing my research."

Buleon excused himself to finish preparing for tomorrow's journey, and Brother Leo, the young brother who had been ruffled by Buleon's reference to the museum, was charged with seeing me back to my room. Upon Buleon's leaving, Leo spoke to his brothers in only French, which struck me as quite inhospitable. I admit to not keeping up. The brothers seemed not to care to keep up as Leo prattled on. I turned my attention to the windows; the mission was on the cusp of darkness.

Upon our leaving the dining hall, the brothers bade me goodnight and retired to the mission house. Leo and I set off for the men's dormitories, but were quickly stopped by the Sister I had seen earlier outside the convent.

This time, I was permitted to look upon her face; it glowed warmly within the bondage of her habit like a pearl in its shell. From her slight lips came forth a few words of French, which had never before sounded so much like music!

She had called Leo away to some imminent matter, and he informed me that she, Sister Marie, would accompany me until his return.

Marie turned toward me and smiled. Her English was as musical as her French. Under the sway of her powerfully blue irises, I spoke to her with a forthrightness I was powerless to check.

"How long have you been in Gabon, Sister?"

"About a year."

"Father Buleon gave a good appraisal of the mission's effort to convert the Gabonese. Is he right, in your estimation?"

Marie blushed; I should not have asked such a direct question.

"Yes, I think so. The Africans are quite impressionable. They must be kept away from the vices of . . ." Marie looked away from me. "Of white men who have lost their faith. But in the confines of the mission, they flourish."

Marie turned back to me.

"Are you here to hunt gorillas?" she asked.

"Oh, no. I am interested in what can be learned from living apes, not dead ones."

"Like Father."

"Perhaps. Why is he interested in apes?"

"Oh, I'm not sure. I know only that he finds them very interesting creatures."

"I aim to study the chimpanzee, primarily. His language."

"Language?"

I could sense her doubt.

"Yes, his language. The races of men have linguistic powers equal to their evolutionary status. There are simple, primitive tongues, such as America's Indians have—and of course your African charges. And there are our own sophisticated languages. It's my belief that among primates, there exists the same range of languages. Very low in most monkeys, and highest in the chimpanzee."

"I had not thought of human speech like that before. My charges have learned French quite well. And as for animals . . . . Well, I just don't know, Professor."

"Do you not find it consistent with your faith that God would endow all his animals with the powers of speech equal to their powers of thought?"

"I'm not certain that I do, Professor."

In the morning, Wolfgang summoned me to the dining hall, where the traders and I were fed a hearty meal before the natives came for their own. McLaughlin, whom I expected to find taciturn as usual, was speaking at length in French to Father Buleon. Their conversation was a mystery to me, for Wolfgang and I sat at the opposite end of the great table, and they held whatever they were saying quite close. At the time, I thought little of this arrangement, but soon enough I would not be able to remember it as anything but conspiring.

I wished Wolfgang the best of luck in capturing—and keeping alive—a gorilla. He likewise wished me the best in living among the chimpanzees and capturing their talk on cylinder.

"I'm taking Olago with me while you're traveling with Ozounge," he added. "But I'll have him back to help you set up your camp."

"Ozounge," I said. "Several of the natives called him that yesterday. What does it mean?"

"Oh—they all call him that. 'Savior.'"

After breakfast, Buleon's team was assembled in front of the church. No one from the mission besides Buleon and I were joining the caravan; the team was a dozen Nkomi men, all of whom were dressed in native attire, save for the packs of provisions they wore across their backs and the rifles a few held at their sides. I was not expecting to find Buleon on such terms with natives who were not being brought into the fold, but I would find that these half-naked savages were essential currency upon leaving the mission grounds.

Buleon marched the team east past the convent, where the superior and the sisters watched us pass. The superior was most marked by her manner of playing sentinel to the sisters, drawing a boundary between the team of men and the sisters with her crossed arms and the enormous whites of her eyes. I searched among the black columns for Sister Marie and found her, but dared not cross the superior's barrier by acknowledging her. Soon the team reached the riverbank, and the convent was lost.

Upon the Rembo Nkomi's banks was a pair of canoes, or pirogues, each one the length of a train car. The Nkomis loaded the provisions and rifles into one, and then Buleon directed me to sit in its center with him. The Nkomis, save the few who would launch the pirogue into the river, joined us. We were launched, and the last men leapt into the canoe. It easily bore the weight of fourteen men and supplies, maintaining an even keel.

For three days, Buleon and I were rowed up the Rembo Nkomi. We passed hours in conversation, but we also passed hours silently watching the shores for signs of apes. These silences were infused by constant, subtle movements and their attendant sounds. The rowers' muscles rippled like the breaking water. The shores teased us with trembling foliage, though whatever stirred the trees and created the music that was to be heard at all times—the euphonic jungle calls that met in so many cacophonous layers to become, like a tuning orchestra, euphonic again—remained hidden.

Being one of two white men surrounded by a dozen Africans could have been unsettling were it not for the command Buleon demonstrated over the natives. During our conversations, he would occasionally call out to one of the rowers, his voice bursting from its usual warm evenness into percussive riffs. From where he got the air needed to generate these barks will always be a mystery. I failed to understand the meaning of any of his entreaties, but each earned an affirmative nod from the addressed native.

Buleon and I had spoken on the first couple of days about the jungle-scape and the dangers of bites and stings and fevers. He was a fount of useful information on the Fernan Vaz region. He was especially informed about the habits of wild gorillas.

As we set out on our final day, Buleon told me that we were blessed not to have rain, nor to have traversed any rapids, yet. That afternoon, as I peered upriver, now vigilantly watching for white water, Buleon inquired into my particular interest in the apes.

"I understand that you are interested in the sounds made by chimpanzees."

"That's correct. I've studied the speech of several monkeys and apes in zoological gardens. My purpose here is to study them in their natural habitat."

"Forgive me, Professor, but perhaps you could enlighten me as to your definition of speech so that I may fully understand you."

"Of course. Speech is the oral expression of thought. An utterance preceded purely by emotion might not rightly be called speech, and a thought unexpressed remains simply a thought. The chain of thought and utterance constitutes speech. Would you agree?"

"I believe so. Am I to understand that you believe monkeys and apes possess speech?"

"Yes. In my studies, I've found the utterances of monkeys and apes to share the attributes of human speech. When they speak, it is addressed to another party. When they have spoken, they await a reply in speech or action. Their speech is certainly of a much lower type, but it's as deliberate as our speech right now."

"I may not give you the reply you desire, Professor."

"I don't know what to expect in the way of your reply, Father. I know you have a curiosity about apes; but I also suspect you hold true the dogmas of your faith."

"You are correct on both accounts—though my interest in apes is not mere curiosity. In my observations of apes, their utterances have been driven by instinct. A male gorilla chases another male from his mate with angry grunts. That is not speech; that is the inarticulate sounding of his biological drive."

"But it is articulate! You have not been blessed with the use of a phonograph to study those soundings. Some of these species speak so rapidly compared to men that it's like the insensible bleating of a bagpipe compared to the melodious tune of, say, 'Swanee River.' The phonograph has allowed me to slow down their speech and distinguish multiple utterances where you believed you heard only one."

"Perhaps you will share these recordings with me upon our return?" Buleon smiled knowingly upon this request. "Be that as it may, Professor, God endowed *men* with souls. How could creatures without souls have minds?"

"Why should God's bounty be so limited? These animals think; that is clear to me. Why should God not have endowed them with the power of expression equal to their power of thought, however meager it may be?"

A rower called to Buleon.

"Thoughts are the soul. Words are the body."

"Hold on, Professor. We are treading into dangerous waters."

The roar and hiss of crashing waters raised as we neared a bend in the river. With quick glances and clipped words, the rowers readied themselves to pass the rapids. There was a sheen of sweat on their dark arms that I did not notice before. Father Buleon's calm, in the center of the rowers' anxiety, did not assuage my fear.

The pirogue rounded the bend; the rowers tightened their grips and drove us into the least of the white squalls. The rushing water pushed and pulled at the pirogue, rolling it side to side as it tumbled forth, bucking against rocks. Sucking pools of foam promised to swallow us should the pirogue be overturned.

More barks from the rowers. Buleon remained unmoved save his hands, which, like mine, gripped the pirogue's sides.

"Good God!" I yelled through the din.

"God is good! He will see us through—in this life or in eternal life!"

"That's not reassuring!"

The most terrible tumbling yet caused an eruption of water to enter the pirogue, against which I shut my eyes. Then the rowers' barks ceased; we had either passed the trouble or been lost to the river and I was not yet conscious of our fate. I opened my eyes to find that we were still alive. With a sudden lunge forward, the pirogue was jettisoned from the rapids.

The first two night's camps had reminded me of camping with other boys back in Virginia. On the sandy banks, the Nkomis built fires over which we cooked our suppers, and Father Buleon and I pitched a small tent, inside of which we shared sketches of monkeys and apes, commenting only on the variety of species before falling asleep. In spite of the fact that the excursion was delaying my true purpose in coming to Gabon, it was a thrilling time being rowed deeper into the heart of the jungle toward an encounter with savages whose nature remained a mystery to me. But since escaping the rapids that afternoon, Buleon and I had not continued our argument, and I swore he looked upon me with only condescension and distrust in his green eyes. I began to feel like a hostage in the caravan and wished I were settled in my cage, my own master. So on the third night, I elected to sleep on my mat around the dying fires with the Nkomis.

"You will be eaten by mosquitos!" Buleon cried, to which I offered no reply except draping my jacket over my head.

When the Nkomis' conversations withered to silence, I ventured to engage them in English.

"Why do you men not belong to the mission?"

One of the Nkomis turned toward me. His chest and shoulders swelled with strength, and his prominent brow imbued him with a great African fortitude. His eyes, however, suggested an intellect not in keeping with his station. I thought he was about to reply, but he made no speech to match his thoughtful stare, so I continued.

"Don't misunderstand me; I'm not suggesting you ought to join the mission. I'm sure you prefer your own customs and find the Spiritans' ways quite strange. I find them quite strange, you know? And I come from a town—a village, if you will—where the Christian religion is the natural state of being. From my youth, though, I found it unnatural. A regular inquisition."

The bright-looking Nkomi turned away, and I did not believe at this point that he nor any of his brothers were listening, but I went on speaking for my own company.

"The Christian religion was not the only one I was exposed to as a youth. My family owned several slaves before the War of Northern Aggression—surely you know about that; your own kind kept slaves just like in America!"

The bright-looking fellow turned back to me as if something I had uttered caught his attention.

"Anyway, the oldest fellow among them—he was called Uncle Jim—he had lived among his tribe until reaching manhood, so he brought with him his tribe's religion. He practiced it until his dying day, though always out of sight of his white masters, save me. I was allowed to see his totems and watch him practice his white arts. Though after a certain age I had little belief in them. I am a rational man!"

The fire had withered to a few glowing embers. Most of the Nkomis had fallen asleep. But the bright-looking one was staring at me in such a way I believed he was finally forming a response; his answer, however, was to lay his head down without a word. Trade had spread the English language among the tribes of Equatorial Africa for so long that I doubted you could bring together a dozen natives and not have a single English-speaker among them. But it seemed that such a group had been assembled by Buleon.

Upon waking, I felt an ache at the top of my spine. It was not the ache of spending a restless night on the jungle floor—the tightness that had eased the previous mornings when attended to with a cup of coffee—for this ache, it was painfully dawning on me, had invaded my every muscle. My blood was cold as a snake's. Putting on my coat did nothing to still the shivering that overcame me quite suddenly. Upon standing, my legs cried for relief. There was no denying that I had fallen victim—and not for the last time—to one of Africa's hellish fevers.

I immediately, though surreptitiously, put a large dose of quinine into my canteen and swallowed every drop. The Nkomis were gathering up their packs and rifles; Father Buleon was consulting a map. There would be no restful hours in the pirogue today, as we were embarking on our march toward the Eshira. We had several days of traversing the dense jungle before we would arrive at their village. My only hope was that the constant marching would aid me in sweating out the fever.

This was a fool's wish!

Beyond the savannah of the riverbank, the jungle exploded from the earth. A feeling of trepidation fell upon my heart at the threshold of that mystery—but it was thrown off by the curiosity that had grown in me since I first set eyes and ears upon our primate cousins.

Buleon, though slight, vigorously led the team into the jungle. Its terrain is thick with vegetation whose fingers stretch from both canopy and earth. Vines hang in clusters from the branches of mangrove trees, while the trees' roots grasp your feet. Being unaccustomed to the jungle-scape placed me last in the caravan. After an hour, we spilled onto a well-trodden, though not very straight, path. Upon reaching this path, I weaved through the Nkomis and joined Buleon.

"Why was the path not cut from the riverbank?" I asked. "It would have saved us a lot of time."

"Men did not cut this path," Buleon laughed. "This is the work of forest elephants. Their straight tusks are made to rend the jungle for their passage."

"Interesting. Any chance we shall see them?"

"Should they hear us, they will run away. You need not fear being impaled upon an elephant's tusk."

I fell to the rear to hide my condition. My shivering made for an unsteady march, which my feet repaid with shoots of pain. Marching on the elephant-trod paths, which we found infrequently, offered little relief. So intense was the shivering that I feared I would inadvertently pull the trigger of my rifle and kill the young Nkomi in front of me! The ache that had started in my spine was now swelling in my extremities. A fire burned under my brain. Even my eyes felt the inflammation. They burned, too, from the thick droplets of sweat coursing into them from underneath my helmet. My skin grew warm, as I was perspiring faster than my wool underclothes could pull away the dampness.

My worsening fever caused my pace to slow further, and the distance between me and the last Nkomi grew. Buleon was quite out of my vision. I occasionally heard his barking in the Nkomis' tongue; each bark was fainter than the last. One by one, the Nkomis vanished from my sight as well, until there was but the youngest one, who looked back at me pitifully from time to time. I gathered enough strength and air to speak.

"Mind you, I might lose the way if you leave my sight." With the little air left in reserve, I forced a laugh.

The boy looked back, though the distance between us and my blurred vision obscured his countenance. I was unsure whether his simple face expressed concern or condolences.

By noon, the young Nkomi had disappeared, and I had fallen upon my knees in exhaustion. My head dropped. I resigned myself to never discovering the wild apes I sought, to never seeing Maggie or Harry again, to returning to the earth in this very spot, to curling in a tight ball and waiting for the bush to overgrow me and the driver ants to whittle my flesh down to my bones.

Chapter Six

It may have been hours or mere minutes that I lay on the jungle floor. Whatever the duration, it came to a different conclusion than I had feared when I was roused by someone prodding my back, urging my response.

My unconsciousness must have restored some strength to me, for I was able to right myself and find the young Nkomi, and behind him, the big, bright-looking one.

"Thank God."

The men helped me up and, draping my arms across their shoulders, began to drag me—my legs being quite useless—through the jungle, though our destination was unknown to me. Surely they did not intend to carry me all the way to the Eshira village.

"Where are you taking me? Blazes, it's no use. I'll be fluent in chimpanzee before Nkomi!"

"Save your energy, Mister."

"Am I hallucinating? Or do you speak English?"

"I am Odanga, Ozounge's interpreter. I speak many tongues."

"Where are we headed? Is the caravan waiting?"

"There is a village close by. You will rest there."

"Did he send you back for me?"

"No. Ozounge was not concerned for your safety. But I will not have a man in my charge dying in the jungle."

"What devilry is Buleon up to?"

"Please rest."

The Nkomis carried me swiftly, and, my fever still sapping my energy, I soon fell asleep in the men's arms.

Some time later, a curious thing happened: I awoke feeling quite able to support myself and told Odanga that I preferred to walk. We marched single file, Odanga in front, myself in the middle, and the young Nkomi in back. I did not check my watch to see what hour of the long midday it was. Nor did I inquire of Odanga our destination. The important thing seemed to be to keep setting one foot in front of the other—to keep moving forward.

The subtle sounds of birdcalls to which we marched was broken by a shrill thrashing to the right of our path. The source was aimed to meet us upon our trail, so we aimed our rifles back.

Then the foliage was blacked out by a shadowy beast of a gorilla. He was the height of a man, but the breadth of three. The creature's roar was one-hundredfold that of his orangutan cousin. He batted Odanga's rifle from his grip, then batted the man to the jungle floor. Paralyzed by fear, the young Nkomi and I failed to get off a shot before the great beast unburdened us of our rifles. The young Nkomi's he tossed aside before batting the boy down like grass; the barrel of mine he treated like a mere ribbon, taking it in his shiny, black hands and tying it into a knot. The combination of strength and agility with which he made the steel into a knot foretold the brutality I faced in becoming his meal: He could neatly tear away any portion of me that he favored, feasting on my flesh before my eyes as I awaited the release of death! Would that he had the mercy—or the craving!—to rip out my heart first!

The beast brought his hot breath to my trembling face. Then, to my astonishment, he spoke:

"Call off the hunters."

"You can speak!"

"You knew that, Professor. The test is whether you will listen."

"The gorilla speaks!" I cried. "The gorilla! The gorilla!"

I cried the beast's name until I was slapped across the face by Odanga.

"Now you are hallucinating, Mister."

When I next became conscious, I was lying on my back, staring at the painted face of a wizened native. Seized by anxiety—for I had never seen this man before—I tried to right myself, but another man's hand stayed me. It was Odanga, to whom I owed my full trust.

I lay still and extended my trust to the old medicine man, even as Odanga escaped my view. The medicine man dipped his first two fingers into a clay jar, wetting them, then reached into a bag fashioned from an animal's skin and caked his fingertips in powder. I did not flinch when he wiped the powder across my forehead and lips; I guessed the powder to be the grindings of some root or bark that the Nkomi believed to have healing properties. It was likely of the same bark white men pulverize to produce quinine! But deceiving the African of his magic was the so-called duty of dogmatic missionaries—not the role of a scientist.

Still, as I lay under the medicine man's spell, I felt moved by his efforts. Underneath his paint, he was not so different from Uncle Jim, the old African I had known in my youth. He, too, was something of a medicine man. And once, we two had made a scene similar to the one in the African hut. I was not yet ten at the time. I was sick with fever and restricted to my bed. During my convalescence, my two most frequent visitors were my mother and Uncle Jim. The old African was charged with delivering to me soup and clean nightshirts. But one evening he also had hidden in his pockets the skulls of several small animals. Having earned my father's trust after many years of servitude and, at his advanced age, not presenting the threat of escape, Uncle Jim was allowed to accompany me in the nearby forests to hunt squirrels and rabbits. Oh, how I enjoyed those hunts! We skinned and cleaned the animals right there in the forest, sometimes starting a small fire over which we cooked and shared the meat. Uncle Jim must have collected the skulls, and while I lay in my weakened state that evening, he blessed them and laid them at the corners of my bed. When it was time for him to leave, he gathered the skulls and hid them in his pockets again. Though the ritual I experienced in Gabon was different than the one Uncle Jim had performed, as each came from distinct religions, it echoed the earlier ritual's shape: Each medicine man believed the natural materials conducted his healing powers to the sufferer. Superstition, of course—but in both cases the medicine man was affirmed by my recovery!

I fell asleep under the medicine man's ministrations, and when I awoke, my fever had subsided. I sat up and surveyed my surroundings: a primitive square constructed of tightly bound bamboo covered by a thatched roof. Over the doorway hung a curtain that was clearly a white man's trade. I regained my legs and pulled back the curtain to find Odanga on the other side. It must have rained during my recovery—though the thatched roof kept me completely dry—for a lane of mud ran on either side of the bamboo hut I had recovered in. On the other side of each lane ran a row of huts. These appeared to be the village's residences. The middle row of structures, of which the guesthouse I inhabited was a part, consisted of common areas: a clubhouse for men, a laundry for women. Odanga wished to introduce me to the village's chief, Rimpano, so I followed him along one of these muddy lanes, earning the stares of the villagers. They were quite used to seeing white men—even the children, who laughed easily at me as my boots sucked at the mud—but they preferred to know the business of their visitors. The chief's house, which was the village's largest structure, sat at the head of the center row of huts.

Deference required Odanga to formally introduce me to the chief, but no introduction was necessary: Chief Rimpano sat upon a throne covered in a patchwork of cotton and wore a skirt of indigo silk. He was flanked by a retinue of dozens. Strong men stood with their spears or rifles at their sides like a small army; women and children were seated at the king's feet. The chief spoke in his tongue, and I in mine, and Odanga interpreted.

"Thank you for your hospitality," I said. "I am afraid that, given the circumstances under which I arrived in your village, I have nothing to repay your kindness."

"Chief Rimpano accepts the gratitude of the English any time," Odanga translated.

Odanga had apparently informed Rimpano of the caravan's purpose and route, for the next question the chief asked was if I were a missionary. I explained that I was a naturalist and had only joined the caravan to become acquainted with Gabon's interior. I considered myself a guest of Commissaire Brazza more than a guest of Father Buleon. Upon hearing this, Rimpano offered me one of his daughters for a wife!

"I appreciate your kindness," I said. "But I must refuse. I already have a wife."

Rimpano laughed, for my having only one wife was a curious thing to him. But he did not press the issue, for I was already in his debt without the gift of a wife.

I was allowed to return to the hut to rest. As Odanga and I were walking, I inquired about the chief's pleasure at hearing of my association with Brazza.

"The chief, like many Gabonese, reveres Brazza."

"And you?"

Odanga paused before continuing.

"I am more cautious in my appraisal."

"Do tell."

"To some Africans, Brazza is the Father of Slaves. To others, he is an extortionist. There is a story among the Nkomis who live above the Ogowe. When Brazza first came to explore Gabon, he traveled up the Ogowe with one message. 'The white man has two hands. One bears gifts, the other death. There is nothing in between. We will go up your river, either bringing trade which is profitable for you, or scorching the riverbanks with our powerful weapons. The choice is yours. Will our path be strewn with gifts? Or will the Ogowe run red with blood?'"

Back in the privacy of my hut, I removed my khakis and my damp and reeking underclothes. I spread the underclothes upon the floor to dry, then lay upon the bedding where the medicine man had ministered to me and covered myself in a blanket; there was no shortage of white men's cloth in this village.

More than once, my sleep was disturbed by the rustling of the curtain and the appearance of small black faces. Upon my waking, the spies would gasp and duck away. Finally, there was a time when the children's curiosity did not stir me, for when I was fully awake, my khakis and underclothes were missing.

I emerged from the hut wrapped in the blanket in the style of a Roman to the surprise of several women and their charges. I could not speak their tongue, so I mimed putting my legs into a pair of drawers. Laughter burst from their faces, for what did these savages know of the wearing of drawers!

"From what tribe did you learn that dance? Or has your fever returned!"

"Odanga! Laugh at me if you must, but help me recover my clothes. Some rascals ran off with them."

I returned to the hut, and a moment later a young woman delivered my khakis and underclothes, which had been laundered and hung to dry and folded. She laid them on my bedding; they were still warm, either from the sun or the woman's breasts. I remained a few moments longer in my toga.

A handful of boys, out of either guilt or curiosity, brought me some mangoes when I emerged from the hut. I sat with them on a pallet of grass in the center lane and bit into one of the ripe fruits.

"Thank you," I said. The boys smiled, pleased that they had pleased the white visitor. "English?" I inquired.

"No," one boy laughed. "Nkomi. You're English."

"Yes, I know you're Nkomi. I was inquiring if you spoke the language."

A couple of the boys shook their heads vigorously. Palm nuts, cotton—the language of commerce was batted my way. I raised my hand to stay them.

"Okay," I said, laughing. "That's very good."

"Are you from the factory?"

"No. I am a naturalist, not a trader."

The boys awaited an explanation, for trader, missionary, and slaver were likely the only words they knew for white men. Along that spectrum, from the trader who was to be courted to the slaver from whom the villagers would seek escape further in the jungle, the boys did not know where to put the naturalist.

"I have come here to study chimpanzees."

Several of the boys looked to the boy who had called me "English" for an interpretation.

"Kulu-kamba," he said, and rose to his feet to demonstrate a knuckle-walk. His friends and I exploded in laughter.

"Yes!" I said. "That's right. "Kulu-kamba. You've quite the resemblance!"

When evening came on, Odanga invited me to take leave of the boys and join him and the village's men around a fire in the village's center. Spits of meat and manioc reminded me how little I had eaten since waking with fever.

"If you are ambivalent toward the commissaire, in what regard do you hold Father Buleon?" I asked Odanga.

"Ozounge is a good man. He cannot be blamed for the situation Brazza and the French created. And Brazza acts decently within the Gabon he has made."

"But you wish he had not made it in the first place?"

Odanga smiled affirmingly.

"What you must understand is that for the Gabonese, people are wealth. Chief Rimpano possesses many men and women, but it is not the same as it was in your country. Though he may be said to enslave them, they are still men and women, and they are allowed the dignities that come with their position."

"Could the same not be said of the slaves in my country? Slaves married and raised families."

"When white masters have possessed Black people, there has been no dignity. I have learned enough to know that American slaves were machines whose backs and families were broken to build up that nation."

I thought of the bicycle again, and the likelihood that men were dying for it, that villages were vanishing for it. Had bolts of cotton not created nearly the same effects in America before the war? Had men not worked mercilessly and, yes, like Odanga said, had families not been sundered? In the shadows of my fond memories of Uncle Jim were dim recollections of a younger, stronger slave who loaded train cars bound for plantations and mines. I recalled him once leaning against the train station, exhausted after his labor, watching with glassy eyes and sullen lips as the cars were pulled away. His pathetic countenance, it occurred to me, was not due solely to his aching muscles; there must have been a wife, perhaps children, too, on a plantation somewhere. Did he dream of hiding aboard a train and finding them? Of bearing them to their freedom in the North? If he had such dreams, the threat of consequences kept him in place. My father was not a harsh master, but if ever a slave would have attempted escape, my father would not have let him forget that he was his property.

I could not come to my country's defense again. I had long held Emancipation responsible for my family's decline, so had looked upon it with great bitterness. But the truth was that since coming of age, I had not suffered any ill effects from it. Hearing Odanga's assessment of

American slavery, I doubted there was any defense of it.

"Brazza's Gabon has utterly changed its people's way of life," Odanga continued. "But, within the Gabon he has created, Brazza has acted decently, in that he has disrupted the slave trade that many Gabonese foolishly rushed toward. I offer my services to Ozounge so that he may purchase Gabonese from the hands of unscrupulous chiefs who dare keep up the trade."

"Is that what he's doing in the Eshira village?"

"Yes. And I would rather they live in Ozounge's mission than suffer at the hands of cruel masters."

I was passed some roasted manioc. My stomach found it agreeable, so I accepted a stick of roasted meat from Odanga. As I brought the meat near my lips and was touched by its steam, I asked him what it was.

"Monkey."

I would have to be sated by manioc that night.

In the morning, I felt strong enough to march with Odanga to a nearby Holt factory. We headed back in the direction of the river, and were fortunate to find an elephant trail that made the going easier. I was still awfully weary, and very nearly was marching in my sleep. My lids grew very heavy, and my footfalls felt less and less in my power. I was simply moving along by some inertia fueled by the jungle's heat.

In my sleepy state, I did not notice Odanga come to a stop, and I was powerless to stop my forward motion anyway, so I came bumping up against his broad back.

"What's the matter?" I asked.

"We must leave this trail."

"Whatever for?"

I regained myself and stood next to Odanga. A rope of vine was stretched across the path and, wrapping around mangrove trees, stretched into the jungle on both sides. Odanga pointed to a bundle of wilted flowers, once red, strung to the vine where it crossed the trail.

"This marks a reserve. No one shall hunt or gather fruits here until the men who designated it remove the boundaries."

"They are keeping it to themselves?"

"No, Professor. It was at risk of being depleted. It is being given a chance to replenish itself."

"Well, surely we can cross it. We'll take nothing."

"I would be at great risk crossing it, especially with a white man. No white man takes nothing."

For several grueling hours, we skirted the reserve through thick, untrodden jungle. Even the powerful Odanga grew weary; he sighed and cursed—or so that is how I took his utterances—at intervals as he eked out our path. At no point did he betray any temptation to trespass upon the reserve, and for that I grudgingly admired him.

We finally arrived at a building that looked very much like the Hatton and Cookson factory on the lake. I knew it must be the Holt factory.

"Oh, thank God," I said to Odanga. "I may finally rest."

An English agent appeared at the door, and seeing my condition, helped me to a hammock inside. As the agent and Odanga helped me into the hammock, I thanked Odanga for not leaving me to the ants and cannibals.

"Rest," Odanga said. "Ozounge will stop here so the men may have a respite. You will rejoin the caravan then."

The agent took my helmet as I sunk into the hammock—and before the thing stopped bowing under my weight, a deep and dark sleep carried me away.

I awakened from uneasy dreams with a great weight on my torso. There sat upon me a young chimpanzee.

"I dread I am hallucinating again."

Having spoken these words, though, I knew I was not. The little brown face was real—and it conveyed to me the chimpanzee's delight in his position; I mean to say he pulled his lips back and exposed his teeth in what was unmistakably a smile. He followed this by caressing my ears and cheeks and, finally, my lips. I reached out and gently brushed my own fingertips across his soft mouth. Speech was not required for us to form the bond we would share for the remainder of the chimpanzee's brief life; touch was our common language.

"I think Moses likes you, Professor."

I turned and saw Wolfgang. I sat upright on the hammock, the little ape remaining in my lap.

"How long have I slept? I haven't missed the caravan? Where is Odanga?"

"Don't worry. He went to catch up with Father Buleon. They'll be through here in a few days, depending on how things go with the Eshira."

Wolfgang invited me to sit at a table, and the chimpanzee leapt from my lap and climbed into the chair opposite me. An agent (a few bustled about now) could be heard in another room of the factory; from the clacking noises he produced, I imagined him to be packaging ivory for shipping to the coast. Wolfgang heated a tin of soup on a kerosene stove and served it to me with some crackers. I thanked him and said I felt quite recovered.

"I don't know that I ought to rejoin Buleon. Odanga said he wasn't concerned about me. He wanted to leave me in the jungle to die!"

"Come, now. Perhaps he didn't know you were suffering from fever. Was that plain?"

"Surely it was plain on my red face! Though, no, I didn't tell him."

"See? Father trying to kill you. That's absurd."

"Is it? I know his dogma's threatened by my work. He told me as much."

Wolfgang, disbelieving, shook his head.

"So have you caught the trail of any gorillas?" I asked. "I have seen them only in my horrible dreams."

"Not yet. Though I did purchase Moses here."

"Moses?"

"A native claimed to have found him on the banks of the Rembo Nkomi, apparently orphaned. Probably his mother was killed by a hunter. Anyway, he was got for a decent price. I was thinking of you and hoping to run into you here."

"I'm afraid I don't have much to offer you."

"Consider him a gift."

Moses was giving my meal a longing look, so I handed him a cracker, which he quite enjoyed. He then spoke for the first time in my presence.

"Uh." (The "u" short and the "h" breathy.) "Uh."

"I think he wants another cracker," said Wolfgang.

I passed Moses a second cracker, which satisfied him.

"That wasn't too hard. Maybe I should get into your line of work, Professor!"

I spent several days in the factory getting acquainted with Moses. He measured about thirty inches; I guessed him to be no more than two years of age. His little tawny face was long, with a pronounced muzzle and brow. The eyes, however, lent him a wizened look; even with the darkened sclera, they were keenly expressive, and, combined with his flexible lips, allowed me to know his present mood. His fine, black hair was long everywhere, except upon his head, where it was shorter and fell into a natural part in the middle, like the combed hair of a young boy.

A chimpanzee's gait, however, will spoil any belief that they are like small humans. Moses, in exploring the trading post, used his long arms like a set of crutches, placing a portion of his weight upon his knuckles as he advanced with his stout legs, the right foot always leading. He would stand upright for a moment to reach an object from the table, and would use his long hands and prehensile feet in conjunction to climb countertops.

The agents were used to seeing chimpanzees accompany men, white and Black, but rarely were the animals allowed to run about the factory freely. It soon became evident that my keeping Moses there for so many days was unprecedented—and unappreciated. The curious little ape had a penchant for interrupting business. I would be heating soup and hear a sudden clacking of scattering palm nuts and the curses of an agent.

Wolfgang left to pick up his gorilla hunt. Moses and I continued to await the caravan. To leave the agents in peace, I took Moses on walks into the jungle—only shallowly, so I would hear the approach of the caravan if it came. Moses leapt ahead of me, exploring the groundcover for insects, or allowed me to pick him up and place him on my shoulders. He rather enjoyed this method of travel—not unlike Harry had when he was the same age.

One afternoon, as Moses and I were walking in the jungle, I heard what I guessed to be the caravan: A number of bodies treading through the jungle toward the factory. I returned to the factory's yard, Moses on my shoulders, and instead of finding Buleon's caravan, found a caravan of at least thirty Nkomis. Pairs of the men were bearing large crates with the name Holt painted on their sides. The leader of this caravan was not a white man, but an African. This man was cordially greeted by one of the Holt agents. The Holt agent directed the porters to carry the crates to the rear of the factory, and I followed. In the rear of the factory were rooms into which African goods were packaged for shipping downriver to the lake and up the coast by steamer all the way to Libreville, where they would be transported by ocean liner to Europe.

The porters removed the lids from the crates, and the Holt agent and his African liaison inspected the contents of each one. I had learned from the agents that it was their practice to advance credit to their African agents in the form of money or goods. Therefore, when the agent returned with his porters, nothing was returned to him; it was the duty of the Holt agent to inspect the delivery and ensure that it satisfied the credit that had been advanced. To this end, the Holt agent was marking a manifest. Curiously, the African also held a manifest—and was making parallel marks upon it!

"I beg your pardon," I said to the Holt agent. "But what is your liaison doing with that manifest?"

The Holt agent looked upon me with exasperation.

"Are you blind, Professor?"

The African continued to look into the crate and count elephant tusks. He paid me no attention.

"Are you saying this fellow reads and writes?"

The African looked upon me now. I swear he rolled his black eyes back in his head.

"Well enough," said the Holt agent. "Now would you mind? We are quite busy."

"Of course. I know the children in the missions learn to read and write. But I never saw a savage come out of the jungle with a manifest. Remarkable."

Buleon's caravan finally arrived late one afternoon. I was enjoying watching Moses play in front of the factory with some boys who had wandered over from the village to make small trades with the agents, when Buleon appeared with his Nkomi entourage. The boys had been one thing, but the semicircle of men frightened Moses right into my arms.

"Professor! I am sorry your fever prevented you from reaching our destination," Buleon said. "But I see you encountered an ape all the same."

He petted Moses, who accepted the gesture with palpable trepidation.

"And I am thankful Odanga was there to save my life while you were busy saving souls." Upon a more thorough count of the natives that surrounded Buleon, I realized he had failed to return with any slaves. "The Eshira drive too hard a bargain for you?"

Buleon smiled. He was frustratingly unflappable.

He allowed his men a period of rest, during which Moses remained in my arms, before we began the march back to the Rembo Nkomi. My strength having returned, and practiced as I was in treading the jungle floor by my brief jaunts around the factory, I found the marching to be quite tolerable. I became adept at avoiding the grasp of mangrove roots and ducking the low-hanging vines. I was able to keep pace with Odanga, who, besides Wolfgang, I trusted more than anyone else I had yet met in Africa. Moses rode my shoulders through the thickest parts and knuckle-walked across the elephant trails that occasionally gave us respite.

Buleon and the Nkomis paid little attention to the caravan's new member. Would that he went unnoticed at the mission!

Upon arriving at the Rembo Nkomi, the Nkomis pushed the pirogue to the water's edge, where we boarded it. Moses sat upon my lap, and was a perfect, though awfully bored, passenger for the three-day trip back.

I did not press Buleon for an apology for his neglect of me nor a confession of his designs to kill me, but I refused to be timid any longer regarding the nature of my work. Moses, sitting patiently between us, became the focus of nearly all our conversation during those long hours aboard the pirogue, and I was incautious in using his language in front of Buleon.

"Uh," I said to Moses around noon of the first day.

"Uh," he said back.

I pulled a banana from my pack, peeled it, and offered half to him.

"What you just saw," I told Buleon, "was me raising the idea of food to him, and his replying, 'Yes, I would like something to eat.'"

"That is clever, Professor. But mimicry and the passing around of bananas is something I have seen many times between native children and captive chimpanzees."

"Surely even you know that chimpanzees are not parrots."

Buleon laughed smugly. "I was not suggesting that the ape was mimicking you. Quite the opposite!"

At the first night's camp, I pitched a small tent that I had purchased at the factory, inside of which Moses and I slept soundly, apart from the scheming Buleon. The following day, Buleon and I passed the hours in the pirogue discussing Moses' features and their apparent uses. When I passed Moses a banana, he did not peel it as a man does, but bit into its center to gain purchase on the peel, which he discarded at our feet. I commented on this interesting habit, but earned no reply from Buleon; he either had witnessed the habit before or was a fine actor. We observed, finally, how the chimpanzee's fingers are quite long, relative to man's, but that the tendons are shorter than the bones, so that he can never lay his hand flat; rather, in its "open" position, the fingers are curled. This clearly was to aid his swinging in trees. I stroked Moses' palm and was moved by our affinity.

"I wonder if the chimpanzee, finding an arboreal life advantageous, evolved so as to have this curled hand."

"I beg your pardon?"

"I am wondering if chimpanzees used to have flat hands, like our own. I mean millions of years ago. Let us imagine that was the case. They would not be as strong of tree climbers, and they would be more susceptible to predators. The chimpanzees who, due to natural variation, had slightly curled fingers would be the strongest climbers. More of that variety would survive and reproduce. Eventually, you would find the situation at present: chimpanzees with very curled fingers living an arboreal life."

Buleon thought on this a moment.

"That is not an unsound idea," he offered.

"That," I said, with betraying enthusiasm, "is natural selection. Evolution!"

I had won Buleon's admission that Mr. Darwin's theory of evolution was "not an unsound idea." I ought to have held on to that victory for the time being, but I could not resist pressing the case further.

"The other possibility is that an earlier iteration of man was arboreal and had curled fingers. Perhaps men evolved to have the more useful hands we possess."

"The idea of man's evolution is quite different from that of apes."

"How so?"

"It's blasphemy."

"Let go your dogma, already!"

"Perhaps I am wrong, Professor. *You* might be an earlier iteration of man, in fact: Your fingers are nearly curled into fists."

I looked down at my hands, which were in fact tightening into fists.

"That is because I want to strangle you!"

After two more days of Buleon's excruciating company, we arrived back at the mission. It was just before the dinner hour. I had made arrangements with Buleon and Odanga to hire the Nkomi entourage to assist me with transporting my materials into the jungle and constructing my cage. I wanted to strike out immediately, but our departure would have to wait until the following morning.

After cleaning up in my borrowed room, I walked to the dining hall. A trader or naturalist joining the missionaries and their charges generally did not warrant much attention, but I, of course, had little Moses at my side, holding my hand as he scooted along. Being used to the presence of chimpanzees, the students were less abashed than the brothers and sisters. Buleon had never brought a chimpanzee into the mission compound before; Moses was a great explorer!

Moses and I sat in a gap in a long table between the students and their teachers. On my left was a young native man who bore a scar upon his cheek; the gash must have split him open from his chin to his ear, which had grown gnarled, likely from the same blow. So hideous was the disfigurement that I could not ignore its presence in my periphery.

The sister whom I had met before my adventure up the Rembo Nkomi asked to join us, and sat opposite me. A student served us—Marie and me, that is. Moses made a dinner of the manioc I shared with him and whatever insects he could find below the table.

"Your pet!" Marie said. "He is so adorable. What do you call him?"

"Moses. An orphan found by the river."

"How terrible. Will he go with you back to America?"

So focused was I on my studies in the jungle that I had not yet considered Moses' future. But Marie's query led me to the insight that I imagined would guarantee the delivery of a phonograph.

"Yes. I believe I know someone who will be very interested in purchasing him!"

Marie called Moses in her sweet, low voice, and he crawled under the table to visit her. He enjoyed her pets immensely.

"Sister, I cannot help but ask," I whispered. "Have you any idea what happened to that poor boy?"

Her countenance revealed that she knew of whom I was inquiring.

"He came here from the Congo Free State. Thousands have fled the cruelties there."

"That scar?"

"A lash from a chicotte. A whip made from the hide of a hippo."

My father's slaves were a docile bunch that never warranted any punishments, but I knew that among slaveholders whipping was the preferred method of discipline. So it went in the Congo Free State.

"It is too terrible to imagine what goes on there."

"I pray it does not happen here," I said.

"So you are a prayerful man?"

"Savages they may be, but the Africans are imbued with the knowledge of their continent's natural history. As a scientist, I would not want that knowledge ruined for all the rubber and ivory in the world."

"I hope that as a prayerful man you would not want the Africans tortured and murdered for any price."

"Yes, of course. Every race is due its dignity."

Moses, having cleared the floor of insects, asked for more manioc with a few "uhs." "Uh," I said, giving him more. He threw it on the floor and pouted. I suppose he wanted plantains.

"I also hope that turning them into Christians does not spoil their knowledge," I said.

"Did you just compare our mission to the Belgian capitalists?"

"I meant no such comparison. I'm only suggesting that the presence of concessionary companies and Christian missions alike have greatly impacted the Africans' natural habitat."

"I would prefer if you excused yourself."

"Sister, I only—"

"Please go away! Your pet may stay. He has much better manners."

Having left Moses with Sister Marie, I walked to the mission building to send a telegram to Mr. Walcott. I found the associate priest and several of the brothers enjoying coffee in the mission building's lower level and inquired after a telegraph operator.

"Mark will assist you," the associate priest said. He called out in French and was answered by the young Nkomi who had greeted Mr. Wolfgang and me upon our arrival at the mission building. The Nkomi appeared from a chamber off the main room; it seemed a reasonable assumption that he lived there, rather than the men's dormitory, so that he could be quick to assist the missionaries.

The young man listened to the associate priest's instructions, then flashed me a smile and bade me to follow him. So follow him I did, up the stairs toward the room that held the telegraph machine. There had been nothing in the priest's demeanor that suggested he was being anything but forthright with me, but I felt as if I were being put on. An African telegrapher!

"Am I to understand you are the telegrapher?" I asked as we ascended the stairs.

"Yes, sir."

"Mark. What used to be your name?"

The young man ignored my question.

We arrived at the desk, and Mark seated himself and readied his fingers at the keys, awaiting my message. At the risk of embarrassment, I stated the recipient's name and address. The young African tapped out the information.

"Where did you learn this skill?" I asked, for the young man had earned my trust.

"One of the brothers taught me."

"Impressive. I'll go on now: Have acquired young chimpanzee, stop. On promise to deliver said animal to Mr. Hornaday upon return would appreciate shipping of phonograph to St. Anne's Mission Gabon, stop. Time is of the essence, stop."

Chapter Seven

Fort Gorilla. McLaughlin had named my cage in derision, but the name had caught on among the Nkomis who were to help assemble my home in the jungle. Odanga had taught it to the men who didn't speak much English, and they delighted in saying it.

On either side of St. Anne's and Hatton and Cookson, Lake Nkomi's perimeter is a patchwork of sandy plains, teeming with colobus monkeys and bushbucks, and fingers of lagoons and marshes, festering with disease. Beyond the perimeter lay the thick jungle. Into the jungle behind the mission, I led, with the aid of my trusted companion, Odanga, the dozen Nkomis who carried my trunks and the crates that held the materials from which my cage would be constructed. Moses knuckle-walked alongside me, and Olago was on my other side. We had set out in a southeasterly direction an hour or so after dawn, and at about ten o'clock, I intuited that the place at which we had arrived was perfectly suited for my work. I say intuited because there was nothing about the spot that explicitly suggested its suitability; the jungle here—and I estimated we were just a few degrees south of the equator—was not less dense or damp. It simply struck me as the place I ought to make my home for the next several months.

Ten o'clock is the beginning of the quiet midday, when every living thing surrenders its motion to the oppressive heat. On this day, my party unfortunately interrupted the wildlife's restful midday. The Nkomis chopped the trees and vines and groundcover with machetes, clearing a rough square on which to construct my cage. I explained the cage's assembly to Odanga. He then directed the other men, and within a couple of hours, they were smiling and wondering over the result. "Fort Gorilla!" they repeated.

Fort Gorilla sat upon a wooden floor, elevated by wooden legs about two feet tall; this was to reduce—though not eliminate—the problem of ants and snakes entering the cage. The cage itself was a cube built of twenty-four three-foot, three-inch-square steel lattice panels; with four squares per side, each side equaled six feet, six inches. The right-hand panels on the south side functioned as a locking door. Every panel had been painted green to camouflage the cage. A roof of thatched bamboo was laid over the top panels by a couple of men who scaled one side of the cage.

The four panels that were to lie over the wood floor I had set aside; they proved to be unnecessary, as the cage felt sturdy enough without them, and I needed quarters for Moses. These remaining panels were attached to form a cube sans roof and floor. A slightly elevated bamboo floor, covered in leaves, and a bamboo roof were hastily made, and Moses quickly had a miniature version of my cage. The Nkomis were delighted by the impromptu construction, and named it Fort Kulu-Kamba. I swung open one panel to allow Moses to explore his new home, and upon his entrance, the Nkomis burst into curious laughter.

"In my country, there are great gardens in which animals live inside cages so that everyone can see them."

Odanga translated for the men.

"Chimpanzees, elephants, and a great many beasts you have never seen."

There was some chatter among the men, and Odanga asked me what beasts they had never seen. I thought on this a moment and recalled the black bears who had frightened visitors to Mr. Hornaday's zoo with their rooftop antics.

"There are bears, for one example."

I stomped my feet and bared my lips in the mammalian expression of dominance, but not knowing what to do with my hands, they flopped in front of me like fins. Oh, I was a terrible bear. Some of the men, including Odanga, laughed at me, so I quickly gave it up.

"When your own country is more civilized, perhaps you will have your own zoological gardens. Then you will see a proper bear."

I stepped into my own cage. There was more chatter among the men, to which Odanga smiled before interpreting.

"They want to know if you are putting yourself on display for the animals here."

"Oh, that's very good. A human zoo."

It occurred to me that I had never explained to Odanga my objectives in his country. I stepped back out of the cage to converse with Odanga while the men rested.

"I am not sure if you heard, or if you heard whether you understood, any of my conversation with Father Buleon on the journey back from the Holt factory, but I am in my little human zoo to study chimpanzees—particularly their sounds—to prove human evolution. Evolution, you see, is the theory that the ancestors of your people, and my people, and all the peoples of the world today, savage or civilized, once existed in a state such as little Moses here now exists."

As I've said, Odanga was very intelligent for his race. His smile suggested that he had followed my explanation. But while the contours of his mouth showed understanding, something in the shape of his eyes revealed his doubt.

"It took millions of years," I explained. "Imagine an early race of men: more naked and hunched over than even the most savage tribe of today. Let's say some members of this race had an advantage—like bigger brains. Those brainy types would know how to live longer, and would produce more offspring; eventually, they would be a dominant race among the early races of men. The other races would die out, with or without the help of the dominant races. It's all led to you and me and Moses, but go far enough back, and there's a shared line."

"That's an interesting theory, Professor."

"You don't believe in it, yet, do you?"

I let Odanga consider evolution and returned to the cage. Being just under six feet tall, I had enough headroom. And having brought so little in the way of furniture, I had ample space to arrange my quarters. I was passed my two trunks and watched by the Nkomis as I opened them and furnished the cage. I set up my kerosene stove in one corner; on this, I would boil water for drinking and desiccated soup. In one corner adjacent to the stove, I unfolded my camp chair, and in the other I placed my trunks, which would serve as writing surfaces. And in the corner opposite the stove, I unrolled my bedding. The whole time, the Nkomis watched with great interest. They had never seen a naturalist so ready to brave their dangerous world!

I felt like singing. And I thought the Nkomis might enjoy a song after their troubles. I removed Pearl from a trunk, and from inside my cage I began to pluck and sing "My Old Kentucky Home." Already a devotee of Foster, I had picked up a love for the song when I briefly lived in Kentucky, in spite of its abolitionist leaning. It was not lost upon me that I was an ambassador—though of what sort I was not yet sure—bringing Foster's song to the heart of Africa, the cradle of civilization.

My performing earned the natives' curiosity, much as it had captured the curiosity of the orangutan, Jim. Moses emerged from his cage to investigate, too. My audience's sideways glances soon turned to smiles, and I was sure everyone—savage and chimpanzee—enjoyed the sight of a white man in a cage singing a strange song to the plucking of a foreign instrument! Only Odanga was not grinning; his earnest countenance suggested that he had detected the song's message and appreciated my tacit agreement with America's abolitionists.

When the song was finished, Odanga sternly called for the men's attention, as he was ready to begin the march to their village. I returned Pearl to her case and walked over to Odanga.

"I don't know if your theory is true," Odanga said. "But I appreciate that it depends upon our shared humanity. I wish all men recognized that."

"Well said, my friend. I wish there were some way I could thank you."

"Your kindness to Ozounge and the commissaire is enough. They have freed many of my brothers from slavery." Odanga thought a moment longer. "Remain kind to Gabon, and it shall always welcome you."

Olago was left behind to assist me. He had brought his own sleeping mat, a rough version of my own purchased by Wolfgang. I granted him permission to enter the cage and stow his mat. Moses climbed in, too, and played upon my trunks.

It was past the hour for the midday meal, of which Olago reminded me by studying the stove. But I was simply too excited to eat. Many times I had wondered if my dream of studying apes in their natural habitat would ever come to fruition. Yet there I was! I was forty-four years old, but felt the exuberance of a man decades my junior. I believed my strength and curiosity would never extinguish, yet I also felt that I could not waste another minute before observing my first wild ape. I peered into the thick jungle, wishing my subject on.

But my reason—and my appetite—won out. Every ape in the jungle, save Moses, was resting at this time. I scooted Moses off a trunk and pulled two cans of fish from it. While I was opening these, Olago plucked a few plantains from a nearby tree. I sat in my chair, and Moses and Olago settled on the floor. I gave Olago a fork; Moses ate the fish with his fingers. Before I took a bite, I reflected on the significance of the scene: My cage in the jungle, which had been a proposal unlikely to gain approval by the Smithsonian and a speculative illustration in *Harper's Weekly*, was now a reality.

After lunch, Moses returned to his cage, where he marveled at the steel lattice with his fingers, and Olago rested on his mat. I could not imagine sleeping, so I decided to write to Maggie—something I had not done since arriving in Liverpool months ago.

Dear Maggie,

I am writing to you from my home in the jungle of Gabon. But I am not alone; I have been provided with a servant boy and have acquired a chimpanzee. The little ape's name is Moses, and you would think him a delight.

Everyone I have met on this adventure has been wonderfully helpful, be they French, English, or African. Except for a mild fever, which was relieved by a single dose of quinine, I have felt perfectly well. I expect the trip to be a complete success and a major contribution to natural history.

I expect to receive a phonograph from the Smithsonian Institution very soon now, as I have promised my chimpanzee to the Smithsonian's zoo. The instrument's arrival will allow my studies to begin in earnest.

I hope you are well in my absence.

Your loving husband,
Richard

Around two o'clock, the jungle began to awaken from its midday slumber. Something rustled in the groundcover before gaining the cleared ground around my cage: an armadillo. His armor contracted as he stood to explore the strange structure before him; and in moments like that, when some small fellow captured my attention, I would notice that the song of insects and birds had risen imperceptibly back to its earlier, busier state. Midday was over. The armadillo, satisfied that he was under little threat, returned to his search for insects.

I spent the remainder of the late afternoon wishing for the appearance of anything simian, but for a couple of hours nothing save a few rodents came in view of my cage. Then, just before evening began, a disturbance in a tree caught my attention. A group of vervets playing above brought a smile to my face; it was only my first day in the jungle, and already it had yielded simian life. Chimpanzees were sure to follow. I was uplifted by my confidence that over the next several months of living at Fort Gorilla, I would not only see chimpanzees, but also record their voices and begin the earnest study of their language.

The jungle's shadows began to deepen around five o'clock. They did not grow with the stealth of the insect- and bird-song, announcing nightfall with frightening suddenness; rather, they grew darker by degrees, striking a heavier shade much like a clock hand strikes a later hour.

To prepare for the night, I put on a pot of water to boil for desiccated soup and opened some tinned beef and crackers. The hiss of the match strike had caught Moses' ear, and he climbed into the cage to investigate. As the water heated, I struck another match, and he panted with excitement at the flame.

"Fire," I said.

I extinguished the match with a flick of my wrist, and Moses reached out to take it from me.

He stared at it, waved it, trying to reignite the flame, but only making the ashes crumble.

"Some cousin, between your kind and mine, learned to harness fire a long time ago," I told the ape. "Soup?"

I had Olago move a trunk to the middle of the cage for a table, at which Moses joined us. I set a bowl in front of the ape and held out a spoon for him.

"Watch," I said.

I demonstrated the spoon's use. Moses immediately imitated me, though he failed to keep any soup in the spoon on its way to his mouth and ended up only licking the utensil clean. I noted the number of attempts before he grew frustrated and tossed the spoon away: five. He consoled himself with a handful of crackers, which he fingered inside his lower lip. He flicked his tongue in there, too, and, his jaw wriggling forwards and backwards, softened the crackers enough to swallow them.

I picked up a few crackers to try it myself. Olago copied me. There we sat, seeing how long it would take for our saliva to soften the crackers enough to eat them chimpanzee-style.

Through the wad of dough in my jaw, I tried asking Olago how he was doing. He grinned around his own wad, showing his big upper teeth. We began laughing at ourselves, acting like apes as we were!

I raised my eyebrows to indicate to Olago that I was going to swallow—then promptly choked! I turned around and coughed the wad through the steel lattice.

"My goodness," I said. "I suggest you chew your food, boy. That's enough experimentation for one evening."

Moses, if he noticed, was not impressed with our mimicry. But it did not escape his attention that Olago and I were enjoying our meat with our forks. He reached for my fork and, when I held it away from him, threw an absolute bared-teeth tantrum. His fit quickly turned to begging, and he persisted with a whimper until I gave in. Once in possession of the fork, he did not use it to lift his meat, but immersed the tines in his soup. He was quite disappointed in the result, and threw away that utensil, too. I feared another tantrum coming, but the good-natured little ape sighed in resignation—much like men do—and finally enjoyed his soup by lifting his bowl to his mouth.

"We shall have to work on your table manners, Moses!"

After dinner, Olago swept the floor (Moses had left cracker crumbs and drips of soup in his place) and I tossed the empty bowls and tins outside the cage; this would generally keep the cage free of ants, and put them in our service cleaning the dishes.

Olago settled onto his mat. Moses, rather than going to his little cage, climbed a nearby tree and designed a small nest of leaves. I stood below him watching as he fluffed the leaves to his satisfaction. At the Holt factory and on the journey to St. Anne's, Moses had always slept on top of me. Perhaps that had been out of fear of the traders and Africans. Now, in the company of only me and the boy, he was reverting to his natural way of sleeping. I bade him goodnight and retired to my own bed, and I would be lying if I said I didn't miss his tender form weighing on my chest! But I would have no trouble sleeping.

When the final stroke of darkness fell, the jungle was a swath of deep blue, pierced occasionally by a star visible through the canopy. The seconds were marked by the bursting of dew drops from their high perches, which served to lull me into a restful sleep that first, memorable night.

Morning came to the jungle as nightfall's inverse: By slow strokes, a soft light extinguished the darkness, each stroke revealing a deeper layer of the surrounding foliage, until, by six o'clock, I could see as far into the jungle as the mangrove trees permitted.

At that time, Fort Gorilla's inhabitants took a walk. Armed for protection with my rifle, I led us in the direction of a spring we had heard bubbling on our way to set up the camp. Moses rode my shoulders, and Olago followed with a clay jug. Aboard the *Ballay*, I had heard that Gabon's interior was blessed with magnificent falls, streams that burst through foliage and mountain and cascaded into clear pools. Misty oases in the jungle miasma. The spring we arrived at was not one of these great falls. The water began just above my head and bubbled down three small shelves of rock before filling a shallow pool of only a few square feet.

The chimpanzee not being a water-loving animal, Moses climbed from my shoulders to the branches of a mangrove tree while I walked to the edge of the small pool and dipped my cupped hand into it. I tasted the cool water. A mere trickle it may have been compared to the faraway falls—but perhaps this spring had slaked the thirst of not only generations of men, but generations of species of men. Perhaps not this very spring—but its cousins, other streams fed by the Rembo Nkomi—had provided drinking water for the iterations of men who roamed these parts of Africa before passing into prehistory. For the species from whom Moses—he whose species had taken to the trees (or had remained in them)—and I had evolved.

We returned to Fort Gorilla, where Moses and Olago were allowed to play in the surrounding jungle; they quickly learned to enjoy each other's company and played like brothers. I asked only that Olago keep from speaking in English or Nkomi, and keep his utterances to imitations of Moses'; in that way, any nearby apes would hear only two chimpanzees at play. During this time, I removed my camp chair from the cage and placed it at the edge of the clearing where I could sit and take notes on the small animals who passed by. From this window on the jungle, I observed an array of birds. I am no ornithologist, but I recorded detailed descriptions and made some sketches to share with a man of that specialty when the opportunity arose.

Just before ten o'clock, I was stirred from my sketching by a rustle in the treetops. I set down my sketchbook and followed the sound, which came from the southeast. Olago and Moses quietly joined me. The rustle revealed itself to be only the group of vervets we had seen the previous day.

Moses then gave a sharp cry that sent the monkeys higher in the trees.

"For goodness' sake, Moses, what is it?"

He repeated the cry. I followed his and Olago's frightened countenances in the direction of the cage. Between us and the cage—not more than ten yards away—was a gorilla! The great black ape had paused from his knuckle-walk and was calculating the threat of the strange trio before him. I was struck with fear of the gorilla standing erect and beating his breast before leaping the short distance between us and rending me, limb by limb. Olago and Moses would suffer the cruel fate of having witnessed the mauling they were due when the beast made dessert of them! For my rifle was on the other side of the gorilla, inside the cage!

But these terrible thoughts were only fleeting; this was not the nightmare beast of my fevered imagination or the mythical creature invented by false accounts of less-scientific adventurers. This fellow had little interest in us, as he was likely in search of a wife. This realization—that the gorilla was quite alone and with an agenda that did not include tasting human flesh—assuaged most of my fear; though I would rather have had my rifle than not. But the gorilla continued to stare at us; his eyes, under his heavy brow, held at the same time his animal instincts and that part of his intelligence he shared with man. Briefly, he turned his attention in the other direction—toward the cage. The situation was brought to a conclusion when Moses made a piercing cry, his lips curled backwards and his teeth bared, which sent the gorilla on his way. His escape into the jungle was surprisingly quiet, his stealth another contradiction to the tales of gorillas ripping through jungles to catch their victims. I took note of his direction—northeast—to pass along to Wolfgang.

After lunch, I asked Olago to take my letter to the mission for mailing.

"But, sir, what about the gorilla?"

"What about him? I don't think you'd make a suitable wife!" I laughed. "Besides, he went in nearly the opposite direction."

Olago was not laughing.

"I promise you won't need it, but if this makes you feel better . . . ." I reached inside a trunk and pulled out my revolver. I tossed it to the boy.

"And you should sooner point that revolver at your own head than point it at an ape. Understand?"

That evening, Fort Gorilla withstood its first storm.

No description of such a storm can fully satisfy the reader who has not lived through one, though I have attempted it in my books. The storm announced itself with a whisper: I felt as much as heard the subtle trembling of thunder, miles away. Leaves and vines answered with their vibrations in the cool breeze. Confident the murmurs would soon turn to screams, I had Olago assist me in hanging curtains on the sides of the cage; we would be sheltered from the rain—provided the whole thing did not blow over!

The thunder and its attendant quaking were soon upon Fort Gorilla. Lightning shocked the jungle with its rending bolts and revealed to me a canopy writhing in great pain. The jungle moaned under the assault. Every animal sheltered itself; Fort Gorilla's inhabitants sat in the cage, which took its lashings with great fortitude, waiting out the hour of the storm.

Moses sat in my lap; he and Olago faced the ordeal with admirable stoicism—they were creatures of the jungle, after all. They were only stirred by the events of the storm's final quarter, when the storm reached its zenith. The sound of the very earth below us being rent had us gripping the lattice for dear life, till we realized it was the splitting of branches we were hearing. Then we brought our hands away from the lattice, should a branch crash against the cage and crush our fingers. We huddled instead, praying for the storm to subside. A few more branches were ripped away, then it seemed as if the storm's thirst for destruction had been slaked.

"I think that may have been the worst of it," I said.

My words were followed by a sound like great bones breaking and a shower of bamboo leaves raining upon us. I held up my hands to protect myself and Moses, who was screaming in fright, and called out to Olago. He brushed leaves from himself and seemed to be unhurt. A branch had walloped the roof and mercifully rolled off before it collapsed. Had the roof been less sturdy, it might have crushed us!

My third day in the jungle was spent fixing Fort Gorilla's roof—a task which took me and Olago most of the quiet midday. Moses followed our activity with curiosity, though he never offered to lend a hand!

To make the time pay with more than just a fortified roof, I inquired about Olago's village. His description matched my impression of the village in which I had recovered from my fever: a chief with many wives and servants, brave men like Odanga to provide for the villagers, and women to rear the children.

"Do you prefer your village to the mission?"

"I am called to the mission only to help Mr. Wolfgang."

"I suppose he prefers you as you are, rather than in the hands of Father Buleon."

"I think he and Ozounge worship different gods?"

"Something like that," I laughed. "So you like accompanying Mr. Wolfgang?"

Olago nodded.

"Does he ever hire any other boys from your village?" Olago was obedient and strong for his age, but there must have been older, stronger boys in his village that Wolfgang could hire.

"No, only me."

"Your father must have great trust in Mr. Wolfgang."

Olago did not reply, instead busied himself with the thatching of bamboo.

Dew drops lulled us to sleep that night, though our slumber was soon interrupted. Contrasted with the splash of dew drops, the crackle of groundcover is a harsh—and in the blue-black jungle night—terrifying sound. I sat up and faced the direction from which the steps approached, though I could see nothing. My first thought was that the bachelor gorilla had returned, but the slow, heavy tread drew a leopard on my mind's eye. His cautious approach was the creeping of a hunt; I believed Fort Gorilla's inhabitants were the intended prey. I reached for my rifle—I now made sure to always know its location—and aimed it in the leopard's direction, resting the muzzle in a hole of the lattice. Olago was awake, too, breathing heavily behind me. The big cat continued its forward tread. I remembered Moses, and prayed that the cat could not scale the tree to his nest and enjoy him for an appetizer!

The leopard stopped in his tracks. A gentler rustling could only have been the flickering of his tail as he prepared to leap. Should he have leapt, Fort Gorilla might have been crushed like a tin can—and there would be only one fate for its inhabitants.

My finger sweated on the trigger as I prepared to fire. But I could not be sure I would hit the beast. I stood to either save my life or hasten my death!

I chose to wait a few seconds longer. This proved to be the prudent move: The cat turned on its feet and bounded into the jungle. The sound of his pads breaking the groundcover faded into the rhythm of dew drops, though I don't believe Fort Gorilla's occupants slept another second that night.

Henry Labouchere would have you believe that those three nights were the only ones I spent in Fort Gorilla. And that the observations I reported in my second book, *Gorillas & Chimpanzees*, were fictions I invented while enjoying the comforts of St. Anne's Mission. The suggestion that the scientific labors I carried out in the dangers of the Gabonese jungle were imagined under the influence of St. Anne's claret has been the greatest affront of my life.

Yet perhaps I could be blamed for aiding my enemies in their slandering, for I did visit the mission more than I had intended—and fostered a friendship with Sister Marie.

In fact, I returned to the mission the next day to assure everyone that Fort Gorilla had weathered the storm. I had allowed Olago to travel to his village, armed again with my revolver for safety, to assure his family that he had survived the storm unharmed, and I had marched to the mission with Moses on my shoulders and my rifle at my side.

The students were in the dining hall for the midday meal when Moses and I arrived. Perhaps they were surprised that I had not succumbed to storm or fever, for they smiled and laughed and asked me to join them. Sister Marie was among the children, though she would not meet my eyes when I looked her way. Was she still upset over our last meeting? Or was she only being mindful of the superior? The superior paced the hall's perimeter, missing nothing.

I sat down at the centermost of the long tables, Moses still on my shoulders, and the children there clung to us magnetically. Brother Leo walked a beat between the tables, complementing the superior's surveillance, so the children at the surrounding tables could only bend their ears toward the storyteller. I proceeded to regale them with my adventures: The bachelor gorilla, the terrible storm, the leopard in the night. It hardly seemed as if it all could have happened in three days!

"It hardly seems as if it all could have happened in three days," said Brother Leo, standing right behind me.

The magnetism broken, the closest children fell back into their seats, the others let their ears relax.

"You come and see for yourself, Brother."

I watched Moses search for scraps on the floor as the hall began to empty of children, though of course there were not many to be found among those well-watched children. Marie, leading a group of girls out, paused by me, so I stood and removed my helmet.

"Good afternoon, Sister."

"Hello, Professor." Her eyes darted toward the superior, who must have been her constant watcher. "I enjoyed your stories very much."

"You were listening!"

A brief—but undeniably joyful—smile overcame Marie's face; a second later she was whispering a goodbye to Moses, who gently hooted in reply.

"Good day, Sister."

I reported to Father Buleon that I had remained quite safe in the jungle and had even observed a solitary gorilla.

"And did this gorilla have anything to say for himself?"

"He was silent on the matter of my making him a good wife. I'll need to observe a family to study their natural speech."

"And a phonograph, correct?"

Buleon insisted I spend the night at the mission. I could enjoy a fine dinner and a comfortable bed before returning to my home in the jungle. I had planned on marching back, but so insistent was Buleon that I allowed myself to be shown to a room where I could clean up before joining the brothers and sisters for the evening meal. I began to have doubts on the matter of Buleon's leaving me in the jungle for dead, for he was not eager for me to put myself back at risk in Fort Gorilla; but the motive behind his hospitality would soon be revealed.

I could not sleep.

In my room was a small desk at which I had done some writing after dinner. When I could write no more, I retired to the bed, expecting sleep to take me in seconds. Instead, I lay awake imagining a family of chimpanzees exploring Fort Gorilla, calling to each other regarding the strange structure they had discovered, and climbing the lattice to the roof, which made a pleasant bed. All that simian activity and I was not there! My rational mind knew there was very little chance my thoughts bore any resemblance to reality, but they kept me from sleep nonetheless. Moses, untroubled as usual, had tucked himself next to me and was sleeping soundly.

Moses and I returned to Fort Gorilla the following morning. There was no evidence it had been visited by anyone, save a couple of snakes curled upon the floor, which I simply kicked aside, sending the beasts into thrashing fits until they found purchase in the steel lattice and slithered through. At the jungle's threshold, they disappeared into the groundcover. Would that they were the only snakes to penetrate Fort Gorilla!

From that threshold, unmolested by snakes or any other beasts, Olago appeared, spear in hand and revolver at his hip. The first time he had left camp by himself, he had been quite frightened, for we had just met the bachelor gorilla. His dark eyes had shone with anxiety upon his return. But this time, his eyes reflected steadiness. The boy seemed taller, too, which I attributed not to his having grown—though he may have shot up a bit—but to his holding himself in a smarter posture.

By the following day, the young man and I and Moses were back to the routine we had developed: After the morning walk to the spring to get the day's supply of water, I enjoyed the best period of observation the day offered; we had the midday meal, after which Olago went fruit gathering and Moses napped while I wrote; as evening approached, I enjoyed another period of observation before preparing dinner and readying Fort Gorilla for the blue-

black night. The pattern was abundantly satisfying to me, and interruptions to it—of which
there were many—were generally unwelcome.
As the weeks passed, I suffered no more fevers.
I improved my diet of tinned meat and desiccated soup with plantains and mangoes that
Olago gathered, and so was always satiated.
The notion that I abandoned Fort Gorilla for
full-time residence in a dormitory at St. Anne's
was indeed slander!

One evening, as Moses sat upon a trunk watching me prepare dinner, he surprised me by
springing to the lattice behind me with a great,
bared-teeth shout. I grabbed my rifle and
swung around, expecting the big cat's return.
Oh, God, I thought, the cage door was open!

My fear was relieved when the thing approaching turned out to be only Brother Leo,
who had drawn his own rifle and was searching
for the beast I mistook him for.

"Thank God," I said. "It's only you. Do come
inside."

Leo, flinching, trained his rifle on the barking ape.

"Cut that out, Moses," I commanded.

Moses hid his teeth behind his lips, but remained clinging to his corner. Leo lowered his
rifle and stepped into the cage. He had never

seen it before, and studied it—though it is not a subject that can be studied for very long.

"So you decided to come see things for yourself?" I said.

Leo handed me a letter, that being the purpose of his visit. It was the letter from Mr. Walcott I had been anticipating.

"We're just about to eat. Would you care to join us?"

Moses whimpered his dismay at my invitation.

"Moses, please. You're not making Brother Leo feel very welcome."

"Thank you, but I prefer to return before dark."

"Afraid you might cross a gorilla? Or a hungry leopard? Step off the plantation once in a while, and those things are bound to happen, you know."

"I have duties at the mission."

"Very well. Another time, then."

When Leo had disappeared into the jungle, I harangued Moses for his behavior—though I could not stay mad at the adorable ape for long. I playfully whipped him with the letter Leo had delivered, and suggested that I would have Mr. Hornaday beat him for such offenses.

So sure was I that Walcott would be amenable to my proposal that I was absolutely crushed by the letter's contents:

I decided at once to telegraph Mr. Hornaday in New York. I arrived at the mission the next morning, and happened upon a curious scene. Wolfgang's Fang and the young man with the scarred cheek were conversing in front of the mission building. I could not understand what they were saying, but observed incredulity on the countenance of the Fang, and the projection of foreboding from the mission man. The exchange aroused in me a greater sympathy than I had ever felt for any Black persons anywhere. I suddenly intuited the subject of their conversation: The mission man was describing the cruelty of the Belgian concessionary companies—I thought I saw him gesture toward his scar—and warning the young Fang of the terror that could one day sweep into Gabon. The barely clothed and sharp-toothed young man surely was puzzled, then, by the other man's adopting white manners—even as he himself had pledged service to an Englishman. If the white man has terrorized you, why have you delivered yourself to them? he seemed to ask. Brazza, Ozounge, they may be our best hope for protection from Leopold. These were the points upon which the men's conversation stalled and my sympathy was most greatly aroused: The Black man, whose dominion is Africa, had suffered to some degree from white men since Europeans first sailed to their continent centuries ago. Not the least of which was the American slave trade, an institution I had come to see as regrettable. That suffering, if the reports from the Congo Free State were true, was rising at a rate like never before. The palm oil and rubber seeker owed the abundant continent and its people a measure of restraint. The sport hunter, whether he seeks ivory from the plains or furs from the jungles, ought to set limits so that the continent's animals remain abundant. The naturalist, like myself, should take only knowledge and what specimens are absolutely necessary to his work. What would happen to the continent and its people should those limits not be respected?

I nodded solemnly to the Africans as I passed them to enter the mission building. I found Mark in the foyer and asked for his assistance with a telegram. In my telegram to Hornaday, I expressed my pleasure in hearing that he was building a new zoological garden for New York and offered my services as an animal collector; I further explained that I had already acquired a fine young male chimpanzee, which I would be happy to deliver upon my return if he would have a phonograph sent to Gabon immediately.

As I was finishing up, Father Buleon and Wolfgang came up the stairs to talk in the sitting room.

"Come by for a respite?" Buleon asked.

"Just sending a telegram. I shall be returning to my camp soon."

"Please sit down for a moment. Have you observed any more apes?"

"Not yet."

Behind his beard, Buleon's mouth twisted into a smile. Into this smile I read not sympathy, but smug satisfaction.

"How's Olago working out for you?" Wolfgang asked.

"Perfectly well. He's really developing into a strong and dutiful young man."

"Smart, too," Wolfgang said.

"Yes, for his race. He may one day be a leader among his people. If we can keep Father's hooks out of him!"

Wolfgang laughed uncomfortably.

"Well, now," he said, "perhaps the young man ought to be converted. Where is he, anyway?"

"He's visiting his village for a few days."

"Is that so?"

"Yes. I sent him home after that terrible storm to assure his family he had been quite safe. And I granted his request to go today."

Wolfgang shifted and sighed as if some blow had winded him.

"I'd prefer he remain with you. Or at the mission."

I had left Moses outside of the mission building and found him hooting and charging among a group of girls led by Sister Marie. The children and their teacher laughed at the little ape's amusing display. I paused before interrupting them; there was no sound in Gabon that equaled in pleasure Marie's laughter, its featherweight and feminine grace. It recalled for me the laughter of the young women who mystified me in my youth—though it was distinguished by its lightness. It was Virginia and Gabon, past and present.

"Your little ape is such a delight," Marie said. She seemed to have forgiven my offenses from the last time we had conversed at length. "Are you and Moses returning to the jungle now?"

"No. I plan on spending the day here and returning in the morning."

"I must be going," Marie said, giving Moses a pet on the head. "Good day, Professor."

Though I had not yet received a reply from Maggie, I wrote her again that afternoon from my room at the mission. I explained that I was now dealing directly with the estimable Mr. Hornaday and that my pet was destined for New York rather than Washington, though I would of course bring her to New York to see him. I relayed the story of the bachelor gorilla, assuring her that I was quite safe from the ape.

I also wrote Harry. Prior to my leaving for Gabon, my son had informed me that he intended to embark on a career in the life insurance business. I was very excited for him, and felt blessed that he had not had to endure the hardships of war. He was beginning adulthood with a sound body and mind and the love of his parents. But I was afraid, too, that he was crossing a threshold, on the other side of which my influence would be greatly reduced.

Why had I waited so long to write him? By the time the letter arrived, he might be totally beyond my influence. With urgency, I assured him of my relative safety and comfort in Gabon, then paused before moving on to what I really wanted to convey.

"Professor?"

Wolfgang appeared in the doorway.

"I'm sorry—you look like you're working."

"No. It's quite all right."

"I thought you might be interested in the race between me and Irish."

"Yes."

"He's not got a gorilla yet, either. But he has reported seeing scores of chimps."

"Where?"

"South of the lake. That's where your cage is, right?"

"Yes. I shall return at first light. Thank you. May I ask you something?"

Wolfgang nodded.

"Do you have a family back in England?"

"No, Professor," Wolfgang laughed. "Since I was a much younger man, I've spent more time in Africa than England. I had a girl when I first came. Was set to marry her. Kept a picture of her in my breast pocket, wrote her all the time. A year later, I surprise her at her parents'. Her face is white as a sheet and her belly is the size of a Christmas turkey. I slap her face and tell her, 'You were a virgin when I left you, but now you're a regular whore.' Her father grabs me and says she's a married woman now, and I'll be off if I want to keep my teeth."

"That's awful."

"So I kept my teeth and came back to Africa."

"I'm terribly sorry."

Wolfgang brushed my condolences away.

"I find the society here quite agreeable. I know plenty of Englishmen here, I've a friendly rivalry with that Irish bastard, and I meet other interesting people all the time. Like this American who's going to speak ape!"

I laughed, for I was beginning to feel a bond with the funny Englishman.

"And the Gabonese are fair peoples. Backwards, but fair. And since you might be uninitiated, I will tell you that the Nkomi women are fine company."

I continued my letter to Harry:

> *I urge you to find a suitable young woman to make your wife. The bonds of matrimony and the rearing of a child—*

though perhaps you will be blessed with many children!—have been the greatest joys of my life.

I shall see you and your mother early next year. Until that time, I will miss you both dearly.

I chose to dine in my room that evening. Luke delivered a tray to me containing half a chicken and roasted sweet potatoes; the portions were more generous than those served in the dining hall, and on the tray was a bottle of claret and a glass.

"Merci, Luke. Tell me—are you enjoying your time at the mission?"

After a moment, the boy nodded. Clearly my question had been a breach of some kind.

"I'm sorry," I said. "I've put you on the spot. You may go."

Though I was not used to such large portions, I ate everything on my plate save the bones; I thought it would be rude not to finish the fine meal I'd been served. The claret proved to be perfectly suited for it, and I actually emptied the bottle!

Set on returning to Fort Gorilla at sunrise, I decided to take a walk around the mission to see what company I could find; you never know what you might learn from Gabon's inhabitants, be they Black or white. Most everyone had retired to bed by this time; surely Sister Marie was asleep by this hour, for how else did her skin remain so fair?

The company I found was Brother Leo, who was sitting on the steps of the mission building cleaning his rifle by lantern light.

"Good evening, Brother."

"Professor. Where is your pet tonight?"

"Oh, asleep in some tree nearby. As long as he has the liberty to go about as he pleases, he's quite attached to me. I suspect the opposite is the case, too: Were I to bind him with a chain, he'd probably become the most disagreeable sort."

"Then leave him his liberty. St. Anne's is not a place for wildness, by ape or man."

"Quite true. I hope we both have been agreeable company."

Leo neither affirmed nor denied that we were, but kept polishing the barrel of his rifle.

"I shall be leaving very early tomorrow. Please give my best to Sister Marie. She's very fond of Moses, you know."

Leo rested his rifle upon his knees.

"Sister Marie has very important duties. Playing concierge to Father's guests—and their filthy pets—is not among them."

"Moses is not—"

"I advise you to leave her alone."

Leo resumed polishing—with extra vigor.

Chapter Eight

Weeks passed at Fort Gorilla uneventfully; rather, events that I have already described repeated themselves without variation. Armadillos, pigs, snakes, and monkeys trespassed Fort Gorilla's perimeter—but no apes. Moses grew. The regimen for a young chimpanzee included hours of playing in the trees, a steady diet of plantains and ants, which he mopped from the dirt with his hands, and lots of sleep in his little nests of sticks and leaves. Olago remained in my service. To prevent him from returning to his village, I invited him to the mission whenever I found myself wanting a respite from the boredom of the jungle. He joined me the first time, and after Wolfgang, who happened to be at the mission, spoke to him, he always joined me afterward. I never asked the boy exactly what Wolfgang had said, though I tried to get it from him indirectly.

One afternoon on a march to the mission, I told Olago I had heard Wolfgang suggest that he might enjoy joining the mission.

"Would you like that?" I asked.

Olago turned back to me briefly, keeping his steady pace forward.

"And leave my master for a white master?"

"You mean leave your father to be Buleon's—Ozounge's—charge?"

"I was talking about the chief. My village ought to be my home. My mother, my cousins—all are there. And most of the time we enjoy peace with our neighbors."

"And the mission is a 'village' of a completely different flavor, isn't it?"

"Yes. The women—why are they so … buried under their clothes?"

I laughed.

"Their habits?"

"I know nothing of their habits."

"No—that is what they wear upon their heads: a habit. They mystify me, too."

"Do you have any wives among them?"

"No. They are wedded to God or some such nonsense."

"Does not Ozounge have wives among them?"

"No. The same goes for him."

Olago faced me again. This time he came to a dead stop.

"How do white men …."

"How do we have children? That is left to the rest of us. I can't explain the religious classes. Myself, I have a wife and son in America."

Moses, who had been following us by leaping from tree to tree, used my stopping in my tracks to climb upon my shoulders. I reached up and petted his small feet; the touch recalled Harry riding upon my shoulders as a child; how vivid was the memory, and what feeling it elicited still!

Satisfied with my answer, Olago started marching again.

"How about your own father?" I asked after a moment. "What does he want for you?"

"My father wants me to be an agent for Hatton and Cookson."

"To straddle both worlds. That must be tough."

"It seems to be my burden."

During my respites, I sometimes saw Sister Marie and would tell her about the goings-on at Fort Gorilla—though I most often told her nothing there was new, but that I was confident that just beyond the limits of my vision into the gauzy jungle chimpanzees were teeming, and it was only a matter of time before they entered my field of observation. Patience would yield a great reward, I said; something she could surely understand.

I always kept an eye out for the watchful superior and Brother Leo. The former I hoped to avoid, for I did not want to be a source of trouble for Sister Marie. The latter I wished to see us! I wanted it known that I would not be intimidated. During this period, however, I did not see either of them, though it is quite possible they were aware of my presence, marked as I was by my helmet and ape and American accent.

If I were away from the mission for very many days, Father Buleon visited, rifle-wielding Leo at his side. Buleon inquired about my observations and expressed sympathy that I had not seen a single chimpanzee, though I believe his feelings were probably insincere. And he always invited me to come back to the mission, though I was already spending more days and nights there than I had ever planned.

If I had a letter or telegram at the mission, Buleon would deliver it. It was in this way that I learned that Moses would not soon be enjoying life in a new home in New York. Mr. Hornaday replied to my letter with great enthusiasm about the New York Zoological Society and his planned zoo. The society would be a great force for animal conservation, and the zoo would be the world's most beautiful and possess the greatest menagerie ever assembled. But it would be some time before he was ready to start receiving animals. The upside was that he wanted to secure Moses. He included a small sum as a security deposit and a contract that promised the remainder upon my delivery of the ape in New York. He was pleased to hear of my acquisition and hoped that I would become a trusted supplier of monkeys and apes.

"Moses, do come here. Uw. Uw."

I had gathered from my weeks with Moses that "uw" was the sound he produced for gaining someone's attention. Upon hearing my call in his language, he hurried into my cage to see what was going on. I laid the contract on the surface of one of my trunks and gave it my signature.

"This contract guarantees you a home in what is to be the world's greatest zoo." Moses looked at me curiously. "You will be under the care of the great conservationist, William Hornaday." Moses' head tilted to one side, as if the ape were wary of the proposition. "You will be housed in a fine enclosure. No savage African or rifle-wielding Englishman will be able to harm you. And in time, you will be joined by others of your kind, and your primate cousins." Moses' head straightened. I know he did not understand me in a literal way, but something in the tone of my promises assuaged the little chimpanzee.

I held out to him my ink pen, which he took and nearly brought to his lips, point first, before I could correct him. Moses failing to work the pen into his hands in the manner of a human—for his fingers, as I have mentioned, were not exactly like our own—I turned the pen upside down in his fist, so he could produce marks with it.

"Now," I said. "Underneath my signature, place your own signature."

With surprising gentleness, Moses inked a crude X on the contract.

"Congratulations!" I shouted. "You are the first animal to enter a legally binding contract!"

Moses burst into joyful laughter! He jumped about the cage, bouncing from trunk to chair. I think the orphan genuinely understood that he had played some role in his future.

"Oh, Moses," I said, petting his soft head. "You haven't even left me yet, and already I'm missing you!"

My happiness waned with the afternoon. The sum Hornaday had sent was not enough to cover the cost of my greatest need; I felt all avenues for acquiring a phonograph closing. Moses could not really understand the day's significance, so returned to his normal, generally contented state. Nor did Olago, being illiterate, appreciate the historic moment. His demeanor, since our conversation about his future, had turned sullen; I believe he had simply grown tired of his duties and living away from his village.

That evening, I took out Pearl and picked out some Foster tunes. Moses, Olago—I know not what effect the alien melodies had on them, for they remained in the tree they'd planted themselves in, whiling away the time picking at their teeth.

The deep-throated cry of my nightmare gorilla returned. An image of the gorilla did not precede the sound; only darkness and the cool breath of night followed.

"Professor!"

Olago was calling and shaking me. It had been no nightmare.

"Professor!"

"Yes, I heard it."

I reached for my rifle and heard Olago scrambling for the revolver; he might have accidentally killed me if he'd remained any longer. I prayed against an episode like the one we'd had with the leopard. But when the gorilla cry sounded again, it was evident it was far away. The gorilla roared once more. I remained awake for some time afterwards, not so much bearing my rifle, as the threat had vanished, but kneading the stock and barrel to exorcise my frustration over those nearsighted fools who were keeping my phonograph from me— and scientific progress from the world.

Upon waking, I found myself alone, and Fort Gorilla's gate opened. Olago had left and taken with him my revolver. I imagined he had gone to his village and would return in time—but he had not returned by the time I next visited the mission—nor did the little thief ever return! I suppose the gorilla's roar had frightened him for good.

When I did return to the mission, I had the good fortune of meeting Sister Marie walking from the women's dormitory to the convent. Moses knuckle-walked ahead of us, expressing curiosity at any passersby. Like a child on a walk with his parents might, he tested how far ahead of us he could wander before being called back by me.

"He's so like a little boy, don't you think?" I asked.

"Oh, yes. I had three baby brothers."

"Are you any more convinced of the affinity between apes and men?"

"My brothers did not walk upon their knuckles!" Marie laughed.

"But surely you must see how close—relatively speaking—the chimpanzee is to you and me."

"I'm sorry, Professor; I see a naked animal. A sweet, adorable pet he may be. But he is an animal."

"As are we."

Marie shook her head, exasperated.

"May we speak of something else?" she asked.

"Of course. Tell me of your family."

All these years later, the music of Marie's voice is what I recall best from that afternoon. Even at the time, I'm sure I devoted more attention to the music than the story it conveyed: A large, Catholic brood, for whom every resource was spread thin; a father who imparted to his children that what few goods they had were blessings from the Lord; a calling to serve those who had even fewer resources; an opportunity to serve in Equatorial Africa, where she believed her influence would be tenfold what it could amount to in France, and which frightened her mother, but won the blessing of her father. What the music conveyed to me is inexpressible in language; whatever its message, it gave me the succor I was promised St. Anne's would give and rejuvenated my patience for the chimpanzees' eventual appearance. I needed nothing else from the mission—not food nor wine nor shelter. Only Marie's music.

"You must see Fort Gorilla for yourself!" I ejaculated.

"Oh! I fear it's not safe for me to venture so far from the lake."

"It's hardly far at all! You would be perfectly safe."

"The superior would hear nothing of it. Even if I could go, there is too much work to be done here."

I sighed in disappointment, which Marie read as doubt in the importance of her work.

"The women here need me," she argued. "I am afraid that perhaps you do not see that the Africans welcome civilization. You may not see them as equal to us, but we are all of us sons and daughters of the same God. They have souls just like us, and it is our duty to introduce them to their Creator."

"Moses has a soul, but I doubt God would make an impression on him."

Before Marie could respond, we were alarmed by the little ape, who had come running back from the corner he had just turned; the source of his anxiety was Brother Leo, whom we saw come around the corner next.

"Moses," I said. "Would you stop worrying over Brother Leo!"

"Good afternoon, Sister. Professor."

"Brother Leo has been to my cage on several occasions," I said to Marie. "Brother, would you tell her that my cage is not really that far in the jungle?"

Leo's dark eyes darted from the ape, to Marie, and finally to my own eyes.

"The sister is not, and never will be, concerned with the location of your cage."

"Please, Brother," Marie said, "do not be cross with the professor. He isn't serious."

"Oh, I am quite serious."

"The impertinence!" Leo shouted.

"Enough!" I replied. "She can make up her own mind. She doesn't need your permission. Now good day to you, Brother." To Marie I bowed. "Sister." Then I scooped up Moses and departed.

I did not ask Marie again. It was a foolish request, was it not? I meant only to share my scientific work with her to sate her innocent curiosity. Our intentions with each other were absolutely pure, as white as Virginia snow. Designs to attract Marie to my cage to satisfy carnal impulses were invented by base traders and spread by that worm, Labouchere! Damn them to hell for implicating a flower like Marie in such terrible tales!

I abstained from visits to the mission for several weeks after that day. My only company being Moses, I went for days without speaking, save uttering "uh" to Moses at mealtimes, and occasionally "uw." In the evenings, I assuaged my need for something other than the jungle's subtle reverberations by plucking at Pearl, though it was a muted kind of plucking, for I did not want to break the jungle's peace too much.

These weeks were disturbed only once. Father Buleon, again followed by Brother Leo wielding his rifle, marched into the clearing one morning as I was boiling the day's water.

"I'm sorry to disappoint you gentlemen—" I overestimated the effort it would take to make my voice heard after such a long respite from human speech and somewhat barked at them. "But I have not perished."

"I did not expect to find that you had," Buleon said.

"I wasn't speaking of your expectations, only your wishes."

This I had meant only for myself, but damned if it wasn't plain to them as well.

"Don't be morbid, Professor. I thought these might be urgent."

Buleon handed me a letter and a telegram. Harry and Mr. McClure. I sighed and stuffed them in my pocket.

"Perhaps you could inform me of what deserves your immediate attention, and Brother Leo and I can spare ourselves efforts like this."

"What deserves my immediate attention would not fit inside an envelope."

"What seems to be the delay in acquiring your phonograph?"

I withdrew the messages from my pocket.

"I must attend to these, if you'll excuse me."

Harry's letter informed me that he was moving to Baltimore to join an insurance firm. He assured me that his mother was fine with his decision, though I knew she would suffer greatly. The letter left me with a pang for the family I had once possessed, but which now felt sundered by my own failings. This deep hurt was joined by a new anxiety that trembled on my skin, produced by McClure's telegram.

IN AFRICA FOR MONTHS AND NO WORD. IF YOU HAVE NOT BEEN EATEN BY CANNIBALS, I EXPECT YOU KNOW SOMETHING OF THE APE LANGUAGE. SEND STORY RIGHT AWAY. WILL FEATURE IN NEW VENTURE, MCCLURE'S MAGAZINE.

I went to the mission that evening to telegraph Mr. McClure that I was indeed alive and would send him a story as soon as possible, though I could not imagine what it would contain. I had pages of notes about Gabon and its jungle, some anecdotes about Moses, but not a single word about chimpanzees in their natural habitat—the very thing I had come to Africa to study!

After sending the telegram, I found myself in a familiar dormitory enjoying a fine dinner and a bottle of claret, when Wolfgang appeared in the door.

"Professor! Mind if I join you for a drink?"

He pulled a flask from his vest pocket and joined me at the small table. He explained that he was having no more luck catching a gorilla than McLaughlin.

"But I'm having a hell of a time all the same," he laughed. "And what about you?"

"I feel as if I'm very close. I have to be. My literary agent is pressing me for a report."

"Tell him about Moses, here."

Moses was sitting in a chair, fingering the inside of my helmet.

"I will; but I need to observe a chimpanzee group in the wild. To see them interact naturally. And hear them speak to each other. Though it appears I won't be able to capture any ape speech I might hear."

Wolfgang passed me his flask sympathetically.

I remember that evening well—it being the last time I saw Wolfgang: We enjoyed each other's company and the whiskey, and shared stories of the strange creatures and natives we had observed in Gabon. I am sure we had a few words for McLaughlin. It was the one occasion on that expedition when I allowed myself to be intoxicated. A right pleasant time, until the conversation darkened.

"Olago still proving helpful?" Wolfgang asked.

"Olago? He's been gone for quite some time."

"What?"

"I'm sorry—you wouldn't have any way of knowing. One night we heard a terrifying roar—a gorilla. One I'd love to see you catch! Anyway, the next morning, he was gone. The boy, that is. Took off with my revolver, too!"

"And he's not returned?"

"No. Come to think of it, there was something different about him the last few weeks. He'd been energetic in his duties and playful with Moses; but then he turned—" I reached for the right word—"listless."

"You should not have let him leave you!"

"I did no such thing. He left while I was sleeping. Look, I'll not hold you responsible for the missing revolver."

Wolfgang's face boiled red.

"Nor will I press you for another servant. I have nothing but respect and sympathy for the natives—but, frankly, your Fang frightens me! Do you always sleep with one eye open?"

"Professor! This is quite serious."

"Oh, I'm sure the boy's just gone back to his village. Or perhaps he's running still!"

Wolfgang left abruptly. I tried following him, but upon rising from the table, my body felt light and pulled in another direction.

Notes of Marie's voice were carried on the breeze, leading me toward one of the women's dormitories. Marie had just escorted one of the young African women there from the convent. I asked permission to accompany her back. She had some cause to be smiling warmly, which may be why she readily agreed.

"I trust that was a happy meeting," I said.

"Oh, yes! The superior has entrusted me with the vetting of marriage proposals—and I have just arranged my first!"

Marie explained that upon their marriage, the couple would be given a plot of land in a growing Christian village further in the interior, on which they would begin their life together.

"I suppose congratulations are in order, for the young couple and for you."

Marie lowered her voice.

"You would recognize the husband-to-be. The young man bearing the scar from the unholy capitalists. Oh, I am especially happy for the way his fortunes have changed."

The sun had sunk below the tree line by this time, leaving the mission grounds in shadow, illuminated by only the fiery glow at the tip of the canopy between us and the Atlantic. We walked slowly; she seemed no more eager to part than I, despite the fact that it was too late in the evening for a sister and a man to be in each other's company. I did not even have Moses, who was the prop with which I could somewhat excuse being otherwise alone with her. The silence of the shadows and empty paths—were they a rebuke to our impropriety, or conspirators in it?

"I'm sorry, Professor—what is it you wanted to see me about?"

"Oh, nothing in particular."

Marie's eyes shrunk and she looked on both sides of the lane. We had finally arrived at the convent's door. We came to a stop, though some motion refused to be held in either of us. Marie searched my face.

"Why do you always seek my company, Professor?"

"Loneliness."

Marie tried hiding her blush by looking at the dirt path.

"And you seek me out to abate your loneliness? You do not seek the company of a Nkomi woman, as so many other men do?"

"Absolutely not. And I do not seek you out for . . . base pleasures."

Marie raised her eyes to mine.

"What are you looking for?"

"Your music."

"I don't understand."

"I would tell you what you mean to me, but language simply fails at the task."

"I must go, Professor. I do not believe speaking to you this way is in the spirit of my vows."

"Nor do I think it's in the spirit of mine—but I still don't want to leave you."

The next morning I awoke with a terrible headache and feared another fever. But after a moment it became clear that I was suffering from the claret and nips of Wolfgang's whiskey. I let Moses out and prepared to march back to Fort Gorilla, determined not to return to the mission until I was ready to mail Mr. McClure his story; I did not care how long it took. I would stretch my provisions to their limits if need be.

When I emerged from my room, Mass had just ended, and les enfants were pouring from the church, the young men in their stark white shirts and the young women in their long skirts. Moses was bounding between them, begging for someone to stop and play. "Uw, uw, uw!" The young people laughed at him, some petting his head as they passed. But no one would stop and play, and the ape whimpered louder and louder, to the amusement of the brothers and sisters. Only the superior and Brother Leo were without joy.

Two boys stopped a second too long to play with the ape. Though it was incumbent on one of the brothers—the offenders being boys—the superior stepped forward with a reprimanding hand; but she stopped and turned her nose up at Moses, her eyes rolling heavenward, as though she could not come one millimeter closer.

"That's enough!" barked Leo, and burst through some of the children to swat Moses away.

The frightened little ape ran from him, and, spotting me, leapt into my arms and crawled high onto my shoulders.

I narrowed my eyes at Leo. The children turned their attention to the ruffled priest. He stroked his beard, tried to regain his composure; he was preparing to say something final on the matter of the American naturalist and his pet. I looked around for Father Buleon, for I thought he would broker some peace between the priest and the naturalist—he saw himself as both, didn't he?—but he must have remained inside the church.

Moses sighted Marie coming out of the church and braved leaving my shoulders to run past Leo and cut through the children to leap into her arms. There is no other word for how she held him: She cradled him, like a mother cradles her child. She had never held him like that, and the picture remains as fresh in my memory as any. She squeezed the ape to her breast and petted him warmly. He had not felt so secure since the last time his ape mother had held him.

It was time to leave. I called "uw," to Moses. He gave an imploring look to Marie.

"Uw," I repeated, to the quiet laughter of some children.

Moses was released from Marie's arms. The children parted, and he slowly knuckle-walked to me. He and I turned to begin our march, when Leo finally spoke:

"This is a mission, not a menagerie."

The day was lost to languorous naps. In the late afternoon, Moses and I emerged from our cages for a quick trek for fresh water. After the evening meal, I felt content to wallow in my camp chair, plucking Pearl until it was too dark to see.

Moses was carousing in the nearby trees, perhaps looking for a late night snack, while I returned Pearl to her case and readied myself for sleep. I had removed my shirt and was splashing still-warm water from the jug on my face when Moses' rustling was disturbed by a most shocking sound.

The report of a rifle shattered the jungle's quiet; a thousand birds erupted from their perches, and with their alarmed calls rose Moses' screaming. The ape's scream was silenced by a second report; the twin blasts echo in my ears to this day.

I grabbed my rifle and leapt from the cage, begging the wayward hunter to stop as I ran in the direction of the blasts.

"Stop! Stop! There is nothing here!"

But the shooter was a hundred yards away by the time I arrived at the place Moses had fallen. My mind determined that the murderer—for he was no hunter!—was running in the direction of the lake; he made no effort to hide his path by softening his footfalls. At the same time, my heart was rent as I pulled Moses to my breast and knew he was gone.

I wept as if I had lost my own child, for the young ape had been my charge for much of his short life.

I carried him back to my cage and laid him in my bedding. A bullet had pierced his heart. Mercifully, he had not suffered. He looked as if he were merely sleeping. I kissed his forehead, just underneath the part of his hair.

"Goodbye, Moses, my child."

The march to the mission the next morning was the most painful journey my body and soul have ever experienced. There simply was no easy way to carry Moses' wrapped-up body; I had to hug the bundle to my breast as I treaded across the jungle floor, which seemed especially tangled that morning. My rifle jangled across my back.

Of course I thought about murdering Leo. For though I did not see Moses' killer, I knew it had to be him.

But my revenge was stayed. What if it were not him? What if it had been a hunter who had lost his way? I say I knew Leo to be the killer—but not beyond a shadow of a doubt. But the larger thought that stayed my hand was that murder in plain sight—for that is how the act unfolded in my red imagination: finding Leo coming out of the mission building and felling him with a blast to his heart, his lifeless body a warning to those who would use violence to subordinate science to dogma—would certainly land me in a French prison, when the only bars I wished to return to were Fort Gorilla's.

I hoped, then, to avoid seeing him while I dealt with the business of Moses' remains. I also hoped not to see Marie, for it would break her heart to know our little pet had perished. On this morning, I was fortunate to have both of these wishes granted, but my third wish—that Wolfgang would be about to help me with Moses' body—would not be. Instead, I found McLaughlin in the doorway of one of the dormitories. He raised an eyebrow, betraying a curiosity he had never shown me—surely brought about by the blood-stained package I carried.

"Is Wolfgang about?" I asked.

"No. That's not his boy, is it? No—it's too small. Unless . . . ."

"What do you mean, 'his boy'? This is no boy; it's my chimpanzee."

"Come inside," he said.

I followed him to his room and laid the bundle on the floor between us, but I did not uncover Moses, yet.

"He was murdered. By a jealous brother, I believe."

"I'm so sorry, Professor. Let's have a look."

"He's not for sale!"

"Take it easy, Professor."

For the first time in our acquaintance, McLaughlin seemed genuinely friendly toward me. He suggested that perhaps he could offer to me whatever I had been seeking from Wolfgang.

"I aim to stay in the jungle for at least another month, perhaps longer. I need Moses transported back to London as soon as possible. I will arrange for a naturalist there to receive him. For study."

"Let me take him for you."

McLaughlin was traveling to London for a respite from the gorilla race; he was not too worried about Wolfgang's chances during his absence. He agreed to transport Moses' remains to London at no cost, for he saw in my countenance the terrible psychic debt I had incurred.

I gently pulled back the sheet to expose Moses' sleeping face. A great sadness clenched me again, gripping my chest tightly.

He was like a child to me.

"Why would someone do this?" McLaughlin asked, as if he had read my deepest thoughts.

"Senseless, isn't it? It's no secret the Holy Ghost Fathers of Dogma would suppress my work at any cost."

"You suggested jealousy as a motive."

"That may be, too. I risked a friendship with one of the sisters who was very fond of the child."

McLaughlin furrowed his brow inscrutably; he betrayed either Christian disapproval or Christian sympathy. Perhaps an uneasy blend of both.

"Professor Snowe will preserve his brains and vocal organs for study. His death will not be in vain—if you assure me he will be delivered."

McLaughlin's face softened. His eyes solicited my trust, and in that desperate moment I gave it.

I knelt down and kissed Moses' forehead for the final time.

Then the miracle happened. The chimpanzees came.

Chapter Nine

Misery set in. I passed the following days going through the patterns I had previously established with Moses and Olago. The hike to the spring was a slog; I felt heavier than ever, the ghost-weight of Moses upon my shoulders. I recorded my observations listlessly, as I could not see much point in them. My appetite was gone. My mind conjured morbid scenes in which I starved myself and was discovered by some future explorer: my cage a vine-covered cube, its door creaking on rusty hinges, myself a skeleton shrouded in khaki and a pith helmet, surrounded by uneaten provisions. What madness is this? the explorer and his native guides would wonder. But no such scene would materialize; rather, I would have to face the undignified scene of summoning from Buleon a team of Nkomis to disassemble Fort Gorilla for its return to America. I could imagine the smug satisfaction in his green eyes.

My savior knuckle-walked into the clearing on the east side of Fort Gorilla one morning as I was boiling the day's water: an adult male chimpanzee whose dark, round face was marked by a strong brow. His attention was drawn not to me, for I remained as a statue, but to a fig tree that had recently fruited. His lips, which had been sewn together mirthlessly, were drawn back slightly to reveal his teeth as he blustered a series of low grunts.

Oh, would that I had had a phonograph to capture this speech—and all the speech that followed! For his grunts brought four more chimpanzees from the jungle! He appeared to be the patriarch of a family of five. His wife had the same strong brow, but a long jaw and pronounced lower lip that gave the impression that she was forever smiling. The single mark against her joyful countenance was one tortured ear; half of it had been torn away, leaving a jagged edge of scar tissue. An infant clung to her underside. I might not have noticed the little fellow were it not for the contrast of his lightly colored face and his mother's dark coat. The oldest child was a giddy female in the range of five to seven years, bounding close behind her mother. The middle child, lagging behind the group as he scanned the earth, commanded the greatest part of my attention, for he was the shadow of Moses.

Husband and wife—the infant clinging tightly!—and children all ascended the fig tree in a flurry of celebratory barks and began feasting on its fruits. Soon, the patriarch was so high in the tree that Fort Gorilla's roof blocked my view of him. I pressed my face against the lattice and looked into the canopy to try to catch sight of him again. Our faces met; the sight of the strange white ape was cause for a new call: Both sets of his teeth were bared as the ape screamed in warning to his charges. They held fast to their branches while he swung down to the jungle floor. When he reached the floor, his hairs were raised in a violent display; he seemed twice the size he was when he ascended the tree!

He paced in front of my cage for a moment, ascertaining whether the curious structure and its strange inhabitant posed a threat. I smiled at him. His heavy brow cinched, suggesting he doubted my sincerity. I had a mango at hand and held it up to show him. "Uh," I said, hoping that if the word held the same meaning for him and his family as it did for Moses, my articulation of it had not suffered by my not speaking it since Moses' death.

The patriarch rose on his feet, interested in the sight and sound I had presented. He came closer to the cage. At the same time, I slowly made my way to the cage's gate and down to the jungle floor, the whole time watching him and holding up the mango as an offering. We met a few feet from the gate, whereupon I said "uh" again. The patriarch took the mango from my hand into both of his, brought it to his muzzle for inspection, and then turned to his family with an "uw."

My heart lifted! He had said "uw," the word I had suspected meant "Come here." He was calling his family forth to share the fruit. Upon his biting into the mango and sharing bits of it with his wife and children, a flurry of sounds came from each ape. Were I to have a phonograph, at that close range I could have captured the sound of this family speaking over one another, a cacophony parallel to the mixed conversations one would hear at a large Christmas dinner. Of very little use scientifically, as the real study of their language would require isolating their speech for close scrutiny, but what a wonderful sound it was!

As a single mango was not likely to keep the family's interest for long, I stepped back inside my cage to fetch a handful of plantains. I brought the bounty outside and laid it before the family. The patriarch approved of this offering, too, and called the members of his family to take their share. Save the littlest ape, who was still a nursling, each grabbed a few plantains and began to eat. Like Moses, they bit into the sides of them to get at the fruit. Their apprehension of me had entirely dissolved!

Watching the middle child bite into a plantain gave me a fresh pang for Moses. But that pang was assuaged by the intense satisfaction of observing this new ape and his family.

The apes, having sated themselves on fruit, began a period of what I can best describe as "play" at the edge of the clearing. The mother lay with her nursling, whom she caressed and tickled. Shadow Moses and his siblings alternately wrestled and petted each other. The patriarch examined the perimeter of Fort Gorilla before treading back into the jungle.

Fearing that he would lead his family away, I returned to my cage for a notebook so that I could record my observations while the chimpanzees still remained. I squatted and opened a trunk to retrieve a notebook and pen. I shut the trunk and, as I was righting myself from my squat, turned around to be met by a man's eyes. Save for the white sclera that encircled brown irises, my every sense was confronted by a dark, simian countenance: a hoarse whisper and earthy odor of breath; a black muzzle and rippling brow that threatened to touch my own.

The warning of the keeper in Cincinnati came back to me: The chimpanzee's strength, relative to his size, is much greater than man's. This adult male could have been the death of me.

I remained at the ape's level.

"Hello, there," I said in gentle tones.

The ape huffed.

"I don't have any more fruit, but I can offer you something else."

I am not certain whether he was assured by my speech or confident that he had trapped me inside the device that was intended to protect me, but he took his attention from me long enough to examine the contents of the cage. He grazed his fingers across a sketchpad, picked up and set down a tin of beef, and poked at my bedding. Finally, his attention settled on the corner where my rifle leaned. Was this an object he recognized? Had he an association between that object and the white man that might never be undone?

"I won't hurt you."

I was able to observe this family long enough to faithfully describe their habits, as they joined me in the clearing around Fort Gorilla for scientific studies, which they enjoyed as games the likes of which Africans had never shown them, and slept in the trees on the east side of Fort Gorilla for a period of weeks. The agility and grace of their climbing and swinging, unrestrained as it was by any of man's walls or fences, was incredible. And the heights to which they ascended! I estimated the patriarch to have climbed fifty feet into the fig tree. Often he and the adolescent siblings sat in the crooks of the upper branches, their brows and lips softening into relaxed countenances. A man's knuckles would turn white holding such a position, but the chimpanzees could not be more at home. Each member of the family, save the infant, found a suitable place in the trees to hastily lay down a nest of twigs and leaves, in the same manner Moses had.

Each night, I returned to my cage and wished for the chimpanzees to remain another day; and for many weeks, they did. Each morning, I stepped out of my cage to join them. My rifle remained untouched.

Though I had no phonograph with which to capture the family's talk, nor any hope of acquiring one, I attempted to learn as much of their language as possible. I followed the chimpanzees like a reporter and wrote, phonetically, the words they spoke to each other and the action or attitude the word described. Afterwards, when the family had retired to the trees for a nap, I would be utterly puzzled as to how to reproduce the sounds I had written. I sat in my camp chair, attempting to speak the words and only tying my tongue. Would that I had Moses to tutor me!

My transcriptions of "uh" and "uw" already being woefully inadequate descriptions of the true sounds they represent, I shall not recall any of my further transcriptions. Though I am confident of the meanings of the words I captured—of the concepts for which they have invented language. Here is a sampling:

Thank you. The chimpanzee can show gratitude. The patriarch was a gracious fellow, who many times thanked me for the fruit and meat and crackers I gave him to share with his family.

I am sick. One morning, I was awakened by a wailing sound I had not heard before. I left my cage in my shirtsleeves and searched the trees for the source of the pathetic cries. Shadow Moses had climbed into his mother's nest, apparently quite ill; I am unsure of the cause. A little ways off, the infant was in the care of his big sister. The young male wailed, to be sure, but he also gave his mother a measured expression that I am sure conveyed to her his feelings of sickness.

I love you. To the child's suffering, the sick chimpanzee's mother responded in low tones with an utterance that any parent would interpret as a loving reassurance.

During this period, I remained undisturbed at Fort Gorilla, writing my article for Mr. McClure between dinner and sundown, vowing not to return to the mission until I was finished. When darkness made further writing impossible, my thoughts turned to Marie. Was she missing my company? Our little Moses? For she had no reason to know of his fate.

I imagined that if I took the chimpanzees' middle child to the mission, Marie would not be able to tell any difference. I doubted anyone could. Leo would think he was seeing a ghost! Those thoughts returned to me nightly as the chimpanzee family and I submitted to sleep.

One restless, rainy night I allowed the lark of marching into the mission with Shadow Moses to bloom into a fully formed plan to take possession of the child, who by this time had made a full recovery. I resolved to steal him during the family's afternoon slumber and immediately take him and my article to the mission. I could not bring him back to Fort Gorilla until his family had moved away, so I would have to place him—as much as I hated to—in Buleon's care for a short time. Upon my leaving Africa, I would take the chimpanzee with me and deliver him to Mr. Hornaday when the time came. Though I regretted the idea of perpetuating a fraud on Hornaday, he would not know that his new ape was not the one who had signed his contract. I ought to have slept soundly that night, satisfied as I was with my scheme, but the memory of my beloved Moses still caused an ache in my heart.

It took me a few days further to finish my article, for I was very anxious about its content. Being my first dispatch from the field, it was important that I convince the scientific community and the public at large that my efforts in Africa were worth sustaining. Readers would have to see evidence that I was learning the apes' speech if I were to expect further support from my benefactors. That being the case, I had to weigh my experiences for their value in the sphere of public opinion. So I began my article with a preface that my report would not thrill with lies, but would enlighten with facts.

Upon reading an article composed in the West African jungle, the reader may expect to be thrilled by encounters with hungry cannibals, bouts of life-threatening fever, and narrow escapes from ferocious gorillas and deadly leopards. But this author has not found in the jungle the same romantic adventures that so many other explorers have had the amazing luck to stumble upon—and survive! I ask the reader, therefore, to be content with some facts about the habits of coastal Africans, their white partners in trade, and most importantly, the apes that inhabit the equatorial region.

I wrote of my peaceful arrival in Libreville and the pleasant steamer trip to the Fernan Vaz region. Then I had to set my pen down for a spell. Figuring that Buleon's plot to leave me dead in the jungle, where any proofs of evolution I might find would be lost to the ages, might rally support from fellow scientists, I decided to carefully record all that had transpired on my adventure up the Rembo Nkomi.

But I later burned these accusatory pages on my stove. I feared that the controversy, rather than ignite support, might only inflame a public that, although more and more accepting of Mr. Darwin, still revered its holy men. To accuse a priest of plotting to kill a man would likely be too salacious—even for Samuel McClure! Rather than risk public upset, I credited Buleon with providing me with much of my information on gorillas, which I had not yet had the opportunity to properly observe firsthand. The remainder of the article was devoted to my learning from Moses and the family I was then observing. I chose not to darken the article's tone by reporting what had happened to Moses, so to the reader's mind, he still inhabited Fort Gorilla with his human master.

The day finally arrived for me to return to the mission, article and chimpanzee in hand. I carefully watched the ape family as they ascended the trees and built their nests—for, like Moses, they built, or at least refreshed, their beds before every slumber. The little female had ascended the highest; just below in the same tree was Shadow Moses. In a neighboring tree at an even lower altitude, the mother and infant bedded together. At about the same altitude, but some distance away in another tree, was the patriarch. The danger of my mission did not escape me. Climbing the tree would put my strength and agility to the test, though I believed I was up to the task. But I would have to pass the parents to reach my target. Furthermore, the little female, who was just above her little brother, was a fitful sleeper. One wrong move could wake her, and her alarm would send the entire family down the branches and into the jungle, never to be seen by this naturalist again.

I treaded quietly toward the base of the tree in which the little boy and his sister slept. Leaning my rifle against the trunk and checking once more that my manuscript was safely folded inside my jacket, I gripped the lowest branches of the tree, just above my head, and placed a boot against the trunk. In this manner, I hoped to be able to thrust myself high enough to reach the next tier of branches and bring a foot to the lowest branches; but the treads of my boots scraped against the trunk and did not propel me into the tree. I needed a stool of some kind. Casting my eyes over the grounds of Fort Gorilla, I found an object of the perfect size and shape: Moses' cage. Since the little ape's death, I had done nothing to the habitat, nor had any of the chimpanzee family explored it. I am sure an unconscious reverence had stayed my hand,

and perhaps the chimpanzee family had sensed that the little structure had once nested a cousin, now lost. But the habitat would have to be disassembled along with my own cage, so there was no use getting sentimental about it. I carried the crate to the base of the tree, climbed it, and was able to easily ascend the tree afterwards.

In a short time, I reached the level of the parents and the infant. On my right, the patriarch slept soundly, assured that his charges were safe in their perches. On my left, the infant was nearly lost in his mother's bosom.

So human-like was this scene of mother and infant! In its presence in the wilds of Africa, you cannot help imagining early man, though beastly compared to us, in a similar posture: mother suckling baby. You cannot help but fathom its repetition in each iteration of man, to your own infancy, though you cannot remember it, and if you have fathered a child of your own, to the scene of your wife bearing your offspring to her breast.

Having gained my new perspective there in the trees, it should not surprise you that my resolve to kidnap the little chimpanzee expired like morning dew. But I climbed on, gently, until I was level with the little fellow, who was not more than a yard from me in his nest. His brown face was so like Moses'! I wondered if perhaps the two were cousins—or even brothers. Little was known about the social habits of these magnificent creatures in the wild, so I believe very much in the possibility of some kind of close kinship.

My hand, claw-like, extended toward the little ape. Imagine the scientific knowledge to be gained! I told myself. But no amount of goading could make me go through with the act. I simply could not do it.

My fingers uncurled, and with the palm of my hand, I sought to pet the creature's fluffy shoulder. Perhaps I touched him ever so gently; perhaps the tingling against my fingers was merely a trick of my senses, heightened as they were in that sublime moment. Either way, the spell was broken when the little female began to thrash about in her nest; the ripple effect, I feared, might be awakening the entire family to my presence. Such a breach of the boundaries the family and I had formed would surely scatter them into the mists forever.

I began descending the tree. The going-down proved more trying than the coming-up, and with each misstep, I was sure I sensed fresh rustlings from the chimpanzees' nests. Shadow Moses stirred; mother and infant, too. Worst of all, there were quakings in the patriarch's nest. Would that I had retained some of my ancestors' tree-climbing skills!

Once I had descended to about six feet above the jungle floor, I flung myself off the tree, cleared Moses' cage, and landed softly enough upon my hands and feet to avoid further disturbing the apes. I regained the bipedal position and, like early man, walked away from the tree as if I had never been there!

My first appearance at St. Anne's mission in nearly a month warranted a warm welcome from the students, who were bustling to and fro as the evening mealtime was just beginning. "Professor!" many of them called. Brothers and sisters nodded cursorily; some wore a look of surprise that suggested they had forgotten I was still residing in the jungle. My eyes searched among the habits for Marie, but were disappointed as each revealed its owner's face.

At the mission building, I found Mark in his room. He was seated at his desk reading, his posture rigid; either the boy was enthralled by some fascinating material—or he was forcing his attention upon a text of terrible obscurity; there was nothing passive about him. It was a Bible on his desk, I was certain. I interrupted his struggling to entrust him with my important mailing and thanked him.

As I shut his door, the shuffling of a child sounded behind me; to my shock, however, the source of the sound was a small female chimpanzee.

"Please acquaint yourself with my chimpanzee, Professor," Buleon said. "But do watch your language around impressionable youngsters!"

"She's yours? How did you come by her?"

"In the same way you came about your own. Mr. Wolfgang brought her to me."

"Under what conditions?"

"Under the condition that I was free to do with her as I wished. And I wish to study her. If you are inquiring about the conditions under which Mr. Wolfgang came to possess her, I did not ask. I suspect he killed the mother; he was eager to board a steamer on the afternoon he brought me the child, and you know what scientists will pay for chimpanzee materials."

"That doesn't sound like Wolfgang. I can see him taking a grown male—but a mother?"

Buleon laughed.

"Traders are occasionally generous; but as a rule they are fierce competitors without regard for African lives—human or animal."

I petted the little ape, and she received me warmly. She could not have been more than a year old, for she was barely over two feet tall! Her face was even tawnier than Moses'.

"You should know," Buleon continued, "that the contest between Mr. Wolfgang and his associate, Mr. McLaughlin, has changed."

"How so?"

"They are no longer trying to take a gorilla alive, for that has proved impossible for men such as them. Now they are out to kill."

Upon leaving the mission building, my rage toward Buleon fell to new depths. He may not have meant to leave me in the jungle for dead, and he may not have pushed the hand that took Moses' life—but he had belittled my scientific efforts at every turn and was now aiming to undermine me as Gabon's eminence on apes! And he a missionary!

Familiar music drew me out of my cloud of anger.

"Professor!"

On the path in front of the mission building, obscured only by the evening's shadows, Marie embraced me—something she had never done before. We were in danger of being seen, but the mission at that time seemed dead save for us. Her breath whispered against my neck; strands of her hair tangled with my whiskers; then she was returned before me at a proper distance. Her ghost stayed upon me, though; I remained still so as not to disturb it, so that it might linger.

"I was worried about you. You've been away for so long."

"Chimpanzees, Marie! A group came right into my camp. They may be there still. They're magnificent."

"Is your pet with them?"

"My pet? Oh, yes, yes."

"You have just come from seeing Father? Then you know about our own pet?"

"'Our own pet'? Yes, I saw her."

"Isn't she wonderful?"

"Oh, yes. Very fine."

As if she were listening to our conversation, the little ape came bounding from the mission building and leapt into Marie's arms.

"Hello, little girl!" Marie cooed. "I want to name her, but Father will not allow it. It is *unscientific*."

"He is no scientist."

Buleon's shadowy presence in the door appeared in my periphery.

"I am not? Do I not live among Africa's flora and fauna and record my observations with shrewdness and diligence so that man's knowledge of the natural world may increase? In our methods, we are not so different, Professor."

"That may be, Father. But my methods are in the service of science—not dogma."

"Science! I will grant that you are a scientist, Professor, but you are a woefully mistaken one."

"Mistaken?"

"Your belief that men and beasts share ancestors is not science! It's totemism! Explain evolution to any African, save those who have accepted Jesus Christ as their savior, and you will find him in complete agreement. He will say, 'Why, yes, I am descended from a gorilla.' And a man from another tribe will say he is descended from a lion! Evolution is not a leap forward in man's thinking—it is a leap backward! Come down off your pedestal, Professor. You are not more enlightened than me; you are as heretical as the most superstitious native of this continent."

"Heresy is the author of progress!"

With that, I quickly bid Marie and the little ape adieu and began marching back toward camp.

"Do as you wish, Professor. But leave my name out of it."

It was a relief and a pleasure to find the same family of chimpanzees sporting about Fort Gorilla upon my return. They seemed not to have taken much notice of my absence, which had been only a few hours, during which they would have nested down and napped for a bit. The cage had been locked, of course, but its exterior seemed undisturbed. I opened a tin of beef to eat inside my cage; as usual, the opening of a can of meat pricked at their attention, though they remained cautious about approaching the cage. They sniffed the salty aroma, then returned to their present activity of mopping up ants. I observed them until dark from my camp chair, which I had returned to a place about ten feet out from the cage. They ate, played, and finally made their nests.

I wondered how much longer they would stay near my camp, for the fruiting tree would eventually be emptied of its bounty. But the fruit and the chimpanzees remained for several more weeks. The rainy season began in earnest. While chimpanzees avoid bodies of water, they do not mind rain one bit. The mother and her children weathered the rain in their nests, looking not at all disturbed by their matted fur. The patriarch, however, seemed to rather enjoy it; from my cage, I watched him many times run through downpours in the bipedal position, grabbing vines and swinging with total abandon, the grace of his regular movements cast off for an ecstatic dance. I would lose him in the spray and foliage; a moment later he would burst back into my vision.

In a moment of great inspiration—and little wisdom—I dared join him. I left my helmet behind so the rain would soak my hair, too. He was already running and swinging; I ran, too— though in another direction so he would not think I was chasing him. I waved my arms wildly and leapt over roots and shook vines.

When he noticed me, it did not matter that I was not chasing him, or that I had not interrupted his dancing; my mere presence during his display so upset him that he charged toward me screaming, his wet fur raised on his shoulders like knives. Before he could clobber me with his thick hands, I jumped back into my cage and shut the gate. He pounded the lattice a few times and cursed me—surely he cursed me in his tongue—before restarting his dance.

The next morning, I made a peace offering with some mangoes. He could have ripped me apart there in the clearing, but something in his man-like eyes told me that he wouldn't. Had he and his family not left days later, I think we would have become great friends.

In the end, it was not the depletion of fruit that caused the family to leave.

The steady percussion of a light rain sounded throughout camp on the fateful afternoon. To that pleasant pattering, the chimpanzees had just settled into their nests, and I had begun to doze in my camp chair inside the shelter of my cage, helmet covering my face, when a great stamping and shouting emerged from the woods to the northwest.

"Garner! Garner!"

The barking of my name shook me from my slumber. I adjusted my helmet and instinctively reached for my rifle.

"Garner!"

I opened the gate and leapt to the jungle floor, raised my rifle toward the barking. In the trees, the patriarch made great shrieks of alarm; his calls were answered with the sounds of the mother and her charges shaking out of their nests and down the branches.

"Stop right there!" I shouted into the woods. I had meant to stop the human intruders, but hoped the apes would heed my words as well.

The men did not stop. Buleon charged onto the grounds followed by Leo. Buleon was unarmed, but Leo wielded his rifle, so I did not, at first, lower my weapon. Buleon did not slow at the sight of it. Was he inciting me to violence so that Leo could murder me? I panicked at the thought of a melee that left Buleon and myself bleeding to death on the jungle floor; I could not move.

I heard behind me a frantic rustling away from the impending human violence and into the jungle four times: mother and infant, Shadow Moses, his sister, and the patriarch.

"You've frightened them away!"

Leo looked side-to-side, keeping his rifle aimed at me.

"They may never come back, now!" Oh, how I wanted to fire upon those fools.

Buleon's hands shoved the barrel of my rifle down and away and thrust a magazine against my chest.

"Whatever is the matter?" I asked. I leaned my rifle against my leg and took a look at what Buleon had delivered. It was the *McClure's* inside of which was my article.

"I asked you to leave me out of your reports!"

I had no idea to what he was referring. I opened the magazine to my article; at a glance, it appeared as I had sent it to Mr. McClure. I had not accidentally included any pages that called into question Buleon's character—though I would wish that I had!

"I had half a mind to call you a meddling dogmatist, an impediment to scientific progress. But I treated you rather kindly, I think, crediting you for your fieldwork with gorillas."

"You treated me as a mere informant! A subordinate!"

"You *were* a valuable informant on the habits of wild apes!"

"Of course I know more about wild apes than you! I have been in Gabon far longer! You had no right to publish knowledge I discovered. It is bad enough that academics diminish my scientific work without an amateur doing the same!"

"Amateur!"

"I am more of a scientist than you will ever be!"

"I will entertain that you are a scientist when you remove that chain from around your neck!"

Included with the magazine was a letter from Mr. McClure.

> *The public is simply wild about your story! You absolutely must write a book about your experiences in Africa. I am sure it will outsell your first book. I've arranged for you to begin drumming up interest immediately upon your return to civilization. Make arrangements right away to be at Prince's Hall, London, on January 16. Bring Fort Gorilla and your pet chimp—I want the audience to see exactly how you made your incredible observations!*

I fell into my camp chair to digest these recent developments. Buleon and I were at an impasse. I feared it was time to settle our affairs. It was likely time to seek another location for the study of apes; Buleon and Leo had frightened the chimpanzee family so much that they would not return for the tree's remaining fruit. And McClure had given me a firm date by which I must return to England. I would have to leave within a few days to make the journey to Cape Lopez, Libreville, Liverpool, and finally London.

I stepped into my cage and retrieved Pearl. My melancholy over leaving Africa was deserving of song, so I plucked and sang "Swanee River." I felt my own heart grown weary so far from home.

Chapter Ten

My hopes for the chimpanzee family's return diminished with every passing hour of the following day. Those hopes were extinguished with the day as night swallowed my camp.

A return to the mission was warranted: I needed to telegraph Mr. McClure and settle things with Buleon. As much as it pained me, a monetary contribution to the mission was in order. If there were any justice in this world, my troubles would have been payment enough for anything I had enjoyed from the mission! After accounting for my travel to London, including transporting my cage, I had very little money left—about a hundred francs. Giving Buleon all the benefit of doubt, I would give him all of it.

Mark greeted me at the door of the mission building. The little chimpanzee was shuffling about his feet.

"Just the man I was looking for," I said. "And hello, little girl."

The little ape followed us upstairs, and as Mark worked the telegraph, she pulled at my pants leg, hoping for my attention or perhaps some little morsel. Once I had confirmed to McClure that I would indeed be at Prince's Hall with Fort Gorilla and a young chimpanzee, I squatted down and petted the little girl. I caught Mark smiling at us.

"She's so much like us, isn't she?" I said.

"She seems happy. Often she seems lonely."

"I imagine she experiences the same range of emotions as you or me. Don't you? Can you believe we were once quite like her kind?"

Mark's face stiffened. He was obviously a sharp child, but he was just a child, and an African, too. His first, tribal beliefs; his earnest study of the Bible; the suggestion of evolution from a learned white man—it was too much for him to reconcile.

"Thank you, Mark. That's all I require for now."

Upon approaching Buleon's door, I heard voices within. I paused. Buleon and Leo. I could not make out much of their conversation, it being on the other side of the door and in French. Commissaire Brazza may have been the topic.

I knocked and was admitted. The little chimpanzee remained outside with Mark.

"Good afternoon, Professor," Buleon said. "Please join us."

I sat in the chair beside Leo. The coward refused to look at me.

"If I might venture to ask, Father—do you worry about the French giving their side of the Congo up to concessionary companies?"

"Gabon is France's possession. I trust it will manage it wisely."

I smiled wryly to myself, though Buleon noticed and inquired as to what I found amusing in his comment.

"You have observed apes almost as much as I have," I said.

"More."

"We will get nowhere pursuing that argument. Shall we agree to avoid it?"

"Agreed."

Father turned his attention to some letters on his desk. Leo kneaded his hands; I've no idea what was in his hot, stupid brain.

I returned to my topic: "Don't tell me you haven't noticed their treatment of 'possession.'"

"What are you talking about?"

"In the chimpanzee family I've observed in the jungle, they have borne out the idea that possession is the right of ownership. When a chimpanzee obtains an article of food, his peers rarely try to dispossess him of it."

"He would put himself at risk."

"Therefore, the possessor owns said article. I'm certain that men share with chimpanzees the source of this behavior. Of this thinking. That we have similarly evolved to enjoy and respect the notion of ownership."

"It is an ape's instinct to protect his food," Buleon argued. "And for the would-be thief, his well-being."

"So you admit he can consider the likelihood of his success or defeat?"

Buleon looked up from the letters and trained his green eyes upon me.

"That does not make him equal to man."

"I agree there, Father. The chimpanzee does not appear to take possession of more than he needs. Men—and nations—sometimes do."

Buleon chewed on this a moment. "Did you learn nothing from Commissaire Brazza? The needs of France and Gabon are mutual."

"Religion for rubber? That's not an even trade."

"You exasperate me, Professor."

"But for both our sakes, I hope things remain as they are. Anyway, I shall be leaving in a matter of days."

"Is that so?"

"I have been asked to give a lecture in London in January."

"How wonderful for you."

I handed Buleon an envelope.

"For your . . ." I had trouble getting the word past my lips: "hospitality."

"Merci, Professor."

I excused myself. At the door's threshold, I turned and told him it was 100 francs.

"I'm sorry—did you say 100 francs or $100?"

"100 francs."

From his screwed-up smile, I could tell that he found 100 francs to be a niggardly contribution. Leo shifted uneasily in his chair, his thick head turning between Buleon and me, before rising and rudely pushing past me.

"Of course, I plan on sending you the balance—the francs to make a contribution equal to $100—after my lecture."

Buleon returned to his letters.

"There is a steamer arriving nearly every evening."

The little chimpanzee was awaiting me outside the mission building. I allowed her onto my shoulders, her slight weight upon my back a warm reminder of Moses. We walked aimlessly about the grounds for a while, for the sky had turned gray and heavy, and I did not care to be caught in a bout of rain on my march back to Fort Gorilla. As luck would have it, I spotted Marie in the convent door. But when I waved at her, she cast her face down and turned back toward the convent. The little ape climbed down from my shoulders and rushed to her before she gained the door again and leapt into her arms.

"How are you, Sister?" I said, catching up to her.

"Oh, Professor—" she searched the grounds. "You really must not talk to me."

"Whatever for? Have I done something wrong?"

"No—I have. I have been in your company too much. The superior was very disappointed to have seen me—"

"Because you once put your arms around me?"

"She took away my vetting of marriages," Marie whispered—angrily, was how it struck me.

"I'm very sorry. I'll be leaving soon, anyway. Perhaps she'll restore your duties once I'm gone."

She whispered again, "I will miss you and your pet. What will become of this one?"

"She's unlikely to survive in the jungle without her chimpanzee forebears."

"Perhaps Father will give her to you."

"Perhaps you've forgotten—Buleon and I see each other as superstitious fools. But only one of us is right."

"You are both hardheaded fools."

She handed the chimpanzee over to me. The animal was sure to remind the superior of me, should Marie be caught with it.

"Goodbye, Professor."

The rain began as the evening meal was getting underway. Wanting to avoid Buleon and the brothers—I did not see Leo among them—and Marie, I joined a group of students. I had mastered neither the nuances of French nor the simple tongue of the Nkomi, but several of the students were proficient in English, having had dealings with traders. From these boys I was able to learn more about their experience at the mission. The boys enjoyed life at the mission; they liked all that St. Anne's provided them: their quarters, clothes, food, and lessons. Luke, the boy who often worked in the dining hall, and Mark, the telegrapher, were there.

"And we will each have a wife," said one boy.

"But only one!" said another, eliciting much laughter.

I asked these boys their names.

"Jean."

"Mathieu."

"John and Matthew. Good heavens—you've all the gospels among you!" This coincidence led me to my next question: How did they feel about surrendering their beliefs for Ozounge's?

The boys were reticent to speak, but a few nodded their heads affirmatively, as if to suggest that Christianity was another enjoyable good provided by the mission along the same lines as their wool pants. Another element of their old lives that they traded to live like white men.

After a moment, the boy called John spoke: "Our families want us to live like Ozounge's people. Your people."

"I wouldn't call myself 'Ozounge's people,' but never mind that. Why do you think your families want that?"

Matthew spoke up: "Your people rule Gabon. But it is our home. We must be good stewards of it. Together."

I molded my countenance to convey to the young man that I agreed with his assessment of the situation and, furthermore, admired his wisdom. The Africans' sovereignty had been eroding for years, and now teetered at the cliff's edge. If Commissaire Brazza were removed, and concessionary companies allowed to take control of the colony, the last vestiges of Gabonese sovereignty would be obliterated.

I had never marched back to camp at such a late hour, and as I approached the clearing, I felt a mix of relief and anxiety. I would not be among the mangrove roots and vines when darkness fell and dangerous beasts lurked; but there was something strange about Fort Gorilla's appearance—something greater than the effect of twilight on what was, admittedly, already a strange place.

Upon entering the clearing, I saw that something indeed was wrong: The gate on my cage was wide open, its lock having been smashed apart. My trunks were upended, their contents strewn about the cage's floor. I climbed into the cage for a closer look. Pearl! Her neck had been broken, and she lay in two pieces, hanging together by her strings. I held a piece in each hand, hoping that she might be repairable, but her head had been trampled. Pages torn from my notebooks littered the cage. I gathered all the loose pages inside the binding of the first notebook I could find; I would have to reorder them in tomorrow's light.

Outside my cage, my camp chair had been smashed to pieces. Several tins had been tossed outside and flattened so that beef oozed out their sides to be devoured by ants.

This was not the work of excitable apes, though I was meant to think that it was. Only one man was capable of such a hateful and destructive act. He knew I was at the mission and knew the location of Fort Gorilla. He had, I was certain of it, exercised his hatred on these grounds before. Were it not for my lecture, I wouldn't have given Leo and his master the satisfaction of having driven me from the jungle; I would have repaired the damage, lived on mangoes and plantains, and remained as long as I wished. As it were, though, I realized that this would be my last night in this particular patch of Gabon's jungles.

A few smashed tins lay on the floor of the cage, attracting ants, so I swept them away with my boot before unrolling my sleeping mat. But some of the damned buggers remained and chewed at my neck during the night. Between the biting ants and the storm that finally erupted and raged for hours, battering the roof and spraying me through the lattice, I slept fitfully.

The storm passed by dawn. I lay curled on my mat well into the appearance of morning's light. My burning neck eventually roused me, so I walked to the spring and assuaged the swelled-up bites with a handkerchief soaked in the cool water.

Upon returning to Fort Gorilla, I satisfied myself that all the pages of my notebooks were accounted for. I returned every item—the notebooks, the two halves of Pearl, my sleeping mat, and a few tins and soup packets that had not been ruined—to my trunks, and began walking toward the mission.

My appearance on the mission ground, had it been noticed by anyone, might have been shocking: Sweat dribbled from the band of my helmet across my forehead; I was in my shirt-sleeves, having left my jacket behind; and I wielded my rifle like a man out for blood. Buleon and Leo would have been prudent to run at the sight of me! But as it were, Buleon was likely attending to business in his office, and the brothers and sisters and their charges were occupied inside the classrooms. I leaned my rifle against one of these and sat down on the dirt to rest. My head fell into my hands. My heart was rent by my current circumstances: I had been incredibly fortunate to have had the company of Moses and to have observed a chimpanzee family in their natural state. And Mr. McClure was affording me the chance to share the knowledge I had gained with an audience in London and a new book. When I first saw chimpanzees in Cincinnati's zoological gardens nearly a decade earlier, I could not have imagined having such experiences! But I felt, too, like an utter failure. I had not managed to make phonographic records of the chimpanzees' speech. I had lost the chimpanzee that I had promised to Mr. Hornaday's zoo. I had made enemies with the most esteemed hosts of the Gabonese jungle—though their dogmatic ways had made that a foregone conclusion. Perhaps my greatest accomplishment, given their ruthlessness, was merely to survive! But they would not drive me from my work in Equatorial Africa. I was determined to return.

A treading across the dirt floor that I immediately recognized as a small chimpanzee's knuckle-walk brought me out of my thoughts.

"Well, hello, little girl."

The little female chimpanzee's jaw jutted out in a funny smile.

I patted my thigh, inviting her onto my lap, but she preferred to rock on her feet and occasionally reach out to pet my knees.

"Tell me, you poor thing," I whispered. "What happened to your family?"

The little ape smiled again. Without a wider knowledge of her kind's vocabulary and better articulation of their tongue, I could not make her understand me. I simply smiled back. She reached up and touched my mustache.

"You're a curious little thing, aren't you?"

She gave a little hoot in the affirmative.

"Your master would not be pleased to know I was speaking to you. But he's not here, is he? How would you like to join me on a little trip? I'll bet you've never seen the beaches in the capital. I'm certain you've never crossed the ocean on a ship."

The little ape bounced in excitement. I am not so foolish to think she understood me; she was responding only to the gentle tones in which I spoke, tones which I am sure her master never used with her.

"And then, you could live in a new home, safe from the spears of savages and the rifles of hunters. In time, I would bring you some companionship. How does that sound?"

She skittered in circles and let out joyous hoots. Her antics gave me an enormous grin.

The previous night, while the storm clouds had fitfully cohered until they had blotted the sky, a plan had likewise formed. Pieces of it appeared to me in my restless moments until it showed itself fully—and it was as foolish as its dreamer must have looked, being sprayed by the rains and bitten by ants! But now that plan shone in my imagination, like the sun that withered the clouds at dawn, as possible—as already realized!

When the students emerged from their classrooms for the midday meal, I searched among the sisters for Marie. Upon spotting her, I raced toward her, the little chimpanzee following, and begged her for a minute of her time. She understandably denied me.

"It is important, Sister."

I scooped the little chimpanzee into the crook of my arm and, with my other hand, gently held Marie's hand. Her palm was cool, but flushed with warmth in mine; her slender fingers curled round mine, holding on for safety. The current that ran between us lent extra urgency to the meeting. I led Marie and the little ape around the rear of a classroom.

"What's wrong, Professor?"

"I must leave right away, Marie."

"Why?"

If I expected Marie's help, I needed to tell her everything, shocking as it might be for her to hear.

"Buleon has tried to thwart my studies from the start. When he and I journeyed to the Eshira, I caught a fever and was left for dead by him. It was only the mercy of some Africans that saved my life."

"That cannot be."

"And our child, Moses. He was murdered by Leo, no doubt on Buleon's instructions."

Marie gasped, removed her hand from mine and brought it to her mouth.

"Are you sure? When?"

"Weeks ago. I kept it secret from you. I knew you would be devastated. Then Buleon and Leo trespassed upon Fort Gorilla and frightened away my subjects. As if that weren't enough, they returned to damage my personal property. And for all this, I have given Buleon every franc in my pockets. And an IOU!"

"Are you quite certain of all this?"

"I'm sure, Marie. You're the only person here I trust. So I'm asking for your help."

"That's impossible."

"But you can—and you must. Think of how the superior's treated you—just for my presence, which you have had no control over."

"Professor, I don't know."

"There is a steamer arriving tonight. I plan to leave aboard it tomorrow, with my cage and all the belongings Buleon did not destroy. And I shall be taking something else as a remittance."

I lowered my chin and nuzzled it against the little chimpanzee's head.

I sat upon one of my trunks in the darkness of an unknown hour, training my eyes on the path from St. Anne's, awaiting the flickering of distant torches. As the black night lengthened, I began to worry that Marie had met trouble. But after some time, an orange glow began to widen as it proceeded up the path; it was the men, their torches hidden by the thick jungle. I came out of my cage to greet them upon their arrival, which was signaled by the flames of a half dozen torches revealing them in the final yards of the path before the clearing.

The four gospels were joined by eight of their peers; these were older, stronger boys. Marie had done well. They were dressed in their pajamas and loafers; the mud that caked their shoes and the cuffs of their pajama pants would betray them to the missionaries, but there was nothing I could do about that. I could not even pay them!

The torches were thrust into the ground at intervals around my cage, throwing what light they could onto our task. I instructed the men on the cage's construction, and we set about disassembling it. Two spry boys climbed the cage and pulled off the thatched roof, which was left in a pile with the remains of my camp chair and the ruined tins. After the removal of the roof, the sides came apart swiftly and were stacked inside the crates. The strongest men pulled up the legs, which had sunk further into the soil after months of the cage's resting upon them.

The crates were sealed. My trunks were packed. I looked at my watch by the torchlight. It was three a.m. There was still much to do before dawn. The march back to the mission would take up to two hours now that the men were loaded down with a full crate or trunk between each pair.

"We must get moving," I said. "Grab a torch."

I led the way. The boy behind me—Matthew—was the smallest of the lot and was struggling with his end of a trunk. I placed a hand on the handle beside his and shared the load, and in this way, we made the trek back to the mission.

Much as I hate to be a harsh master, I kept our stops brief and urged the men on, citing the necessity of loading the crates and trunks onto the steamer before daybreak.

"I don't want the brothers finding you missing from your beds."

"The sister said your leaving was a secret," said Matthew. "But she did not say why."

"Father finds my work here to be heretical to his religion. Your religion."

"Do not all white men follow Jesus?" John asked from somewhere in the pack.

"No. I cannot subscribe to a religion that commands men to worship one God—and then commands him to worship three!"

Matthew furrowed his brow; perhaps I had a convert to science!

"Let's just say Father has made conditions here impossible for me."

"But why must you leave under cover of darkness?" Matthew asked.

"Because I'm taking something of his with me as payback."

We reached the mission before 5:30 a.m. and, sticking to the perimeter rather than going directly through the grounds, arrived at the steamer shortly before six. Daylight was mounting the jungle to the east and spilling onto the lake. The sky was blessedly clear. The English steamer captain was on deck drinking a cup of tea and admiring the lake's calm surface when my entourage laid their trunks and crates at the foot of the loading dock. I thanked the men for their help.

"Now please," I said, "hurry to your dormitories."

"What in heaven's name is going on here?" the captain asked.

"Give me a hand, will you?" I called to him.

"What's the rush? The steamer doesn't leave for hours."

"For all the francs in my pocket would you leave as soon as I'm ready?"

"Depends how many francs are in your pocket."

The captain came down the boarding plank and eyed my crates.

"What's all this?"

"The makings of a great cage. They're not that heavy. Come on and grab the end of one."

The captain helped me pick up a crate, and we began to move up the plank. As we loaded the crates and trunks, I kept turning an eye up the road toward the mission; Marie should have arrived by this time. It would be quite easy, she had said, to take possession of my prize; enjoying the relative safety of the mission, the little chimpanzee nested in the crook of a small tree in front of the mission building. Marie would find the little girl there at first light and bring her to the dock.

The captain and I finished loading and stood at the base of the plank sopping our brows with our handkerchiefs. The sun had crested the canopy and shone across the lake's surface.

"What's this?" the captain said.

I turned toward the mission; the image to which the captain referred was the most incongruous of all that I had yet experienced in Africa: Marie half-running down the road from the mission, cradling the small chimpanzee, who clung to the sister's neck to steady herself against the unsteady journey; though she was some distance off, a flushing of her eyes and mouth showed that she was calling to me; but her steps and her calls were buried under a series of scats and barks exploding some distance behind her. She tripped, righted herself, the little ape keeping hold of her neck. When she was but a few meters from the dock, I ran toward her and embraced her. She let the little ape climb into my arms and tried to gain her breath.

"I know who you are!" the captain said. "You're the American who talks to apes!"

"What gave it away?"

"Father is coming, Professor. He became suspicious when I came around the mission building bearing bananas at this early hour. He's shouting such terrible things about you. You must hurry!"

Buleon's barks were coming down the tunnel of mango trees at intervals—and growing closer.

"Let's go," I commanded the captain.

"Sorry, Professor—there's a handful of traders expecting passage to Cape Lopez."

"Please," Marie implored the captain, "help the professor."

"You will be paid for your trouble," I promised.

The captain sighed. I do not think he would have relented were it not for the appearance of Buleon; though he remained some distance from us, he was a formidable sight: Silhouetted by the sun, his black cassock flared like a demon's wings and his barks pierced us, even as they were becoming intelligible.

"Professor! Do not help him, Captain! He was sent! By the Devil! To perpetuate! Heresies!"

"Please!" begged Marie. Still she hugged herself to me and the little ape.

The captain looked upon us, pity filling his countenance.

"You don't look like you were sent from the Devil. You look like a regular family man to me. Get aboard."

Bittersweet music, a chord whose notes were half laughter and half cries, burst from Marie. She embraced me so tightly that the little girl between us had to escape to my shoulders. I put my arms around her back and whispered to her, "Thank you for your kindness. I am truly sorry for whatever trouble I have caused you."

"Goodbye, Professor."

Our embrace was broken; I rushed up the plank, which the captain promptly raised. The steamer engine thundered below and the stack coughed a rebuke to the raving priest.

"That is my ape! You are a heretic, a liar, a leech, and a thief! You will pay, Professor!"

Buleon and Marie shrank as the steamer moved deeper into the lake. Unable to bear watching Marie grow pitifully smaller, I turned my gaze to the jungle south of the mission compound. Somewhere in there was my chimpanzee family. I bade them goodbye and swore that one day I would return to their lands.

Chapter Eleven

Being at sea for several weeks that winter kept me ignorant of what the press was reporting on my expedition. Mr. McClure, surely, was touting my arrival in London and subsequent lecture. But what misinformation had my enemies in Gabon telegraphed under the Atlantic? Rather than dwelling on these unknowns, I prepared my lecture, and, once it was satisfactory, permitted myself to relax, to build a reserve of energy for the task that lay ahead in England and America—the task of reversing my present course and returning to Equatorial Africa.

Upon boarding the Liverpool-bound ocean liner, I was forced at several points to explain my young chimpanzee, whom I had begun calling Susie, and the importance of her receiving the utmost care. I had to fight to keep her in my room and out of the hold. When pressed whether she was trained to use a water closet, I lied and said of course, then promptly showed her how it was done. I also took her to the deck daily for brief bouts of exercise; after only a few moments, the harsh Atlantic winds would send us below deck.

On the morning of December twenty-fourth, I awoke with seasickness and the realization that, for the first time ever, I was spending Christmas away from Maggie and Harry. Susie rolled around on the foot of the bed, perhaps struggling with her own nausea, oblivious to the day's special meaning. When she looked at me, she cocked her head to one side, as if to inquire about whatever troubled me.

That morning and afternoon passed like all the others. But when we entered the dining hall that evening (by this time, Susie went in my arms or upon my shoulders everywhere, and no one gave us a second glance), we were greeted by a party of revelers and a magnificent Christmas dinner: plump geese and roasted parsnips and stewed pies. Brandy. A gentleman pulled out two seats; Susie would have her own, her face just clearing the table for the enjoyment of the revelers. I enjoyed everything on offer and passed bits to Susie to her great satisfaction. "Uh, uh!"

Yes, I absolutely missed my family. I imagined Harry had come home from Baltimore, and that he was taking his mother to the

Christmas Eve service. That part would be the same. But when they returned, it would be to an empty home. The darkened home would remind them that their dear husband and father was somewhere on the Atlantic. What's he doing right now? they would wonder. Maggie would climb into a cold bed. Did her thoughts turn to me at night?

I would see them soon enough. After London, after New York. It would be the better part of a year that I was gone. I hoped to convince Maggie to join me upon my return to Africa.

As for Christmas? I know the party was for the Christmas holiday—but it felt as if it were a celebration of me and Susie. We were interviewed and toasted until the last partygoers retired. And why not? My accomplishments were worthy, my enemies be damned!

Would that things continued in that vein in London and New York!

Our arrival in Liverpool on January fourteenth did not draw any pressmen, for which I was glad, considering the humiliation that met us upon gaining passage on the London-bound train. Susie had ridden upon my shoulders as we approached the ticket window, where my request for a first-class ticket was met with a look of incredulity by the station agent.

"I'm sorry, sir, but I don't think I can permit your monkey on a first-class car."

"First of all, she's an ape. And, second, she's no more than a babe in arms."

"Even so, I don't think the first-class passengers will appreciate her presence."

"Look, I am Professor Richard Garner, just returned from Africa. And I am *not* second class."

"*You* may have a first-class seat, Professor. Your pet may not."

Rather than argue further with the stubborn agent, I purchased a second-class ticket and boarded the carriage, crouching so that Susie would clear the top of the doorframe. Before we could take our place on either of the hard benches that lined the carriage, we were met with an audible blend of curious delight and cautious distance. The men elbowed each other, and the women whispered together, ensuring that all aboard were aware of the young chimpanzee atop my shoulders.

I sat in a corner of the carriage, and Susie moved to my lap. She clutched my lapels as the train lurched forward and started its rocky passage to London. Our journey had barely begun when the man across from us recognized me and set off a chain of remembrances of my articles in the English press. I introduced my young charge to my audience. The men joked whether they ought to remove their bowlers upon meeting the little lady, and a few did. When the laughter died down, the men's countenances turned serious, though the inquiries that followed showed little understanding of my discoveries to date. Had I taught her to speak? "I intend to learn *her* language, not instruct her in *ours*." Could I speak "ape?" I indulged our audience with a lesson on "uh," which it quickly found tedious. After the passengers returned to their newspapers, the man next to me leaned in to quietly inquire whether African women really walked around with their breasts bared.

"Until they find Jesus."

Liverpool was soon behind us. Susie peered over my shoulder and out the carriage's rear window. The notion of a window had been foreign to Susie until then, but she clearly understood that she was viewing the world outside of the moving carriage. In that strange frame were scenes of English countryside. The landscape shared more kinship to Gabon's jungles than the deck of an ocean liner or the streets of Liverpool, but winter had dulled the stretches of green and stripped the trees of their leaves—effects that she had never seen and which rendered the picture unfamiliar, dead.

That evening, we departed the train at Piccadilly, where the Junior Athenaeum Club had invited me to stay upon learning of my lecture at Prince's Hall. Piccadilly was quite bustling at that time, though a bout of dense, London miasma prevented anyone from seeing more than a few yards. Passersby, upon coming within proximity to catch the sight of Susie riding my shoulders, gave us all kinds of strange looks, but the Athenaeum men expressed nothing but delight to meet me and my chimpanzee companion.

A half dozen of these learned men invited me to enjoy dinner with them. The dining hall was deep and wide, built for grand affairs. The seven men and one ape seated around one end of the table, being waited upon by one servant, produced a comic effect. The gaslights were kept very low to reduce that effect, but the result, in my mind, was that every man looked, in the shadows, like his own Mr. Hyde.

Susie was given a seat next to mine and a pillow to sit upon so that she could reach her plate with ease. None of the men sat beside her. Her goblet was filled with water; the men and I enjoyed a fine brandy. There was much laughter at the sight of the little ape stuffing her bread inside her lower lip to soften it with saliva before swallowing. Her silver sat untouched.

"Perhaps," began one of the men, "when you are through instructing your ape in speech, you can teach her to use her silver!"

"Very good," I said, simply to humor my hosts. "Though of course it's their language I'm interested in learning. It's doubtful the chimpanzee's vocal organs could produce the phonetics of English—"

"Wait a moment—are you teaching her American English? Or proper English? I do think that's an important consideration."

"Yes, a very good one," I said. "I've sent the remains of a young chimpanzee to Professor Snowe for him to put his anatomical eye on the brain and vocal organs. I'm very interested to hear—"

"Did you hunt that chimp yourself?"

"No, I did not hunt apes."

"Then she was bought from a savage?"

"She came to me by an English trader."

"Proper English it is!"

This earned a roar of laughter, which was doubled when Susie spilled her goblet.

"Might you have any fruit for her?" I asked, though I doubt I was heard.

"In all seriousness," one of the men said as the laughter subsided. "Your idea of studying apes from a steel cage was brilliant."

"I appreciate that. It indeed allowed me to observe chimpanzees in the wild for an extended period." I believed I finally had their earnest attention. "I would venture that I have spent more time among chimpanzees in their natural habitat than any man—"

"How many times did your cage save your life from wild beasts?"

I waited a moment to answer. The men were too deep into their cups at this point to be enlightened on anatomical differences in humans and apes.

"Once, in the black of night, my servant boy and I heard the footfalls of a leopard as it approached the cage. It prowled so close that its breath whispered in our ears." My voice lowered; the men leaned in, rapt by the tale. "I aimed my rifle through the steel lattice; but the great cat's intuition warned it of the grave danger, and it turned around and leapt away."

The men applauded.

"Another time, we heard the thunderous cry of a gorilla, not far from the cage. The depth of its call would chill you to your bones."

"Looking for human flesh?"

"No." I gave a wry smile. "Looking for a wife!"

More applause. And calls for more tales.

"I'm afraid those were the only times I felt threatened by the jungle's beasts. Otherwise, things were quite peaceful, save one terrible storm."

"Never barely missed being gored by one of those great elephants?"

"Never found yourself in a cannibal's stewpot?"

"Come now, Professor. Half a year in Africa and that's all you've got? I daresay it sounds like you preferred the company of monks to the company of monkeys!"

Before Susie and I were shown to one of the club's rooms, one of the Athenaeum men handed me a package from Mr. McClure containing over a dozen reviews of *The Speech of Monkeys* and a brief letter. "It's a mixed bag," McClure warned. "But it's clear your book whetted appetites for a follow-up to your African explorations!" While Susie explored the suite, I read every review. The general theme that emerged was that my application of the phonograph to the study of primate utterances was "clever," "brilliant," "ingenious," but that my interpretations lacked scientific rigor. One particularly biting critic suggested that my "technological equipment" was in another league than my "mental equipment." The most frustrating review, however, was by Professor Morgan. My experience with the professor at the BAAS meeting had left me feeling quite ambivalent toward him, and his review, which held me in the same estimation as the other critics, extended that ambivalence. He used the review as an opportunity to promote his law, suggesting that my recordings of primate speech could be compared to his own observations of the cheeps of baby chicks, and that in both species distinct sounds could be explained by the simplest of external referents and emotions. I had violated his law in interpreting greater reasoning in some cases of primate speech—though what authority did this supposed law hold? Does not the size and complexity of the brain of a primate prove its greater mental faculties over that of a simple chicken? Morgan, like many other critics, praised my methods of experimentation with the phonograph, though his praise felt especially condescending. What I truly lacked in the eyes of these critics was not scientific rigor—but scientific breeding! It clearly threatened the BAAS and America's armchair scientists that a modest Southerner could arrive at such groundbreaking conclusions.

In his letter, McClure also expressed regret for his absence from my lecture. He had hoped to come, but business kept him in New York. "Give them a real show!" he urged.

I composed a few messages for telegraph. I assured Maggie and Harry that I had arrived safely in Liverpool and was now in London, where I was to give a lecture about my African expedition. I added that I hoped they had had a happy Christmas. I informed McClure of the same. My last message was to Professor Snowe, in which I reiterated my interest in Moses' vocal organs and requested his presence at my lecture.

I saw that Susie was settled in a chair, her sights aimed at a window; Piccadilly had vanished in darkness and miasma, leaving the little girl to dream about what lay outside. She was soon asleep. I passed the rest of the night rehearsing my lecture. In spite of the indifferent reception Susie and I had received upon arriving in England, I was sure that the lecture would be an item of great interest in the English press—and that McClure would see that the American press took note, too. I had no doubts that I would excite London's scientists with my discoveries with wild chimpanzees and secure support for a second, longer expedition to Equatorial Africa. I took a last look at Susie before I turned in; the little ape stirred, restless, for a moment, her mind fluttering with dreams, then settled, a resigned breath on her lips.

The next morning, I left Susie asleep in her chair and walked down Piccadilly for breakfast and a look at the *Times*. An article about my lecture was small and deeply buried, giving me some anxiety. Next I walked to Prince's Hall. The hall was in the center of a beautifully sculpted stone building with shops on either side and a royal art gallery above—a distinguished place for Mr. McClure to have arranged my English lecture. My trunks had been delivered there straight from the train, and I had hoped to find my cage in some stage of assembly. What I found inside shocked me: Fort Gorilla had been completely assembled on the center of the stage with Fort Kulu-Kamba stage right and an empty side table stage left. It was not that a crew had assembled my cage so quickly that surprised me, for its assembly was quite easy; it was the manner in which someone had decorated it. There were skins and skulls, and even a few tusks, hung about the cage. An elephant gun leaned in one corner. The viewer would believe he was seeing the abode of a well-outfitted hunter!

A man appeared from the wings. By his flat cap and loose trousers, I knew he was part of the crew. He carried a wooden case.

"The monkey talk's tomorrow, sir. I'm afraid you can't be in here right now."

"I'm Professor Garner."

"Beg pardon, sir?"

"I'm Professor Garner. The . . . monkey professor."

"Oh, I'm sorry. Didn't mean no disrespect."

"What have you got there?"

The man set the wooden case on the table and began working its top off with his fingers, and I recognized the handle with sudden clarity. It was the very same phonograph lid that had sat upon Mr. Moriarty's desk. The man opened the phonograph and produced the horn from his rear pocket. The instrument's presence, after its absence in Africa, reignited my contempt for the small-minded fools who had stood in my way—Moriarty, Langley, Morgan, that devil Buleon—with greater force than I had ever felt.

The man held it out to me and removed his hat in deference.

"Go ahead, Professor. I'd hate to damage your instrument."

Upon returning to the club, I had telegrams from Mr. McClure and Professor Snowe. McClure expressed delight at my safe return and excitement for my lecture. He had informed "EVERY LAST EDITOR IN LONDON" of the lecture and its significance. I recalled the small notice in the *Times*, but McClure's promise to have drummed up an audience reassured me. Snowe's message, however, sent me into a rage. "NEVER RECEIVED ANY SPECIMENS FROM YOU. MY REGRETS DOUBLY FOR YOUR LOST SPECIMENS AND YOUR LECTURE." McLaughlin! It seemed the Irish bastard had kept poor Moses' remains for his own gain!

I stomped to my room and found Susie awake in the chair, as if she had not moved, reaching across herself to scratch her shoulder. I regained my calm and took the little chim-

panzee in my arms. The second loss of Moses
made me hold her more tightly.

She climbed upon my shoulders so that we
could take a walk and get her something to eat.
At the club's door I was surprised by the smiling countenance of Mr. Walcott.

"Charles! What are you doing here?"

"Looking for you, Richard."

Walcott was actually in Piccadilly to visit
the Geological Society of London, housed in
nearby Burlington House. He had seen the notice about my lecture in the *Times* and had
come looking for me at the Athenaeum Club.

Walcott reached up to pet Susie's shoulder.

"This must be the chimpanzee you've
promised Mr. Hornaday?"

"Yes. I would say we dine at the Criterion,
but I don't think they'll allow this little girl inside."

"Perhaps they'll reconsider after she proves
to be the star of your lecture."

Afternoon sun cut through the miasma, giving Susie and me our best look at London, yet.
The little girl crawled down from my shoulders
and walked alongside me, peering past the tops
of buildings toward the clear sky as if she were
catching the blue in an opening in the jungle
canopy. Passersby kept their distance; the only
people who came within yards of Susie were bicyclists—the first I had seen since returning
from Africa. These were not the bicyclists I was

used to seeing occasionally on the roads, the young daredevils upon high-wheelers. Now there were men of all ages riding upon the new "safety" bicycles, whose design appeared to allow any able-bodied person to mount them—though I daresay I had little interest in the idea. For there were women upon these bicycles, too, their knickerbockered legs pedaling under the folds of their dresses as if it were the most normal thing. The outfits of these men and women did not suggest any sort of club; rather, these were folks going about their normal routines—men venturing to and from their offices on their lunch hours, ladies calling upon one another. Pneumatic tires ensured their comfort and imbued them with grace. But their swift passing by Susie frightened her back into my arms. She climbed back to my shoulders, from where she could keep better watch of the bicyclists. We found a grocer's, where I purchased bread and salted beef for Susie, though she was still too shocked by the bicyclists to eat.

We eventually found ourselves in front of Burlington House. The great brick-and-stone structure reminded us of the Castle. Its many wings housed various learned societies, and I imagine that even a man as esteemed as Walcott was intimidated by the place. I asked Walcott what brought him there.

"Java Man."

"I beg your pardon?"

"You've not heard? An amazing geological discovery was made while you were away. The Dutch anatomist Dubois unearthed several bones on the island of Java—part of a skull, a molar, and—this is the really fascinating thing—a femur. Do you know what's being said about this femur?"

"What?"

"That it suggests standing upright." Walcott leaned in close and whispered, "It's an early man, Richard." He turned his attention back to Burlington House's façade. "Dubois is calling it the 'missing link,' though I imagine that's somewhat reductive."

"That has been my argument," I said. "There have likely been many forms of man—and other apes—that have evolved along similar lines that split from one species millions of years ago. This 'Java Man' is only one of those early forms, unlikely the species from which both men and apes evolved."

"I don't disagree." Walcott turned back to me. "But don't you see what this discovery means? It means the study of human evolution is rightfully in the hands of geologists."

"I don't think a few old bones gives geologists a monopoly on evolution."

"I'm sorry, Richard, I don't mean to belittle the work of naturalists like yourself. I'm sure there are contributions your kind can make yet to the study of evolution." Walcott turned back again to Burlington House. "But we have the materials. Do you have the materials, Richard?"

The next evening, Susie and I arrived at Prince's Hall an hour prior to my lecture. I suggested to the manager that I needed to make a few slight adjustments to my cage. I removed the elephant gun and the tusks and carried them backstage. Fort Gorilla still presented a somewhat false image with the leopard skin hanging about one wall and the phonograph sitting to one side. So I sat backstage among the elephantalia (to whom did it belong?) and worked the misplaced elements into my lecture notes: My African servant boy and I had faced a terrifying leopard from inside of Fort Gorilla one night. Without the cage separating us from the great cat, we would surely have been its meal. A strong argument for the efficacy of the cage as a means of studying the jungle's creatures in their habitat. The phonograph. My first, brief expedition to Equatorial Africa was merely to explore the feasibility of observing chimpanzees in the wild; that having been proved an unqualified success, I planned to return with a phonograph to capture the chimpanzees' language for further study. I would have my materials.

As I revised my lecture, a small roar of Londoners began to fill the hall. McClure's efforts had paid off. Susie had begun to entertain the manager by rolling on the floor, practically begging for attention, which she constantly required of me, so when I felt my notes were ready, I took a brief walk among the seated gentlemen and ladies. A writer from *Punch* introduced himself and began shooting off inquiries: "How did you find Africa, Professor? Have you brought an ape with which to converse tonight?" In due time, I told the excitable young man.

The faces of the pressmen and the society gentlemen and ladies were unfamiliar to me, save for Mr. Walcott and Mr. Labouchere. I had expected Labouchere's presence, for he had been keenly interested in my expedition. I greeted him and expressed my gratitude for his presence.

"Of course, Professor. I have high expectations for your lecture."

At the appointed hour, I walked proudly onstage. A podium was set in front of my cage, which, along with the smaller cage and the phonograph, had generated murmurs of speculation as I waited backstage. Susie remained in the wings with the manager; when called, she would provide the evening's most significant visual element: a fine specimen of man's closest kin. As I approached the podium, the hiss and thrum of warm applause rose and filled the hall, crested in the sculpted ceiling, and settled back into the seats, leaving a vacuum for me to project my insights, to enlighten the assembled ladies and gentlemen upon the rudimentary language of the chimpanzee—to affirm that, the chimpanzee being in a state of developing language and thought, man had once been in such a state prior to evolving to the races of men that inhabit the world today.

I began modestly, by recalling the incident in Cincinnati's zoological gardens when I first witnessed monkeys using rudimentary speech. It was that remarkable observation—upon which no naturalist had yet remarked—that led to my phonograph experiments in Washington and New York with monkeys, and in Cincinnati with chimpanzees. "My early results, however, were immature; to prove beyond a shadow of a doubt that language—the vocal expression of thought—was a natural element of the primates, I would have to study them *in their natural habitat*. Africa. The Atlantic coast of Equatorial Africa, to be precise. For centuries a port for the slave trade, this region is now the French colony of Gabon, governed by the peaceable explorer Pierre Savorgnan DeBrazza. With the blessing of the commissaire and a Catholic mission, I was permitted to construct my cage in the jungle for a period of about six months, from which I observed—*I lived amongst*—the inhabitants of Gabon's jungle. From the driver ants that made the jungle floor crawl, to the great birds that announced daybreak with their calls. And between earth and canopy, a great many monkeys, and yes—apes. A lone gorilla in search of a wife."

The gorilla's air of mystery and danger still intact in society's imagination, my admission drew a gasp from the assembled ladies and gentlemen.

"My greatest achievement, however, was living amongst a family of chimpanzees for a period of several weeks. A husband and wife, clearly, and their three children: The eldest was a fickle female; the middle child was a sweet male, who earned my sympathy as he fought an illness for a period of days; and a baby, who rarely left his mother's breast. This family ate and played and slept in the fruiting trees surrounding my cage; when the trees bore no more fruit, they moved away. But during the weeks they lived in the perimeter of my home in the jungle, I was able to discern many of their words.

"Yes. They did speak to one another. They offered each other fruit and expressed gratitude. They shared feelings of ill health. They expressed love.

"My guest tonight was not a member of this family, but was orphaned when an unscrupulous hunter killed her mother. So I have adopted her, and will carry out what language studies I can with her. Susie, would you come out here, please?"

When Susie knuckle-walked from the wings, there was another gasp from the audience, and several ladies hid their eyes from the naked chimpanzee.

The writer from *Punch* said, "It's all right, ladies. It's a little girl!" to much laughter.

Susie leapt into my arms, and I carried her in front of the podium for the audience to have a better look.

Another pressman asked the whereabouts of Moses.

"He is elsewhere at this time."

"In Piccadilly? Should we keep an eye out for him?"

More laughter.

The *Punch* man spoke again, opening a contest between several pressmen and me. "What have you taught this one to say?"

"She is not a parrot."

"If your ape won't speak, will you play a cylinder for us?"

"I would be delighted to, if I had any cylinders to play."

"Where are the cylinders you made?"

"I did not produce any cylinders—not on this expedition, anyway. I plan to return to Equatorial Africa—"

"No cylinders?"

Since the *Punch* man had spoken up, my spell on the audience had been broken; its tone had descended from a sizzle of whispered awe to a good-humored guffawing and now to a precipice—the anxious nudging and inquiring right before everyone knows the perceived danger is real, the theater is on fire.

"I never claimed to have produced any."

"Wasn't the purpose of your expedition to prove that apes could speak?"

"As I said, I studied the speech of a family of wild chimpanzees."

"But why did you not produce any cylinders?"

"Because a coterie of fools prevented me from having a phonograph!"

My terrible agitation sent Susie leaping from my shoulders and drew the most frightful gasp yet from the audience; their alarm had not entirely sounded when it began anew upon hearing Susie's anxious call through her bared teeth. Susie did not bark again, to my relief, as the manager was eyeing me from the wings, looking quite ready to lock the ape up. She pursed her lips and sought a resting place on the nearby table, clutching the phonograph.

All that remains in the public's memory of that lecture are the resulting image and the lie that it suggested: The chimpanzee, half hidden by the phonograph's horn, gone mute.

Chapter Twelve

Upon our arrival in New York, Susie and I found conditions much the same as they had been in London. Passersby met us with surprised countenances; bicyclists weaved through the pedestrians and carriages with the same abandon. It may well have been a trick of my mind, but it seemed that bicyclists filled the streets in even greater numbers than they had in London. If every metropolis in Europe and America had bicyclists coursing through its arteries, all those tires should have made Equatorial Africa the richest place on Earth. But I had seen and heard enough in Gabon to know that in Equatorial Africa, wealth, like rubber, flowed in only one direction.

We took a room at the Fifth Avenue Hotel. The desk agent, upon learning that I was the esteemed naturalist returned from Africa, was quite cordial, and though they could not hide their curiosity about Susie, the bellhop and elevator operator were efficient in seeing me and my guest to our suite.

Susie explored the suite while I returned to the lobby to telegraph Mr. McClure's office. When I returned to the suite's sitting room, Susie had toppled the coat rack and was trembling in a chair.

"Good heavens, little girl, what happened?"

I extended my arms, and the little ape leaped into them and threw her arms around my neck.

"You're okay, little girl. Did you think that coat rack was a tree?"

A short time later a bellhop appeared at the door and said there were some men from the press in the lobby inquiring about me. I had only telegraphed McClure a moment earlier. What, the bellhop asked, would I like him to tell them?

"Tell them we shall be down shortly!"

Susie held my hand as we walked to the elevator. With the same dignity with which he had delivered us to our floor, the elevator operator, a young Black man, took us to the lobby. He did not remark upon my chimpanzee companion.

I had lived among Blacks in slavery as a youth, and among them in their villages in Africa—and both states had seemed natural to me. But now I did not know how to regard this elevator operator, a free Black man in America. His kind had the peril of slavery behind them, but, since Emancipation, remained largely in a state of servitude, a state which, given their nature, I doubted would ever change. I pitied the young man when I contrasted him with the great Chief Rimpano, with his wealth and wives. Yet the place of Chief Rimpano and his sons was not that different. They were powerful enough to have survived the Atlantic slave trade, but now they faced the threat of enslavement by colonists. I had seen the threat incarnate in the young man bearing the scar of the chicotte. To be Black was to live in a vice, between a deadly past and a frightful future.

I tipped the young man generously and bade him a good day.

Upon reaching the lobby and setting off a flurry of activity among the gathered press—there must have been two dozen pressmen, all shouting—Susie was frightened back into my arms. "Come to Papa," I said, soothing her. She bared her teeth in agitation, but hid her face in my shoulder. I begged the men to compose themselves and petted Susie's back to calm her down. She settled enough that her anxious grin melted, and she was able to face the menagerie of pressmen without trepidation.

I asked the assembled pressmen if Samuel McClure had alerted them to Susie and me taking up residence at the Fifth Avenue Hotel.

"Give us credit, Professor. Do you think the arrival in the city of a man with a pet chimp could escape the press?"

Though I was holding court in a sitting area—no one was sitting, however—to one side of the front desk, several guests checking in or passing through were drawn to the assembly. The lobby was filled with pressmen and curious onlookers.

"Is your pet always that affectionate?"

"Toward me, yes."

"Did you capture her yourself?"

"No, she was not captured. I rescued her after a hunter slayed her mother."

"In *McClure's* it was reported that you had a male chimp. What became of that pet?"

"That orphan perished, tragically, while I was still in Gabon."

"What happened?"

"Perhaps you would like to know more about Susie, here."

"Have you learned the chimps' language?"

"Several words of it."

"So you can converse with your pet?"

"To a small degree. Identifying the chimpanzees' words is one thing; producing them is quite another."

"Give us your best chimp yell!"

"I don't think the lobby of the Fifth Avenue Hotel is any place for such a demonstration. I wouldn't want to frighten the guests!"

There was much laughter from the press-men and the guests, but the laughter quickly died to a question from a reporter who had not yet spoken.

"How do you answer to the report in London's *Truth*?"

"I'm sorry—I haven't read that one yet."

"It suggests that your piece for *McClure's* was a fabrication."

"I beg your pardon?"

Another reporter: "Did you abandon your cage after only three nights?"

"What on earth are you talking about?"

"Exactly how many nights did you spend in your cage?"

"I would have to refer to my field notes to give you an exact number, but it was for the better part of several months."

There were shouted questions about my relations with the missionaries, which I addressed with nothing but gratitude for the missionaries' hospitality. I wanted to avoid another disaster like what had occurred at Prince's Hall.

"Why were you without a phonograph?"

"I never claimed to have had one! Look—I have already made arrangements to acquire a phonograph for my return to Gabon, the details of which I shall be sharing with you gentlemen soon. Good day!"

The London press, the New York press—where was their reverent curiosity? Why had I been met with such hostility? And my reception would hardly be improved at my next appointment: the office of Mr. McClure.

Upon entering McClure's office, Susie, who was riding my shoulders, elicited a gasp from Mrs. McClure and Miss Roseboro, for they had never seen one of man's primate cousins without a barrier of steel bars between them.

"It's all right, ladies," I assured them. "This little girl is perfectly harmless. She's quite friendly, in fact."

Susie came down from my shoulders and knuckle-walked among the desks, looking curiously at the women, for I am sure she recognized them as females and was more comfortable in their presence than in the gathering of excited men we had just left; she likely carried with her the terrible memory of men slaying her mother.

Mrs. McClure knelt down to the ape's level and extended her palm, as you might show a dog you were friendly. Susie stroked her hand. Miss Roseboro became comfortable enough to kneel and pet Susie's shoulder. A deep sigh of pleasure filled the room as Susie rolled on her back; she wanted to be tickled, and the ladies indulged her.

McClure's door burst open, and the man's face was particularly animated, his eyes large

as they sought the reason for the sighs of soft
laughter. The ladies were startled. Miss Roseboro busied herself; Mrs. McClure continued
tickling Susie.

"I'll watch her while you gentlemen speak."

"Thank you, Dear. Come on back, Professor."

McClure and I sat in his office, and he tossed
a copy of *Truth* across his desk. I opened it to
the table of contents and searched for my name,
or Gabon, or apes.

"I'll save you the trouble, Professor. It claims
that you tossed up your cage in the back yard of
a mission and after three nights were driven
away by mosquitos."

"That's what a reporter at the hotel said."

"Have you already talked to the press?"

"Briefly, in the hotel lobby."

"Did you deny it?"

"Of course! What else is in here?"

As McClure talked, I scanned the article, and
in that way the depth of the betrayal set in. The
accusation that I had abandoned Fort Gorilla
after three nights was reported by "a missionary." This unnamed source claimed that, "Garner's study of the ape language made him incredibly thirsty, for he drank several bottles of
claret while enjoying the comforts of the mission." This devil went on: I saw no chimpanzees
save the two youths who were captured by
hunters. The details of my writing were invented as I lay up in my room. Upon my depar-

ture, I failed to make a contribution to the mission equal to the debts in food and drink and rooming that I incurred. Of course there was no mention of my promise of remittance. The grossest of the accusations was that I had "looked lustily after one of the sisters"! All of these lies were corroborated by "a Hatton and Cookson agent."

"This is preposterous! Slander!"

McClure sat on the edge of his desk and massaged a palm with the fingers of his other hand. He narrowed his eyes at me.

"Richard, understand that I wish I didn't have to ask you what I'm about to ask you. But it's not only your reputation on the line." He lowered his face toward mine. "Is there any truth to these accusations?"

"I didn't come here expecting to be interrogated," I said, looking away from him. "But I understand your need to do such." I turned back toward him and adopted an earnest tone. "What I have reported to you is absolutely true."

"Don't play games with me, Richard. I ask if there is any truth to the accusations printed here."

"There is none."

"Readers are hungry for true stories about the unknown wilds of the world. I need to have confidence in you as a man who can deliver those stories. Truthfully. If there's anything you've misrepresented, anything at all true in those accusations, we can deal with it."

"There is nothing to those lies."

Mr. McClure had me write a response to *Truth* for his magazine. In my response, I answered to every accusation. My cage was constructed in the jungle, at least one mile from the mission's perimeter. I had never claimed anything to the contrary. I spent over one hundred nights there—not three!—and fewer than twenty in a dormitory at the mission. During my time in the jungle, I spent a period of several weeks observing a chimpanzee family. I left a small contribution and promised to send the remainder in a reasonable amount of time. And in no way were my manners toward any of the missionaries—especially a sister!—anything less than forthright.

My defense pleased McClure, as it struck a cool and collected tone and met *Truth*'s accusations with nothing but facts. Its original composition contained a few unmeasured jabs at the despicable men who had wronged me, but McClure edited those out, demanding I stay on the higher ground.

I was interviewed several times during my stay in New York, and each time the accusations in *Truth* were raised, I repeated the facts I had set out in writing. Though with each successive interview, it became more difficult to maintain the restraint McClure had asked of me. In what would be my final comment on the controversy until this testimony, I unleashed on Labouchere to a particularly pushy reporter: "His attack is too mean-spirited to deserve any answer besides a swift punch in the face!"

The Bronx Zoo not being ready to receive animals at this time, Mr. Hornaday met Susie and me in our hotel room. Since our return from Mr. McClure's, Susie had grown sullen. She was uninterested in eating, save the occasional piece of fruit, and seemed unable to shake the chill from the trip back from the Morse Building. She sat in a chair and shivered and pulled at her hair.

When I admitted Hornaday to our room, she took little notice. Hornaday was quite pleased by her, though. He knelt down and took the little ape into his arms and studied her face, which she turned toward neither him nor me, but toward some ghost in the room.

"She's very fine, Professor."

"I thought you would find her an excellent addition to your new zoo."

"In due time. How did you come to possess her?"

"There seems to be little regard for apes by anyone over there. Savage Africans and ruthless English hunters kill apes without mercy, and there is little anyone can do about it. The little male I had promised you was murdered."

"For meat or sport?"

"For spite."

"Spite?"

"Yes."

"And who was spiting you?"

"A Frenchman. On the whole, white men are doing far more harm to Africa than its native peoples. And regarding apes, if they remain unprotected, I fear what will happen to their numbers."

Hornaday nodded earnestly. His eyes remained on Susie, but I imagined his thoughts roamed to the orangutans he had taken. To his buffalo. He turned his attention to me, narrowed his eyes.

"You're taking quite a beating in the press."

"Do you doubt me, too?"

He set Susie down in her chair and took a seat for himself.

"I take you at your word. I've no reason to doubt what you have to say about Africa, do I?"

"You should join me when I return! We'll find more specimens for your zoo."

"Thank you, but the zoo needs me here. And I need a trustworthy supplier in Africa. You should be that man."

"I'm no mere collector. I'm a scientist."

"Of course you are. Just consider it."

Since it would be some time before Mr. Hornaday was ready to take Susie for his new zoological gardens, I visited the Central Park Zoo to inquire about housing Susie temporarily. We met a keeper one sunny afternoon in front of the Armory. He led us to the cage where I had studied capuchins.

"You do realize that capuchins are native to the forests of South America, and my chimpanzee is from Equatorial Africa?"

The keeper rolled his eyes.

"I saw that, you know? Would you prefer I throw her in with the bears?"

He suggested that there was another option and led us to the Armory's basement. When my eyes adjusted to the basement's darkness, what came into view were cages of various sizes, laid out haphazardly, with only small aisles to walk between them. You would not know what animals surrounded your ankles save for the shadows they cast in the dim gaslights, their labored breathing, the shuffling of their pads or hooves against steel wire. The menagerie's reek was more potent than anything I had encountered in the densest jungle. Susie clutched my neck and trembled as we followed the keeper. He finally stopped at an empty cage and said my ape was welcome to stay inside it.

"I don't think so," I said. "This basement isn't fit for any animal."

"This is temporary housing. When more housing is built outside, some of these fellows will move out there. Or if an animal out there dies, someone from here gets his home."

"I don't doubt it's the case that more often an animal spends his last night down here. This place reeks of death."

Susie and I returned to the Fifth Avenue Hotel, where Mr. McClure was making it possible for us to remain. But I felt as if I were in purgatory; I wanted to go home to write and plan my return to Africa, but Susie, I am sure, did not want to be submitted to the hardships of the trip. Her shoulders were picked bare by this point, and her eyes appeared dull, as if they had lost their depth. I, too, felt somehow shadowy, insignificant.

When we boarded the elevator, the same elevator operator was there.

"We'll be staying here a while," I said.

"Very good, sir."

"If you have questions about Susie, here, or any of my work, you may ask. I'm sure you've heard talk of it."

"Very good, sir."

Two floors passed.

"Are you telling me you know nothing of my work? There are implications for your people, you know."

"I am aware, sir. It's just . . . no one ever asks an elevator operator his opinion."

"Well, perhaps they should. Surely your people have an opinion on such matters."

For the first time, the young man looked in my face.

"We have opinions on many things," he said with a smugness that surprised and, in some respect, delighted me.

"Exactly! Your people must engage with the big questions. Your most inquisitive minds, your greatest thinkers will pass their traits into new lines!"

The young man turned his gaze forward again, but the smugness remained upon his mouth.

"And one day we'll be like you?"

"See? You already have a basic understanding of evolution."

Something sounded from that man's mouth: slight, airy. I'll be damned if he didn't laugh at me.

We had arrived at my floor.

"Good heavens. Look at me, fishing for compliments from *you*."

Susie and I stepped off the elevator. Before the young man had shut the gate, I turned around to apologize. But I didn't know the right words. I looked him in the eyes—maybe the first time I had ever looked a free Black American in his eyes. Something passed between us, an understanding (or misunderstanding) I remain unable to put into words.

My attention returned to Susie. Near the elevator bank was a pot of ferns.

"What do you think, girl?"

I grabbed the stems and pulled them from the soil, making a great mess on the floor, which I swept under the pot with my shoe. I carried the stems back to our suite and laid them on the settee.

"I know it's not a proper nest. But surely it's better than that chair you've been sleeping in."

Susie climbed onto the settee and poked around at the leaves. Thinking she might mimic me, I ruffled the bedspread in an exaggerated kind of way, until it was a great heap. Then I kicked off my shoes and lay upon the heap, letting out a great sigh. I damn well felt like sighing, considering everything. I swear Susie sighed, too. At this point, though, I no longer felt I knew the little ape's mind.

"We'll get through this, sweetheart."

My suggestion that Labouchere ought to be struck in the face drew an immediate reply in *Truth*, including an insistence for evidence to support my claims. Labouchere remarked that my threat had induced him to construct his own steel cage in which to protect himself from me! "I have chained a gorilla to the cage as a further measure to keep Garner away, for the Professor will avoid contact with those beasts as long as he can help it!"

The argument was spread in the English and American press. Mr. McClure came to the conclusion that there was no point in further rejoinders with Labouchere. I was to maintain that I was entirely truthful in my accounts and suggest to any who inquired about evidence to await publication of my next book. McClure had turned the controversy into a campaign!

The only other bright spot in my return to civilization was seeing my son. I had written to Maggie and Harry upon my arrival at the Fifth Avenue Hotel and finally received a letter back from Harry. He informed me that his mother preferred not to join me in New York, but to wait for my return home. He, on the other hand, would be arriving the following weekend.

Upon his arrival in New York, I left Susie on her settee-nest and went to the train station to meet him. The changes that had come over him since the previous year were remarkable; gone were his schoolboy's shirts and trousers and straw boater, and in their place was a dark wool suit and a smart bowler. Upon his upper lip was a mustache. With a firm handshake and a pat on the shoulder, I conveyed my pleasure at seeing him grown into a man.

We walked back to the Fifth Avenue Hotel for lunch. It was an extravagance I could barely afford, given how long my furlough in New York had run, but Harry deserved only the best.

"How are things in Baltimore?"

"Very fine. Business is good. And I have some very good news."

"How's your mother? Did you go home for Christmas? Has she paid you a visit?"

"My room in Baltimore is no place to receive visitors, but I did visit her with my—"

"And how is she?"

Harry paused, gazed at his soup.

"She misses you dearly. She's very lonesome without you."

"I wish you had gone into business in Washington."

"I suggested she take in a boarder, perhaps a widow with whom she could have a friendship, but she refuses. The savings you left her have run out."

"I'll give her more, then. I'm making a good income from my writing."

"I've been supporting her since Thanksgiving. But I won't be able to once—"

"You don't need to support her! If she would've told me she needed more money, I would've sent it to her long ago."

"She doesn't need you to send her more money." Harry looked up at me. "She needs you to come home."

"I am, as soon as the Bronx Zoo can receive my chimpanzee. I cannot return to Gabon without being one-hundred percent prepared. You know that bureaucrat Langley cut me off—"

"She needs you to come home for good!" Harry looked around, embarrassed by his outburst. He lowered his voice. "I've written letters of inquiry on your behalf to several schools in Washington. One is very interested in speaking with you about a position as a science teacher."

"Son, I appreciate that. But my future is in studying apes."

"You're determined to go back?"

I hesitated, gave credence to the idea that Harry was right, and that I ought to return to Washington for good. I could still study apes and support Maggie as a writer and lecturer—and a teacher if necessary. But I would be relegating myself to the despised league of armchair scientists, would I not?

"Yes. But your mother could come with me. I know she doesn't care for Washington—and Gabon is nothing like Washington."

Harry shook his head.

"Well, I hope you can wait until after the wedding."

"What's that?"

"I've been trying to tell you: I'm getting married."

"That's wonderful news, son! You must tell me all about it."

Harry filled me in about the young lady and their plans, and for a while it was very pleasant being in each other's company. I felt so proud of him—and elated that I was gaining a daughter! As he spoke, I imagined him and his wife arriving at the house in Libreville where Maggie and I would live: The four of us—no, five, for our daughter-in-law would have a babe in her arms—relaxing on the veranda as a breeze played its music across the savannah's tall grasses.

"And will you be here for the wedding?"

"Yes, I promise not to leave before the wedding. You know, I had urged you toward marriage in one of my letters. Marrying your mother and raising you has been such a blessing."

"If your marriage is such a blessing, why do you seem so ready to throw it away?"

Harry and I spoke only out of necessity as I saw him settled in his room. I nearly asked him if he wanted to come to my suite and meet Susie; I was thinking of a decade earlier when he and his mother and I visited the Cincinnati Zoo and entered the mysterious monkey house. The little rhesus society and the alien mandrill had aroused only a passing intrigue in Harry and a minor fright in Maggie, and it was not fair of me to hate them for their reactions; but a profound desire to know more of man's evolution through contact with our primate cousins was born in me. I felt then as I do now: destined to follow that desire at any cost. Maggie and Harry did not have to share my passion, but I expected them to respect the demands of fulfilling it. Maggie—I would propose to her that she move with me to Gabon. Perhaps she would see it as a great adventure! She would be cared for one way or another. Harry—he was a man, now, would probably be a father himself soon. He did not need me. Nor did he, on that night, care whatsoever about the chimpanzee I was fostering.

I stepped into the shadows of my suite, expecting to hear Susie moving about. But the door's closing echoed around the rooms, finding them still. I knew something was irrevocably wrong. My eyes adjusted to the darkness. Susie lay upon her nest of ferns. She was limp as I picked her up.

I was too late; her body lay in my arms, but her soul was in Gabon.

Susie's passing gave me the resolve to return to Gabon as soon as possible. News of her death did little—nothing—to my standing in the world's eyes, for it was and remains a common occurrence for apes to perish in America and Europe. My reputation was still a matter of debate, due to that filth-slinging Labouchere and his "sources" in Gabon; besides Buleon's and Leo's distortions, I guessed that Wolfgang had told lies about me, perhaps for some perceived slight regarding the boy, Olago.

Mr. McClure met any bad press with a bout of good press and helped see to my return to Gabon within a year's time. Fort Gorilla did not go back with me, for after my troubles with Labouchere, it carried with it the whiff of scandal. Instead, I had a modest house built in Libreville. From there, I take a steamer to Cape Lopez and explore the territories of the Orungus and Nkomis and there observe both chimpanzees and gorillas. For several years I hired Odanga as a guide. With that intelligent and trustworthy man I enjoyed true friendship. I do hope he is well, wherever he is, though I fear he is not.

I never travel south of the Ogowe.

My writing and supplying the Bronx Zoo with primates earns me enough to live and study as I please. To be perfectly frank, supplying primates to Mr. Hornaday is my main income. Only a fraction of my essays get published, and the royalties from my books are but a pittance. It's charitable of Mr. McClure to continue handling my work. But I keep it up, for though I may not live to see it, I know my theories will be held in high regard one day.

I employ the help of a few Mpongwe men and a young woman of that tribe as a housekeeper. I even purchased, for companionship, an English Foxhound I called Bubu from an Englishman. I raised him from a pup; he was a good dog. Purebred. He's gone, now. Maggie has never joined me there.

I wrote to Marie, and when my letter went unanswered, I wrote to the superior to inquire about her whereabouts, but she replied only to say Marie was no longer at St. Anne's. She could not—or more likely would not—tell me what had become of her. I have written to every Catholic mission I know of, all the way to Zanzibar, but have never found her.

McLaughlin paid me a visit in the summer of 1900. Commissaire Brazza had been recalled by Paris less than two years earlier, and Paris had allowed concessionary companies to parcel Gabon and the French Congo after the fashion of the Belgians on their side of the Congo. Wolfgang had predicted the expulsion of English and German traders, but it turned out quite worse than that.

McLaughlin had heard that I was living in Libreville and ferreted my address from a Mpongwe contact. I was quite surprised to find him at my door one morning; I had long suspected him of mistreating my property and my good name. But I bade one of my servants deliver us tea on the veranda.

"To what do I owe the pleasure of this visit?"

"To the Compagnie Coloniale du Fernan Vaz."

McLaughlin explained that the French, claiming to own the soil upon which Hatton and Cookson was built, had arrived at their doors with arms and seized the factory and all its goods. It was happening all over the region: The Holts, the German firms—every one was taken over by the company.

"We stood no chance against the frogs. There is nothing to do but flee."

"Sorry to hear that. Where will you go?"

"Home for now. To wait out the war in the south."

As we enjoyed our tea and the afternoon— the sun was bright and hot in the yard, but a mild breeze cooled us under the umbrella—I felt some sympathy for the trader. I had been driven from the Fernan Vaz region by the terrible designs of Buleon and Labouchere and, I suspected, Wolfgang; and now McLaughlin had been forced out as well. It was the first time I had any fellow feeling for the man. I was moved to forgive him for any offense.

"You may tell me now with impunity: What became of the chimpanzee remains I entrusted you with?"

McLaughlin narrowed his eyes, begging further explanation.

"They went missing upon their arrival in your country. I have long suspected that you sold them to some armchair scientist for a handsome price and kept it all for yourself."

"I did no such thing. The remains were delivered as you instructed. No payment exchanged hands. The gentleman promised to pay you when you arrived in London."

"Professor Snowe claimed you never delivered the remains!"

"And you trusted this 'armchair scientist' over a Hatton and Cookson man? I thought you had a great deal more respect for men who braved the boundaries of empire than those who stayed home growing fat on the wealth we produce."

"You're right, my friend. I'm sorry to have doubted you."

"I never spoke to any journalists, either, should you suspect me of that."

"I did not. I believe your associate Wolfgang did that."

"Don't be so quick to blame him. The claim may have been a fiction."

"The truth may never come out. Whoever won the race between you two?"

"No one. I supposed we will never declare a winner now that we're being tossed out." McLaughlin smiled. "Hatton and Cookson men will be fine. It's the Compagnie that will find itself in real trouble. The Gabonese are wise enough to know that what's happened in King Leopold's Congo will repeat itself here. The administration will demand taxes, and the only way the Gabonese will be able to pay them will be to sell rubber and ivory to the companies for the companies' prices. And the companies will require impossible quantities and inflict brutality when they're not satisfied. The moment our African agents saw the French usurpers, they fled to their villages—and I don't doubt they have persuaded their chiefs to pack up and run. The banks of the Rembo Nkomi are probably already deserted.

"On my way out of Fernan Vaz, I stopped to wish Father Buleon farewell. I found him deeply saddened by the brutalities. He said to me, 'France has stripped the Gabonese of everything, and now hunts him down for a centime.'"

"Then I daresay that it is the Africans who will find themselves in real trouble."

Despite Wolfgang's prediction that an American naturalist would not be welcome in Gabon once the French expelled the traders and took over the factories and began the process of draining Equatorial Africa without regard for its natural history or even its peoples, I have been allowed to remain in my home in Libreville and employ Mpongwes and generally carry on as I please. Often, a native, knowing my interests, will bring me a captured monkey or ape and negotiate a price for it. Cotton cloth, rifles and ammunition, even Virginia tobacco—these items were prized by the natives for a few years; but upon Commissaire Brazza's recall, the natives' needs changed.

As the new century began, Gabonese men began showing up at my door ever more frequently with monkeys and apes—some in pitiful shape—asking for protection in the form of employment. When I said that I could afford no more help, I was asked for money; if the men could not meet a concessionary company's demands for rubber, the only way to stay the violence against their women and children—and themselves—was in francs. I had little money, but occasionally I would take pity on the animal and the man.

One rainy afternoon, I answered my door expecting to find such a case, and was surprised to see an old friend.

"Odanga! Please come in."

My old friend looked as hale as ever, though his countenance was heavy with sorrow. His every feature was flattened of its former expressiveness. We took tea in my dining room, where I listened to his incredible story as the rain rattled against the roof. It had been over five years since my visit from McLaughlin, and I admit that in that period, in my little house in Libreville and on my jaunts into the jungle, I was generally insulated from the brutality of the concessionary companies. The men who came to me looking for work or to sell a primate were reminders that the companies were exploiting the Gabonese, but these men usually said little about the situation; I now know this is because the traumas were often unspeakable. When Odanga visited me, I did not know the depths to which the colonists had sunk.

I did know that Pierre DeBrazza had recently been sent back to Africa by the French government to investigate allegations against the colonial government and the concessionary companies. Odanga said that as Brazza traveled, the administrators put on a good show for him, and that he was witness to one of these facades.

"I had traveled to a colonial post Brazza was visiting to share with him what I had witnessed. When I entered his room to speak with him, I was shocked by his condition. Underneath his powerful eyes, his cheeks were

sunken; his face revealed a man of great re-
silience coming to his end.”

“The poor man. I wish I could see him
again.”

“That evening, colonial administrators
forced some of the locals to put on a perfor-
mance for Brazza and his wife and his men. I
quietly took my place in back of the audience of
administrators, and could not believe what I
saw: The lead dancer was miming a man in
shackles! The administrators could see nothing
but barbarism, but I read in it the revelation of
a slave camp, run by those very administrators!
I looked toward Brazza to see if he were reading
the man’s dance, too. But I could only see the
back of his chair. I feared that his attention was
too weakened to receive the message. I began to
back away from the gathering, when suddenly
Brazza shot up in his chair; from what reserve
he gathered the strength, I do not know. He
bade the dancers stop and shouted for the administrators to take him to the slave camp immediately. There was a commotion as the administrators tried to dissuade Brazza, and the
dancers fled to their village. Brazza would not
be satisfied, he said, until he had been taken to
the camp and seen to the slaves’ release.”

“Incredible. And what did you do?”

“I fled. And I am fleeing still.”

Odanga believed that Brazza’s report would
be suppressed, that nothing would change.

"But why leave now, when Brazza is in a position to fix the colonies?"

A nervous laugh escaped Odanga's lips.

"You've not heard? Brazza's dead."

The natives kept coming to my door.

In one instance, a Mpongwe man showed up with a scared vervet cradled in his arms. The little creature quite trembled; what horrors he held in his little black eyes I could guess at: The man chasing him through the jungle and tossing a net over him, separating him from his society; being stripped from his arboreal world and made to traverse the savannahs in the man's rough hands. Who knows how long it had been since the fellow had last enjoyed any nourishment. I could give the poor thing some fruit and let him regain his strength and wits in the trees around my home. Bubu was used to monkeys. And I cared not if the little fellow ran away to find his kind; vervets were not particularly interesting to me.

"I hope you didn't trouble yourself too much about this little fellow," I said. "For I can't offer you much for him."

The Mpongwe said nothing. His silence, so different was it from the usual palaver of one of these encounters, drew my attention from the vervet's eyes to the man's: scleras the yellow of rotting wood, pupils poisoned to black.

I told the man to wait a moment and went inside to retrieve a few francs for the monkey. I returned and held the money out for the man. He took the money in his right hand and tucked it into a pocket of this cloth skirt.

The Mpongwe laid his arms into mine to hand over the vervet. The dry knuckles of his right hand scraped against my left palm; the sensation in my right palm was not quite right: something blunted, covered in scar tissue. The Mpongwe pulled his arms away, and I saw: His left hand was completely gone. It was the mutilated and scarred knob of his wrist I had felt. I had heard rumors of the practice, but I did not want to believe them.

"The French have already asked too much of you, my friend. But I think I can offer you a bit more."

I pulled all the francs from my pocket and handed them over.

"Thank you, Professor."

The Mpongwe turned around and slowly walked away. Would that I could have paid the debts of all like him. Though they were not debts. It was quite the other way around. The French owed them all the land and lives they had stolen. Will it come to pass that the Gabonese will again be stewards of their land? I cannot tell. But I was not filled with confidence by the dead walk of the Mpongwe, his mutilated arm dangling at his side.

Acknowledgements

Man in a Cage grew from a brief mention of Richard Garner in *The Gap: The Science of What Separates Us from Other Animals* by Thomas Suddendorf. In two paragraphs, Suddendorf summarizes Garner's rise and fall as a naturalist and suggests that his greatest legacy might be inspiring Hugh Lofting's Dr. Dolittle. I was so intrigued by the image of Garner in his cage that I immediately wanted to write a novel about him.

Many other books provided essential background for the novel: *The Simian Tongue: The Long Debate about Animal Language*, by Gregory Radick; *Missing Links: The African and American Worlds of R. L. Garner, Primate Collector*, by Jeremy Rich; *Mr. Hornaday's War: How a Peculiar Victorian Zookeeper Waged a Lonely Crusade for Wildlife that Changed the World*, by Stefan Bechtel; *The Autobiography of S. S. McClure*, ghostwritten by Willa Cather; *Brazza: A Life for Africa*, by Maria Petringa; *Between Man and Beast: An Unlikely Explorer and the African Adventure that Took the Victorian World by Storm*, by Monte Reel (about Paul Du Chaillu); *Congo:*

An Account of a Century of European Exploration and Exploitation in the Heart of Africa, by Richard West; *Colonial Rule and Crisis in Equatorial Africa*, by Christopher Gray; *The Spiritual in the Secular: Missionaries and Knowledge about Africa*, edited by Patrick Harries and David Maxwell; *Civilizing Habits: Women Missionaries and the Revival of French Empire*, by Sarah A. Curtis; *In the Shadow of Man*, by Jane Goodall; and *The Speech of Monkeys* and *Gorillas & Chimpanzees*, by Richard Garner.

I'm grateful to several people for helping *Man in a Cage* come together: Sarah Layden, for providing valuable feedback on a draft of the book; Angelo Maneage, for designing a brilliant cover; Jeff Chon, for the chimp-on-a-penny-farthing concept; Alan Good, publisher, editor, and book-cheerleader, without whom, *Man in a Cage* wouldn't be in your hands.

I'm especially grateful to my family: Sarah, for her unyielding love and support, and Lucy and Will, for their endless curiosity. They are my light, my home, my world, and make everything I do shine brighter. I hope that this book returns some small measure of that brightness to them.

Patrick Nevins lives with his family in Columbus, Indiana. *Man in a Cage* is his first book.

Other Malarkey Books Titles

The Life of the Party Is Harder to Find Until You're the Last One Around, Adrian Sobol
Forest of Borders, Nicholas Grider
Teacher Voice,
edited by Alan Good and DeMisty D. Bellinger
King Ludd's Rag,
a zine series featuring long short stories
Faith, Itoro Bassey
Music Is Over!, Ben Arzate
Toadstones, Eric Williams
It Came from the Swamp,
edited by Joey R. Poole
Deliver Thy Pigs, Joey Hedger
Guess What's Different, Susan Triemert
White People on Vacation, Alex Miller
Your Favorite Poet, Leigh Chadwick
Pontoon: volume 1, edited by Alan Good
Don Bronco's (Working Title) Shell,
Donald Ryan
Fearless, Benjamin Warner
Thunder from a Clear Blue Sky,
Justin Bryant
Un-ruined, Roger Vaillaincourt

malarkeybooks.com